Praise for *Holding Court*

"Miller has written a timely Washington thriller that feels ripped from today's headlines."
—Brian Freeman, bestselling author of *The Bourne Sacrifice*

"Both suspenseful and thought-provoking, Alan Miller's outstanding debut novel plumbs today's headlines to tell a twisty story filled with desperate characters and a ticking clock."
—David Housewright, Edgar Award-winning author of *Something Wicked*

"Ride along with Supreme Court Justice J.J. Richter as he hops on his motorcycle for the ride of his life in *Holding Court,* Alan Miller's new mystery, which deftly spans the corporate world and the highest levels of the United States government with intrigue and suspense at every turn."
—Dr. Roxanne Meshar, author of *Living a Luxury Life* and *God Is Not Zeus!*

"Holding Court is a well-written suspense novel framed around the kidnapping of a Supreme Court Justice involved in a high-profile ecological court case. The storyline in this volume is captivating as it incorporates several puzzling incidents involving the White House, the FBI, drones, lies, murder and more. I guarantee that once you start reading *Holding Court,* you will not want to put it down. Based on the engaging structure of this book, I highly recommend it to everyone, especially readers of suspense."
—Dr. Chaunda L Scott, Professor of Human Resource Development, Oakland University, Rochester, Michigan; author/co-author of nine books

"Alan Miller has written a thrilling political murder mystery centered on that important, but secretive institution, the Supreme Court. It is a compelling story told through the eyes of smart and talented characters a reader comes to really like. Miller educates his readers as he takes them into the inner sanctums of the Court and the minds of its justices."

–Hon. Paul Anderson, Minnesota Supreme Court Justice for 20 years

"Holding Court is a compelling page turner that keeps you hooked as you untangle the story behind the kidnapping of an aging Supreme Court judge, an environmental crisis that threatens all of us and a blossoming love story. With nuanced, fascinating characters and Alan's sparkling and fast-paced storytelling, this absorbing thriller will keep you reading!"

–Judith Ruskay Rabinor, PhD, author of *The Girl in the Red Boots: Making Peace with My Mother, Befriending Your Ex After Divorce: Making Life Better for You, Your Kids and Yes, Your Ex.; A Starving Madness: Tales of Hunger, Hope and Healing in Psychotherapy.*

"One of the best new voices for a political thriller to come along in a while. Holding Court is an absolute page turner with its elegant mix of intrigue and at times serendipitous twists and turns. Alan Miller does not disappoint with his timely story of a missing justice and a reporter's exhaustive search for him. Can't wait to see it on the screen."

Cellin Gluck, motion picture director, *Persona Non Grata*

"Holding Court is a breezy, entertaining thriller in the style of Tom Clancy and Scott Turow. Filled with realistic DC and Supreme Court insider knowledge, the story explores what would happen if a Supreme Court Justice was kidnapped. Mort Ahrens, a young and insecure *Washington Post* reporter, makes a great protagonist. He suspects that he doesn't really deserve the dream job he's fallen into, and definitely doesn't deserve his girlfriend, but he surprises himself—and everyone else—on both counts. Find a comfy chair, kick back, and enjoy the ride!"

Shawn Otto, award-winning novelist and screenwriter

HOLDING
COURT

CALUMET EDITIONS

Minneapolis

Second Edition December 2022
Holding Court. Copyright © 2022 by Alan Miller.
All rights reserved.

This is a work of fiction. All of the characters, names, incidents, organizations, and dialogue are either the products of the author's imagination or are used fictitiously.

10 9 8 7 6 5 4 3 2

ISBN: 978-1-959770-13-8

Cover and book design by Gary Lindberg
Author photo by Wannapa Raker

HOLDING COURT

ALAN MILLER

CALUMET EDITIONS
Minneapolis

For the love of money is the root of all evil.
1 Timothy 6:10, King James Bible

For those who treasure our Constitution and Bill of Rights,
and who are willing to fight to maintain it

Also by Alan Miller

You Can Make a Difference
My Name Was Toby

One

⸺ ⚜ ⸺

Travilah, Maryland, Tuesday, June 15

At dawn, a light spring rain fell, and the grass sparkled like a sea of diamonds. A man in blue jeans and a plaid shirt casually descended the wooden steps of a well-tended, single-story house and headed for a small barn. A golden retriever followed him sniffing for the right spot to pee. The man's shoulder-length mane of silvery hair caught the early sun.

Lugging a heavy briefcase, he entered the barn, pausing to admire a gleaming Harley Road King. He patted the passenger seat affectionately and then crossed to a weathered 4x4 Chevy open-backed truck that sat next to a Subaru Forester. The dog expectantly watched him open the passenger door and toss in the briefcase.

"Not today, old girl," the man said, patting the dog's head and handing her a biscuit. After easing himself into the seat, he turned the ignition key. The engine sputtered and screeched. Nothing. He tried again. Same result.

A large pool of oil had seeped into the dirt floor. "Double damn!" he yelled. With a sigh of resignation, he grabbed the briefcase from the passenger side, stepped to the Harley and snapped open the metal saddlebag. Frustrated, he stuffed in the contents of the briefcase. The retriever trotted over to him, cocked her head expectantly and received another treat.

1

The man pulled off his boots, slipped on some yellow rain trousers, then eased back into the boots, grabbed gloves and a black helmet, and mounted the Harley. His foot slammed down on the kick-starter, and the Harley offered a husky purr, like a contented mountain lion. He put on the helmet.

The retriever watched him sit there for a minute. "Damn," the man said again. Turning to the dog, as if to explain what was going on, he said, "Forgot the mask." After switching off the ignition, he dismounted and walked over to the 4x4 and retrieved an N95 face mask. After taking off his helmet, he paused again and then said to the dog, "One of those mornings, girl. Don't need the mask on the bike." He stuffed the mask into his pocket, pulled on the helmet and slammed his foot down on the kick-starter.

Twenty-two miles to the south, the District of Columbia was already stirring, but here in Travilah most of the wealthy residents were still asleep under lush comforters. The town had grown up around the man's property, and what was once a simple home in the country now sat in the middle of a luxurious community.

With a last glance at the retriever, he guiltily handed her a larger biscuit. "Boy, are you getting spoiled," the man said as the dog clenched the treasure between its teeth and turned back toward the house. As the bike eased out of the barn onto the long driveway, the man reached back to make sure the saddlebag engraved with the initials J.J. was closed.

J.J. had been making this trip for decades. The young saplings he'd planted along the driveway had become sturdy evergreens, and the emerald arborvitae hedges along the perimeter had grown thick and shoulder high, offering the house some privacy. J.J. took a deep breath as he snapped down the visor, relishing the crisp air and the solitude of the morning. He prepared to push through the affluent community onto River Road, curling down the Potomac and then cutting over to the Clara Barton Parkway and into the nation's capital. River Road to Massachusetts Avenue offered a more direct route, but leaving the Clara Barton at Canal, taking the Whitehurst Freeway to Virginia Avenue, and then Constitution Avenue was more scenic, which he appreciated.

Plus it offered the closeness of the sleepy Potomac. Traveling behind the White House and across the Ellipse had always sent tingles down his spine as he anticipated approaching the gleaming white majesty of the Capitol and behind it the building that had been his second home for more than thirty years, the United States Supreme Court.

But this morning was going to be different.

A white panel truck was partially blocking the end of his long driveway, and an orange traffic cone was diverting traffic. A person was lying under the truck on the wet blacktop, arms under the vehicle next to the exhaust. J.J. approached on the motorcycle.

"Need help?" he asked.

The man beneath the truck slid out and stood up revealing a tall, powerfully built man in unmarked coveralls and a painter's cap. A Barak Obama mask hid his face. As he spun toward the motorcycle, a larger man wearing a Ronald Reagan mask burst out of the van with a white cloth in his gloved hand. He quickly circled behind the Harley and grabbed J.J. from behind.

J.J. instinctively snapped his head backward. His helmet smashed into the face of the abductor with a sickening crack.

Blood spurted from the man's nose through the Reagan mask, pouring a red stream down the front of his white coveralls. He dropped the cloth and groped wildly for his face. "Jesus Christ!" he bellowed. "He broke my fucking nose!"

Furious, the Obama guy expertly swung the flat of his hand, striking J.J. high on the chest and sending him sprawling to the roadway. Without missing a beat, he scaled the Harley and landed squarely on top of J.J.

Alerted by the noise, the dog charged up the driveway and leaped, grabbing the assailant's arm and tearing the fabric. J.J. was kicking and thrashing on the blacktop.

Obama tried to shake off the retriever while yelling to his partner, "Forget your nose! Stick the dog!"

Reagan yanked at his bloodied uniform pocket and grabbed a syringe with his free hand, bit off the cap and jabbed it into the dog's neck. J.J. was still thrashing beneath the weight of the other attacker.

"Now get the damn judge!" Obama shouted, struggling to keep J.J. pinned.

"Hold him down, dammit!" Reagan yelled as he yanked another syringe from his pocket, pushed J.J.'s helmet up and plunged the needle into his neck. Within seconds, both the dog and J.J. were unconscious on the blacktop.

The second assailant, a Black man, pulled off his Reagan face mask. His partner, who was White, also unmasked and quickly inspected his arm, which was still intact. He jumped to his feet, yanking open the truck's rear door. Together, the assailants picked up the unconscious cyclist like a sack of grain and slid him carefully into the back of the truck. After turning J.J. onto his stomach, they fastened a plastic tie on his wrists, tied him up with a rope and threw a tarpaulin over him so only his head was uncovered.

The entire event had transpired in less than a minute.

The White man tossed the unconscious dog onto the shoulder of the roadway, scooped up his mask from the ground and turned to his partner. "Let's get the bike," he said.

They slid a metal ramp to the ground and wheeled the Harley into the truck. Leaving the traffic cone, a torn piece of bloody fabric, the white cloth and a motionless dog, the truck leaped forward. The light rain continued.

About two miles down the road, the van stopped momentarily, and an arm flung J.J.'s cell phone into the river.

The Black man pressed a cloth to his nose, soaking up the still-oozing blood. The driver carefully drove within the speed limit, occasionally glancing in the rearview mirror to check the unconscious form under the tarpaulin. He looked at his partner and said, "Tune into a news station—just to make sure we're home free. And stop worrying about your damn nose. You'd never win a beauty contest anyway."

"He'll be out like a light for a while," his partner said, fiddling with the radio. "You were right. That propofol is incredible. Even a mild dose. Job like this kind of reminds me of the old days."

"In the old days, if you were caught by surprise like that, you'd be dead."

4

"Can't you go a little faster, for Chrissake?"

"Sure, and when we get pulled over you can explain that we've got an unconscious Supreme Court judge in back."

After scrolling through several stations, the Black man found a news station. An announcer said, "...still baffled over a triple killing in North Potomac last evening. Three young men gunned down on a quiet street. Police will hold a press conference later this morning. It was the first multiple homicide in North Potomac in recent memory."

The driver squinted and said, "He said 'North Potomac.' Weren't you there last night, Brian, to visit your mother in that old folks home?"

Brian muttered, "Oh, shit."

"What'd you say?"

"I said, 'Oh shit!' And it's not an old folks home, it's senior housing."

"'Oh shit' because…?"

"Because there's something I should have told you. Those three punks tried to rob me when I left my mother's place and was walking to the van. They had a knife, maybe a gun—and I, uh… I dispatched them. That's how I got this cut on my side." He put a hand on his side.

The driver shook his head and said, "Another thing you didn't mention to me. Time to get honest, my friend. So, three guys were trying to rob you?"

"Actually, I was driving away from Mom's place and saw these guys robbing an old Black guy."

"Holy shit. So, you weren't even being robbed. You could have just kept driving. Are you crazy or what? You killed three guys the night before this operation? You could have blown the whole thing! Where is your brain?"

"You have no idea why my mother's living in that home."

"This is no time for riddles," the driver replied. "What does that have to do with anything?"

"It has everything to do with it. My mother's there because she can't live on her own since my pop died a couple of years ago. He was mugged. Killed with eight bucks in his pocket. Eight fucking dollars. By two hoods on the street."

5

"So?"

"So, I promised myself that if I ever got the chance, I'd avenge him. Well, last night those punks were settin' on this poor old Black guy, and I got my chance. Balance the ledger… know what I mean?"

"You had to kill all three?"

"At first, I only saw two of 'em beating the old Black guy, but then I saw the third one running for their car. Probably to get a gun, maybe to get away. I had no choice."

"Jesus. I should've done this job alone."

"What's done is done," Brian said. "No sweat. Clean hit. Just like we were trained. And what would you have done without me today? Probably blown it."

"Jesus, Brian. Three guys. Night before a job."

"I had no choice. Four quick shots. No witnesses."

"No witnesses? Where was your brain? And you got stabbed?"

"Just a flesh wound. It was nothing. They had a knife. I had no choice. They just didn't know my background. It's cool, Mateos, really. Just get us there so I can fix this fuckin' nose."

"The last time it was *nothing* we got kicked out of the Secret Service in Cartagena because you tried to stiff that hooker."

"I offered her a hundred bucks. I was drunk, fell asleep. She didn't perform."

"Right, and here we are. That was also some *nothing.*"

"Don't forget that I saved your ass twice."

"Keep reminding me. Story of my life," Mateos said. "I partner with a black Boy Scout."

"After all we've been through together, last night was nothing. Look, I only agreed to this crazy deal because you set it up. Twenty years in stir if it blows up."

"And if it doesn't, you get that bar on a tropical island you've always wanted," Mateos said. And then, as if trying to convince himself, he added, "We're almost home free. No-brainer."

Two

The white van traveled at twenty miles an hour down Main Street in Great Capcapon, West Virginia, a two-lane blacktop road. On both sides of the street were several vintage buildings, relics from the town's halcyon days when the Baltimore and Ohio Railroad maintained a depot there. Those days were long gone, and the few hundred residents in West Virginia's Eastern Panhandle either worked in Berkeley Springs or at the nearby Capcapon Resort State Park.

"We're almost there," Mateos said. Then, nodding over his shoulder at the covered figure in the rear, he added, "As soon as we get him situated, you can take care of your *beautiful* nose. And I can get my head examined for trusting you. Again."

"C'mon," Brian said, "this is a great spot, only an hour from the snatch. And I fixed up the old house tight as a drum. Remember, you're the one who insisted on this adventure."

"Ten million each is what insisted on this adventure."

"Well, you practically forced me, don't forget. In a couple of weeks, when we're rolling in that cash, maybe I'll be thanking you. Now, I'm just nervous."

"Just don't find another way to fuck up."

About a mile from what passed for the center of town, they pulled into a dirt driveway leading to a ramshackle two-story house with flaking paint, set back about fifty yards from the road. A red barn with a rolling door on pulleys sat about eighty yards from the house, its entrance wide enough for two vehicles. The scraggly lawn was blotchy, and the property, which covered several acres, was surrounded by pines and featured a large willow. There were no other homes in sight.

"The back door unlocked?" Mateos asked.

"Like you said, there's never anyone around here," Brian said.

"What about the rental guy?"

"He won't be around. Six months cash up front for this white elephant. He thinks I'm an advance team scouting for a possible new resort. Practically peed in his pants."

"We'll get His Honor set up in the basement and put the bike in the barn with your rental car and my Lincoln. When everything's secure, I'll head back to DC to the office like nothing happened, and you can take it from there. Not that anybody has been knocking down our door with business. Food is no problem, right?"

"No sweat. I bought breakfast stuff, and there's a place in Berkeley Springs where I can get us meals and bring them back. He'll be downstairs, locked up tight as a drum. Not going anyplace."

They parked in back, took the tarp off the still-unconscious jurist and carried him carefully up the back steps into the kitchen. In the corner, a door led down to the basement, and from the door you could see all the way through to the front door. They negotiated their heavy cargo down the stairs and laid J.J. on a canvas cot.

"He'll probably be out for another hour or so," Mateos said.

"And madder'n hell when he wakes up," Brian added.

"Just make sure he's okay. He'll be woozy, but he's our meal ticket."

"Piece of cake."

They left the unconscious Supreme Court Justice J.J. Richter in the darkened basement.

Upstairs, Mateos said, "I'll let them know our status so far. Shit, I can practically taste the money."

He took a burner phone out of the pocket of his torn uniform. He called a number, and a voice greeted him. "The deed is done," Mateos reported. "Went like clockwork."

Three

Slightly after noon on the day of the abduction, Danni Rose sat at her desk at the American University Law School in DC. A diminutive, thirty-two-year-old assistant professor in environmental law, Danni had become one of the most popular members of the faculty in only two years. Her somewhat spartan office was dominated by a bookcase overflowing with law books. A basketball perched on a table beside her desk was adorned with numerous autographs. Wearing a Syracuse University sweatshirt, jeans and sockless loafers, she was having a conversation with Melissa Sparrow, one of her best students in the just-concluded semester.

"I read that you're going to debate Professor Barker from Georgetown on that water preservation case," Melissa said.

"I'm really excited about the opportunity to go up against one of the very best," Danni said. "He's won a bunch of cases in the Supreme Court." A light blinked on Danni's desk phone. "Excuse me, I should take this."

Melissa started to get up, but Danni gestured for her to stay.

She picked up the call. "Professor Rose," she announced, then listened for a few seconds before saying, "Lucille, how are you? How's everything in the halls of justice?" Danni put her hand over the speaker and whispered to Melissa, "It's Justice Richter's law clerk."

After a few more seconds, Danni's face deepened with concern, and she said, "What do you mean, didn't show up in court this morning? J.J. is always the first one in."

She listened for a few more seconds and asked, "Did you try his house?" Then, another momentary few seconds listening, and she said, "…left on the Harley? Good God, I hope he didn't have an accident. Yes, I'll get on it right away. And call me as soon as he shows up, which I'm certain he will." With that she hung up the phone and turned to her student.

"Melissa, we'll have to pick this up later. I've got to trace down a missing septuagenarian." Melissa looked somewhat confused, nodded, got up and left without a word, closing the door on her way out.

Danni pulled out her cell phone and speed-dialed a number. She waited impatiently. "C'mon, J.J., pick up," she muttered before disconnecting.

Immediately, she called another number that picked up, saying, "Hi, LeAnne, this is Danni Rose. Is the chief free?" She listened for a few seconds. "Triple murder?" she said. "Unbelievable. But if I can have just a half minute. It's probably nothing, but Justice Richter didn't show up in court this morning, and he apparently left home as usual." A pause. "Sure, I'll wait."

A minute later, Chief Travis Anderson of the Montgomery County Police picked up. "Danni? Travis here—what's this about J.J.?"

"Hate to bother you," Danni said, "but it's not like him to not to show up in court, and I'm worried."

"Did you check with your mother?" Travis asked.

For lack of another word, Danni's mother, Helene "Chickie" Rosen, was the "significant other" of J.J. Richter, the senior associate justice of the Supreme Court. J.J. had been widowed more than a dozen years ago, and Chickie's husband had died in a bizarre accident about five years later. Chickie and J.J. had been brought together by Danni at a New Year's Eve party and had been inseparable ever since.

"No, you're the first call I made… after calling his cell," Danni explained to Travis. "I got nothing. I'm thinking maybe an accident?"

Danni could hear Travis say to someone on his end of the phone, "LeAnne, Justice Richter has gone AWOL. Check all the hospitals between Travilah and the Supreme Court, will you? And check the precincts and the locals to see if anyone has any information. Thanks."

Travis began speaking into the phone again. "LeAnne is on it, Danni. He probably had something personal that he didn't want to advertise. You know J.J."

"Thanks, Travis. Unlike him, but you're probably right. I'll call Mom."

Again, Travis spoke off-mic to another person. "Jim, give LeAnn a hand for a minute and see if we can track down Justice Richter. Just what we didn't need at the moment."

Travis Anderson was chief of the thirteen hundred-member police department for Montgomery County, Maryland, and was speaking from his office in Gaithersburg. When Danni called, Travis's office was crowded with his chief deputy, Jim Steves, several command officers and his admin, LeAnne. He and Justice Richter had become close friends when they were both recipients of the Congressional Medal of Honor and were thrown together for a Fourth of July ceremony. That was more than a decade ago.

"I'll dispatch a patrol to J.J.'s house," Travis said to Danni, "just to make double sure it's nothing."

"Thanks again, Travis," Danni replied. "Now you can go back to your triple murder."

"Thanks. That one is a complete mystery," Travis said. "Hope we solve the J.J. disappearance a lot easier."

Danni called another number. "Mom, it's Danni," she said. "Is J.J. with you by any chance? Or do you have any clue as to where he might be?"

Chickie Rosen was CEO/President of Rosen-Billings Enterprises, one of the media giants. She had taken her daughter's call in her company office in nearby Alexandria, Virginia.

"What do you mean, where he might be?" Chickie said, alarmed. "Isn't he in court?"

"He left home this morning but never showed up in court. I called Travis, and his office is checking hospitals and other authorities."

"My God," Chickie said. "Something must have happened. That's so unlike J.J. I honestly have no idea where he could be. What do you want me to do?"

"Nothing at the moment. Just stand by. I'm going over to the court."

Next, Danni called J.J.'s home and got the housekeeper. "Lupe, it's Danni. Look, I know the justice left as usual this morning, but we can't find him anywhere. Travis is sending a patrol car to the house just to check, so don't get upset when he pulls in."

"Lady from his office call and say he not there yet," Lupe said. "He still not there? I going to take Connie to the vent. She come home like drunk—walk funny, flop around house. But I wait now."

Lupe had been with him for over twelve years—had been there even before his wife, Meg, succumbed to cervical cancer. In the intervening years, she had become Richter's protector, her hulking presences and dexterous hands in the kitchen an almost comical juxtaposition from the five-foot-eight justice.

"I'm sure it's nothing," Danni said, "but I just wanted to alert you before the police arrive. Relax—I'll call you as soon as I find out anything. Do me a favor and look at his schedule in the office and see if there's anything for today."

"Sí," Lupe said, and was back minutes later. Danni reached into her bag and was about to make another call when Lupe came back on the line. "I see nothing for today."

"Thanks, Lupe. And don't get nervous when the police arrive."

"Dios mío," Lupe muttered before she disconnected.

Four

Next, Danni called Mort Ahrens a little after one. Mort was at his desk in the *Washington Post* newsroom when his cell phone sounded its distinctive ringtone, the "Cavalry Charge." His cubicle was one of many in the newspaper's "bullpen." His personal cell phone—stashed in a pocket of his jacket, which was draped over the back of his chair—was strictly for calls from Danni, family members and close friends. His work mobile sat on his desk next to an old-fashioned land line. He reached back, dug out his personal phone and looked at the screen—Danni.

Mort was not a Robert Redford look-alike, at least not the Redford from *All the President's Men.* He was more of a Mr. Average—five-foot-eight with unkempt sandy hair, large tortoise-shell glasses, a rumpled blue shirt with the sleeves rolled up and a fashionable but unintentional one-day growth of beard. All around him, the other reporters in the investigative unit of "WaPo" were hunched over their computers, chatting on their phones, or staring off while contemplating the obstacles to completing their current assignment.

Mort was blessed with a photographic memory oddly conjoined with a knack of forgetting the unimportant things in life. His first thought upon looking at the Caller ID was *What did I forget to do today?* He started running through the possibilities. He wasn't supposed to drop anything off anyplace. He had turned off all the lights at home and lowered the air conditioning. He hadn't walked the dog because they didn't have a dog… yet. But he was certain the call was about something he was responsible for. It was always that.

"Danni," he said, "what's up?"

"J.J. is missing," she said, her voice an octave higher than usual.

"What do you mean *missing*?"

"He didn't show up in court this morning. He'd never miss a day, especially now. I got the call from Lucille, his law clerk, who had called the house and spoken with Lupe. J.J. left as usual this morning, and she checked the garage. He left on the Harley but never got to the court. What could have happened?"

Mort agreed that J.J. would never miss a day in court, especially at the end of the term. Mort's heart skipped a beat, because he knew something that Danni didn't know—in fact, something no one else but J.J. knew. It involved J.J. getting involved in Mort's life. And Danni's too. If that was the reason J.J. didn't show up at court, Mort knew he was really in deep shit.

"Did you check the hospitals?" he asked.

"Of course," she said impatiently. "I called Travis. He's checking all that. So far, nothing. He's sending a car to check the house anyway. Plus, he's up to his ears with a triple murder."

Mort's heart was now in his stomach, which wasn't strong on the best of days. He was nervously grasping for suggestions. "I read about those murders," he said, "and I was going to give him a call, but I figured it was chaos there. Christ, we were all together just last night. Maybe he had a doctor's appointment he wanted to keep quiet?"

"Nope. Lupe looked."

"This is weird," Mort said, "and certainly out of character. What about your mother? Could he be with her?"

"Spoke to her. She's clueless."

As usual, Mort thought, I'm the last one she calls. But Mort knew where J.J. was headed sometime during the day. It was to get J.J.'s deceased wife's wedding ring out of his safe deposit vault at the bank. He was doing it for Mort. Well, in reality he was doing it for Danni, whom he thought of as the daughter J.J. never had.

Probably at lunchtime, Mort figured, J.J. would stop at the bank to collect the ring. Could he still be there? But why didn't he show up as usual in the morning? And Mort couldn't say a word about it or Danni would go ballistic. It was already early afternoon.

"Something is very wrong," Danni said.

"Calm down," Mort said. "It's only one o'clock, for God's sake."

"Don't be so dense," Danni snapped. "I think it's got something to do with these last few weeks of the term."

"Want me to shoot over to the court and see what I can find out?" Mort asked.

"Where do you think I'm heading?" she said angrily. "But no one in his chambers even has a clue anyway."

Mort began to wonder where he was on Danni's priority list. She had already touched all the bases. Almost.

"What would be helpful," she said, "is for you to use your resources there at WaPo—confidentially, with people you can trust—to see if anyone can suggest something. But keep it quiet. The last thing we want is to raise an alarm if there's nothing alarming."

Her tone was a bit condescending, like she might have been talking to a six-year-old. No, maybe a four-year-old. Bottom line, though, Mort knew J.J.'s disappearance might have been the result of his conversation with J.J. last night and a suggestion the justice had made by volunteering to do a favor for Mort.

Danni had no tolerance for stupidity—with Mort in particular. And Mort managed to forever put his foot in it. With her students, on the other hand, Danni had the patience of a saint, and they loved her.

"Then I'm heading to Gaithersburg to Travis's headquarters," Danni continued, "unless J.J. shows up."

"Okay, I'll nose around and meet you there," Mort said.

Danielle Rose was now an assistant professor. She and Mort were unofficially engaged, but she refused to wear a ring because her first fiancée, a medical resident named Jerry Stone, had previously given her a ring. But while she was wearing it, she caught him cheating with a nurse. End of ring, end of Stone. Then there was that quick second

15

relationship with a Supreme Court law clerk. That one hadn't lasted long enough to even shop for a ring.

Rings were bad luck, she had decided.

Danni used to be Danielle Rosen, from New York. Her classmates at Syracuse Law nicknamed her Broadway Danni Rose, like the Woody Allen character, and she dropped the "n" from her last name because one of her profs suggested that a Rose would smell sweeter than a Rosen when looking for a law firm position after graduation. Danni, a brilliant five-foot-two-inch bundle of energy, had also been an All-American point guard who led the women's basketball team to its best season ever. A five-foot-two basketball player—imagine.

Mort and Danni were 'unofficially' engaged without a ring and shared a prohibitively expensive apartment in Georgetown. With their combined salaries, they could afford it. And *she* wanted Georgetown, so Georgetown it was.

Mort, on the other hand, was on WaPo's Investigations Desk, part of a team that had been involved in some exciting stories including impeachment #1 of the last president. He had never ceased to be amazed that he was with the *Washington Post*, let alone part of an award-winning, Pulitzer prize-winning team. Eight hundred WaPo reporters—he had really lucked out, in his mind. His tendency to diminish his own worth was the focus of frequent discussions with his shrink.

Despite Mort's denigrating self-appraisal, he had graduated college summa cum laude, given a valedictory address on the foundations of democracy that was quoted in the *New York Times*, possessed a photographic memory and a flare for writing and won several hundred thousand dollars on *Jeopardy*. Nevertheless, he still looked in the mirror each morning filled with insecurity.

If Mort's fraternity brother, Al Carr, hadn't sat on a spike at the *Syracuse Post-Standard*, Mort couldn't imagine where he'd be today. While both of them were attending the Newhouse School of Communications at Syracuse, they had also been moonlighting at the P/S. Mort was a junior at the time, Carr a senior. The paper called them junior reporters—in other words, glorified copyboys.

Carr had been at work one afternoon when he'd forgotten he had put the spike used for saving stock market data on his chair. He sat on it. Another two inches and he'd have been a soprano. Mort was at his desk at the D.O.—the *Daily Orange*, Syracuse University's student newspaper—where he was the features editor, when he got the call that Al was being rushed to the hospital. Talk about making an ass of yourself.

Mort dropped everything and raced downtown to cover for Carr. Shortly after arriving, a call came in that a teenager had gone missing in Camillus, a small village about twenty miles west of Syracuse. The staff reporters were all on assignments, so the managing editor sent Mort to cover it. Probably a nothing story. Turns out the girl stayed missing for two weeks, and it was now Mort's story, so he spent a lot of time in Camillus nosing around.

Mort learned from a friend of the missing teen about a guy in his twenties who was infatuated with the missing girl. The friend had never told anyone about this fellow because she didn't want to get him in trouble for no reason. Mort became a sleuth, did some surveillance and hung around the village for two weeks following the "suspect" into a grocery store where he purchased some women's sanitary napkins. Mort put the two pieces together—sanitary napkins and single guy living alone—and discovered the abducted teen was being held prisoner in the guy's home.

He notified the authorities, and the physically unharmed girl was freed. Mort had broken the story—an exclusive with national coverage—and it won all sorts of awards and the headline, "Cub Reporter Solves Kidnapping," which was a little better than "Glorified Copyboy Solves Kidnapping." A few weeks later, one of Mort's professors told him the *Washington Post* had noticed the articles and wanted to interview him for a job when he graduated. Thus, Mort had ended up as a reporter on the *Washington Post* thanks to the spike in Al Carr's ass.

Five

The previous night, Mort had sat in on one of the annual Law and Order presentations given jointly by J.J. and Travis. These events were so noteworthy that WaPo had done a story about them several years earlier. It was because of Danni, of course, that Mort was able to call the senior associate justice of the Supreme Court "J.J." rather than "Your Honor," or "Sir." Danni had been invited, but she was busy doing prep for the televised debate on CNN about the world water crisis with a professor from Georgetown Law School. Mort went in her stead, leaving her surrounded by articles and notes.

J.J. and Travis were as close as two men can be, even with thirty years' difference in their ages. Maybe it was a father and son thing. Someone had gotten the idea that it would be great to feature two Medal of Honor winners—J.J. and Travis—in the annual festivity. The duo presented a surprising contrast—on one hand, a five-foot-eight, seventy-eight-year-old Caucasian justice of the Supreme Court; and on the other, a six-foot-two, forty-two-year-old African American heading a major police department. J.J. was from Wyoming while Travis was the youngest of three boys and credited his mother with getting him out of Detroit so he didn't end up in jail like his two older brothers.

Mort had parked in the crowded lot and was about to walk to the entrance when he saw J.J. pull up in his red 4x4 and park in one of the VIP spaces. J.J. climbed out of his truck wearing a western hat and blue jeans, a western shirt and a Bulldogs team jacket. As he started for the entrance, an officious security guard with a too-large blue uniform jacket and a badge displayed prominently on his chest, rushed over to the justice gesturing and shouting.

"You can't park here, fella, it's for the VIPs."

"I understand," J.J. said, "but I'm a VIP tonight, so that includes me."

"Don't be smart with me!"

Travis arrived just then. He flipped on the flashers of his drug-forfeited Lexus and rolled down the window. "Trouble here, officer?" he asked.

"This guy is trying to park his truck in a VIP space," the security guard said... and then noticed the golden eagles on Travis's collar and stuttered, "Si... sir."

Travis called over to his friend, "Are you causing trouble again, J.J.?"

"You know him?" the guard said, looking at J.J., who was thoroughly enjoying the entire exchange.

This was typical J.J.—a liberal curmudgeon of the first order and probably the most well-known and beloved member of the court, with a conscience as big as the Constitution, a passion for the law. He frequently arrived at the court on his Harley, the bane of other jurists who showed up in chauffeured sedans, limos or expensive personal vehicles, some with US marshals for protection. His brethren on the court ate in the justice's dining room on the second floor; J.J. preferred the public cafeteria on the first floor on those rare occasions when he stopped for a lunch break. First in, last out had been his policy for over three decades.

Travis turned to the guard. "Say hello to tonight's speaker, Associate Justice Richter of the US Supreme Court."

"I'm so sorry, Your Honor," the guard stammered, stepping aside.

J.J. parked and turned to Mort, who had arrived on the scene. "Danni finally kick you out?"

"Just trying to improve my knowledge," Mort said.

"Better off trying the library."

J.J. and Mort walked toward the large entrance of the reddish brick building with "Winston Churchill High School" emblazoned above the entrance. As they passed the guard, J.J. casually said, "It's just J.J. when I'm not on the bench."

Typical J.J.

Mort took an aisle seat about halfway back in the auditorium and watched Travis take a chair on the podium behind the lectern.

***

The auditorium was about two-thirds filled with a mix of parents and students, many wearing Bulldog tees, sweatshirts and team jackets. As J.J. was winding up the presentation by taking a few questions, a young woman raised her hand. J.J. pointed at her and said, "Yes, ma'am?"

"What do you do if you haven't disposed of all your cases by the end of June, when you said you adjourned for the summer?"

"Well," J.J. replied, "we have a tradition of disposing of the entire calendar of cases by the time we adjourn. And we do. Once in a while, we might go a few days into July, but that's only happened once in my thirty-two years."

"Even a case like that big water energy case everyone's talking about?" the woman asked.

J.J. smiled. "You've been doing your homework, haven't you? You mean National Association of Water & Environmental Security, which we refer to by the acronym 'NAWES,' versus The Environmental Protection Agency et al?"

"That's the one," she replied. "The media's been making a big fuss about it for months."

"And well they should," J.J. agreed. "It's one of the most important cases on our calendar since the abortion and gun rights cases. Although, by the time cases get to us, they're all important to some aspect of our society. But that case, too, will be decided before we break for the summer. So keep watching."

The water energy case was one of the most hotly contested in US Supreme Court history. It rivaled the cases regarding abortion, voting rights, the separation of church and state, even the Second Amendment guns rights cases. With only weeks to go in the Supreme Court term,

the court's decision was still in doubt. J.J. Richter led the progressives who argued to reverse the lower courts and sustain the government's position. Associate Justice Anthony Battaglia led the opposition, in favor of sustaining the lower courts. Several justices apparently had not yet reached a final decision.

Six

As Justice Richter was making his concluding remarks, Mort had noticed Travis, who was seated behind the speaker, suddenly glance down and pull his cell phone. After staring at the screen, Travis scribbled a few words on a note pad and then stood and handed the note to J.J. at the lectern before rushing off the stage.

J.J. stopped his remarks. After reading the message, he told the audience, "Chief Anderson apologizes for his hasty departure, but he has an emergency. That's another difference between his side of the law and mine."

As Travis passed by Mort in an aisle seat, Travis leaned down and whispered, "Triple killing in North Potomac."

The newspaper reporter in Mort kicked into gear, and he hurried after Travis and into the parking lot. Mort knew North Potomac for reasons of absolutely no importance—hiking trails. Danni was an exercise nut. Every day it was either the gym, racquetball, or a pickup basketball game when she could find one. Then, for relaxation on the weekends—hiking. Mort hated hiking—you could tell that by his appearance—but it's what Danni wanted to do on weekends, so Mort went along. He probably knew the hiking trails better than the squirrels.

On some weekends, Danni and Mort would go skeet shooting at one of the half-dozen ranges close to their Georgetown apartment. As a teen-ager, Mort and his dad had done skeet shooting. It was *not* his favorite sport, though. That was watching a game on TV—any game

23

would do—with a beer on the sofa with his shoes off. His memory of skeet shooting was a black and blue shoulder from the recoil of a shotgun.

Danni, who took to any sport and usually excelled, came to love skeet shooting after Mort introduced her to it in a moment of weakness. She became good enough to be competitive. So, they had become occasional weekend skeet shooters. The Winchester break action shotgun with two parallel barrels lived in the trunk of his Subaru secured in a leather case with high velocity shot pellets.

* * *

North Potomac was about eight miles from the high school, so Mort planned to take Route 190 past J.J.'s home in Travilah, then Piney Meetinghouse Road into North Potomac. Sitting in his car, waiting for Travis to exit the parking lot, he decided to call in the killing to the desk at WaPo and found that they had already dispatched several reporters and a photographer to the scene. No sense speeding all the way up there since other reporters would beat him to the scene. Besides, he wanted to seek J.J.'s advice on a nagging question. What better time than now?

Mort planted himself beside J.J.'s 4x4 to wait for the justice to arrive at his truck. A few minutes later, J.J. extracted himself from several admirers and approached.

"So, what did you think? Was it worth your evening?" J.J. asked.

"More than I imagined," Mort said. "Fascinating, in fact. But if you've got a minute, can I pick your brain?"

"Not sure there's that much left to pick, but shoot."

Mort leaned up against the 4x4 and said, "Well, you know that Danni and I are engaged. But in my mother's eyes it's not official until I buy her a ring. And Danni says rings are bad luck because of her past experiences. But I want to try again, so do you think I'm wasting my time, or is it worth a shot?"

J.J. paused, nodded that he understood the dilemma, then suddenly snapped his fingers and said, "I know the sad story about the cheating doctor. But that was years ago. Time she got over it. And we want your mother to be happy and make it official. There's a solution, though—one I'd like to be a part of."

Mort leaned forward with anticipation. "And?"

"You know how much I love Danni," J.J. said. "From day one that I met her. And I know how hard-headed she is. And so damned smart. The only law clerk who could beat me in an argument with her logic. To say nothing of basketball. So, here's my proposal."

J.J. put his hand on Mort's shoulder and explained. "Tomorrow, I'll go to the bank, where I've got Meg's wedding ring in the vault and get it out. Give it to you. She'll never say 'no ring' when she realizes that it was Meg's. And it would make me very happy. If Meg was still alive and had met Danni, I know it would have made her happy too. How's that?"

"You would do that for us?"

"For Danni," J.J. said, his eyes twinkling. "You're just lucky she picked you. I still don't understand that one."

Now, with J.J. missing, Mort could only wonder if the trip to the bank was the cause of his disappearance.

Seven

J.J. awoke slowly without any idea of how long he had been unconscious. He tried to push himself to his feet in the dim light but fell back onto a mattress atop a narrow bed or cot. He felt around, and his hand found a floor covering, coarse and stiff to the touch. An indoor or industrial grade carpet perhaps? The small cot reminded him of his days in the service decades earlier.

"What the hell?" J.J. muttered. His eyes began to focus as he remembered stopping the Harley by the crippled van. He checked his body for broken bones and bruises, but everything seemed to be in place. Whatever drug they had used on him had left him woozy.

He pushed himself to his elbows and looked around. The nearly barren room was about twenty by fifteen feet and windowless with unpainted walls. Next to the cot was a card table and single chair. At the far end of the room, stairs led upward to a door at the far end. A basement? There was a musty smell. The room had not been used recently. He noticed another doorway at floor level, this one with no door.

The doorway led to a tiny bathroom with toilet and sink jutting out from the wall on metal supports. No shower or tub. A medicine cabinet had been removed and replaced with thick boards nailed into the wall. On the sink he found a cellophane wrapped plastic cup, a wrapped toothbrush, a bar of soap and an unused tube of Colgate toothpaste.

So, they planned to have him for a while.

He was still in the same clothes he had been wearing when he left Travilah, minus the raingear. His boots had been replaced by slippers, but his pockets were empty, and his watch and wallet were missing.

Thirsty, he reached for the cup and turned the faucet. It made a grinding noise and emitted a small trickle of brown, brackish water. He let it run, and after a few minutes the water started to clear. On the doorjamb, a large bath towel hung from a carpenter's nail. On the far wall a locked door—probably to the furnace, water heater, perhaps a slop sink, he thought—had been replaced by spackled-over plywood nailed solidly in place.

Back in the main room he noticed that on the cot lay a thick, army-surplus blanket and a pillow. There was also a washcloth, a package of undershorts, a package of T-shirts, several polo shirts, and sweatpants with no identifying marks. The light came from two ceiling bulbs hanging from wires at either end of the room.

J.J. shook his head. "And they all settled down for a long winter's nap. Bastards!" If he had been the target of a killing, it could have been done right there in Travilah with no witnesses.

J.J. moved to the stairs and angrily shook the wooden handrail attached to the wall on one side. It was firmly bolted to the wall. "Where are my papers, my court things?" he shouted. "What the hell is going on?"

Hugging the wall, he crept up the creaking stairs. At the top he confronted a thick, solid wooden door with a smaller "doggie door" at the bottom. Too small for a man to squeeze through. J.J. pushed on it anyway and found it locked or bolted from the other side.

He moved around the room, running his hands over the bare walls. The panels had been securely nailed into place with large carpenter's nails. He spotted two small cameras, secured at opposite ends of the room near the ceiling. He tried listening for any exterior sounds but there were none.

Where were his captors? If today was the same day on which he had been abducted, he was probably within a reasonable distance from Travilah, perhaps even holed up in DC.

He cursed himself for stopping at the disabled van. Travis had lectured him many times about safety, and he had refused a driver or a security detail like some of the other members of the court had. He just couldn't think of any enemies who would go to such a length.

He crept back down the stairs, slumped on the cot and dozed off.

Eight

Awakening to footsteps on the floor above, J.J. climbed off the cot and moved toward the stairs, surprised when the doggie door snapped open, and a plastic tray slid through it.

"Dammit," he yelled at the open door. "What the hell is going on? What do you want?" There was a pause, as if the person on the other side of the door was deciding whether to respond.

The door slammed shut and bolts snapped back into place. On the tray, J.J. found fried chicken, mashed potatoes, green beans, a roll, a piece of cake and a cup of coffee. No milk. The utensils were plastic, the plate and cup paper. He realized for the first time that he was starved. This was a better meal than he'd get in prison. He wolfed down the food. *Dinner*, he thought. It must be evening, or at least late in the day. That was a clue. Upstairs, he heard what sounded like a toilet flushing.

J.J. ate everything, carried the tray back up the stairs and banged on the door. After several seconds, the bolts snapped open, and a hand yanked the tray out so quickly J.J. couldn't tell whether it was male or female, Black or White.

"Hey, do you hear me?" J.J. barked. All he got back was the sound of bolts locking the tiny door shut.

Ransom? he wondered. So close to the end of the term, his absence might throw everything into chaos. The current president had previously stated he would never pay a ransom in a kidnapping, but when it came to a Supreme Court justice, the public clamor would be deafening. In any event, Chickie would not idly sit by, and she had the backbone and capability to pay a ransom.

The end of the term was only a week away, two at the most. What if one of the justices was ill or unable to participate in the final decisions? Even up to the last day of the session, circulating draft opinions could still swing some justices from one side to the other.

Anthony Battaglia, leader of the conservative bloc, had already announced his retirement due to a diagnosis of pancreatic cancer. J.J. and Battaglia had locked horns for decades, and he would sorely miss that conflict, but despite their differences they were friends, not unlike RBG and Scalia a few years back. Battaglia had often reached out to J.J. after Meg's death, and the few times J.J. was induced out of his home was at the invitation of Anthony to attend a Wizards or Nationals game where they never talked business. He would sorely miss Anthony from the court.

J.J. had to find a way to escape. "Dammit," he muttered, "it's got to be that NAWES case. That has to be the reason." The world's water usage could turn on that one decision. Someone connected to that industry had to be involved. It meant keeping him cooped up at least until the court adjourned for the summer.

He was certain the case wouldn't be carried over until the next term. The chief justice would not countenance that. It would reflect on her leadership. But when the case was finally decided, then what? Would they just open the door and let him wander out from this unknown location?

Unlikely, because there would be too many clues. Most likely, they'd truss him up, drug and blindfold him again, then drop him far away from this spot. Maybe even torch the house to destroy clues.

But he couldn't let that happen.

J.J. carefully scrutinized the room. It was well secured, a professional job. He could find no possible escape routes, and even J.J., a slender and fit seventy-eight-year-old, couldn't squeeze through the doggie door.

What about a shower? He couldn't go two weeks without showering—or even two days. Or could he? That might present his chance to escape. He remembered the two men who had captured him—tall and well-muscled. The two cameras at either end meant he was also being surveilled, his every move scrutinized. They were probably the men who were holding him.

He pounded on the doggie door and listened, then heard faint footsteps. "My pills! If you want to keep me alive, I've got to have my pills," he lied.

The bolts slid open, and the tiny door opened. "What pills?" a male voice asked. "Can you hear me? What pills?"

"The pills that I take first thing every day. The pills that keep my heart beating, that's what pills."

"Don't know anything about any pills," the voice said. "What kind of pills? How come they weren't in your saddle bags?"

"I just told you," J.J. said. "I take them at home before I leave for court. Except the nitro. I have some in my chambers in case I get *another* heart attack." He emphasized the word *another* and heard the voice mutter, "Shit."

"You went through my things?" J.J. asked accusingly. "That's another federal crime on top of kidnapping. Tell you what. Let me out of here and I won't press charges. Save you twenty years of your life. Minimum. What say?"

There was no answer.

J.J. had never had a heart attack, and there were no nitroglycerine pills in his chambers, but the lie was the first thing he could think of to create a subterfuge that might, somehow, get word to the world of his whereabouts. And if these kidnappers were being paid to keep him out of circulation for a week or two, their plan would probably be destroyed if he died. He was literally worth more alive than dead. Also, the killing of a Supreme Court justice carried the death penalty.

"What's the name of your pills?" the voice said.

J.J. did take two medications. "Simvastatin for high cholesterol and Valsartan for high blood pressure," J.J. called out. "And the nitroglycerin for heart palpitations. But the most important one is Diogensamine. That's the experimental one."

"Wait a fucking minute! I'm not a stenographer."

"I know what *you* are. I hope you're getting well paid."

"I'm slipping a pen and paper through the door. Write down those names and then I want both the paper and the pen back."

The paper looked like part of a torn register receipt from Angus and Ale restaurant. Now, if he could figure out where Angus and Ale was located, he'd have a clue as to where he was. J.J. jotted down the name of the two actual drugs and thought of how to spell the nonexistent "experimental" drug. He knocked on the door, and the same hand grabbed the pen and paper and bolted the door without a word.

Imprisoned at age seventy-eight somewhere near the Angus and Ale restaurant. How had Sen. John McCain endured captivity for over five years under even worse conditions?

A few minutes later, the doggie door opened, and a different voice called down to him. "We'll get your damned prescriptions. I looked them up, but I couldn't find Diogensamine." He spelled out the word and then said, "Do I have the right spelling?"

J.J. smiled. "You won't find it anywhere except in my bathroom. I told the other guy it was an experimental heart drug. It's from some laboratory overseas. I get it right from my doctor. I take it in the mornings with my other pills. First thing every day, with water."

He heard a whispered "Shit" between the kidnappers, then another question. "So where do we get it?"

"You probably can't. But you better find a way if you want me to stay alive."

The doggie door slammed shut. If they went to the Travilah house in search of the mythical medication, there was a chance that something good might happen.

But then he remembered that Lupe would likely be at the house when they arrived. What would happen to her?

Nine

As Mort drove toward Gaithersburg to meet with Danni, Travis and whomever they had gathered, he felt some of his usual guilt. His agreement to J.J.'s plan for the engagement ring was undoubtedly the cause of J.J.'s disappearance, and it was happening when Travis was consumed with a triple murder case.

He called Danni on his cell phone, and she answered. "Doesn't Travis have enough on his plate with that triple killing?" Mort asked.

Danni snapped back. "A Supreme Court justice disappears on his watch—practically family, to boot. He's got a whole department to solve that other case. J.J. is special."

Mort didn't mention anything about the availability of the Supreme Court Police, the Capitol Police, the US Marshals, the Secret Service or the FBI. Danni and J.J. had a special bond between them ever since she'd clerked for him, then moved into his home to chauffeur him to court after he had broken his ankle. That, and the fact that her mother and J.J. were now a couple.

Mort's cell phone rang, and he saw the call coming from the WaPo.

"Ahrens," he said.

"Ahrens, Ginsberg here. Where are you right now?"

Mort almost crashed the car. Steven Ginsberg was the managing editor of WaPo. They had never actually met except the day Ginsberg had given an introductory pep talk to the staff after he was named to his position.

"Mister Ginsberg?" he stammered.

"Yes. Where are you? They tell me that you have some sort of personal relationship with Justice Richter. Correct?"

"Yes, through my fiancée. She used to be his law clerk. I was with him last evening, in fact."

"Last evening? Well, where the hell is he today? We got a tip that he's missing."

Mort was now in a state of panic. The word was out. Suddenly, he had to pee. He didn't say anything.

"Ahrens, are you still there?" Ginsberg asked.

"Yes, sir."

"Well, drop whatever you're doing and find him. I want you on this story. Capisce?"

"Yes, sir. I'm on it."

"And keep me informed. Report directly to me."

"Yes, sir."

"And it's Steven. We're not in the goddam army."

"Yes, si… Steven. Got it. And I'm on it."

Mort made a U-turn and headed back toward DC. He called Danni again, got her voice mail and left a somewhat incoherent message.

Ten

A Montgomery County patrol car entered J.J.'s property, slowly drove down the driveway and stopped near the porch. A young officer exited the squad and knocked on the door. Lupe opened the door, listened to a question and pointed at the garage. Connie, the golden retriever, watched listlessly.

"He always like that?" the officer asked.

"She most times bark like crazy, but today she dopey," Lupe replied. "I have to take her to the vent when we hear from the judge."

The officer went into the garage, looked around and then bent down in front of the 4x4. A puddle of oil was on the floor. He took off his gloves, dipped one finger into the fluid and smelled it. He stood up and walked out, got back into his patrol car and drove back up the driveway.

As he was about to exit the driveway, he stopped his patrol car and got out. An orange road cone was lying on its side. He bent down, fingered it briefly, then picked up a torn piece of white cloth. He got back into his car and radioed in.

"This is Dempsey at the judge's house." A pause. "No, patch me through to the chief. He wants to know about this." Another pause. "Chief, Roger Dempsey here, Patrol 6, at Judge Richter's property. His truck either leaked or was drained of oil, and there was an upended orange road cone, like they use during construction, just outside the grounds. I also saw a torn piece of white fabric which I left in case you want to call forensics. Oh, and the judge's dog is lying around like an overdose case. The maid said she's usually a great watchdog."

Travis had his phone on speaker. His office was crowded with four other officers and LeAnne, his administrative assistant. "Sounds suspicious—worth following up," he said, "unless J.J. surfaces very soon. You did good, Dempsey. I'm thinking it's time to call the FBI."

* * *

Back at his office, Mort took an address book out of his desk, thumbed through a few pages, picked up his office phone and dialed. He had never gotten used to keeping contact details on his phone. He preferred the old-fashioned system and only kept very important numbers on his speed dial.

He got a receptionist and said, "Special Agent Fisher," then "Mort Ahrens of the *Washington Post*." It took over a minute, but finally he was connected.

"Craig, Mort here… No, I'm fine, and it's not anything earth-shattering, but Justice Richter didn't show up at court this morning, which is very unusual for him, and everyone is in a tizzy. So I wondered if there was anything you might have heard?"

Fisher responded matter-of-factly. "They check all the usuals? Accident, hospital and so on?"

"In the process," Mort said, "but I thought you might have a thought. If not, I'd appreciate your keeping your ears open."

"He's up there in years, but a feisty guy. No secret liaisons you know of?"

"Not a chance. He and Chickie are like glue."

"I'll ask around, but don't count on anything coming from here."

"Just a thought. Let's you and Marjorie break bread one of these days."

"Just name it," Fisher said. "Our dance card is wide open. And we have a good sitter."

Mort's next call was to the public relations office at the Supreme Court. He hesitated before making the call, because Danni said she was heading to the court, but he decided to go ahead with a different tack. He had met Jennifer Harouche, the PRO, at the court on several occasions, thanks to Danni.

"Jennifer, Mort Ahrens here. I'd like to set up an appointment to speak with Chief Justice Treller about Justice Richter... assuming he doesn't surface soon."

"Mort, I don't think that's possible right now. We're in the last few weeks of the term, the place is crazy, and J.J. is not even officially missing."

"Assuming he doesn't show up by tomorrow... well, Danni's convinced he's been kidnapped, and it has something to do with the end of the term. I only need a few minutes of her time."

"I don't think it's possible, Mort. She doesn't have a minute to spare."

"I've been assigned to the story, Jennifer, and I'm just giving a heads-up. Won't look too good for the court if I write that the chief justice refused to make a statement about the disappearance of the senior associate."

After a prolonged silence, Jennifer said, "Give me a few minutes, Mort. I'll check with Her Honor."

While he was on hold, Mort pulled up some information about the NAWES case on his computer and scribbled some notes. Then he did a fast Google search for information on NAWES and its home location.

Jennifer finally came back on the line. "Mort, she can give you a few minutes first thing tomorrow morning. Be here at eight-thirty."

"Jenn, you're a doll, see you then."

* * *

Mort's next call was to the headquarters of NAWES, the National Association of Water & Environmental Security. NAWES was the lead plaintiff in the case contesting the authority of the Environmental Protection Agency and several other governmental agencies to impose restrictions and regulations on the use of water for the nation. NAWES was an amalgam of all the corporations in the energy industry and was funded handsomely by contributions from those organizations.

The President and CEO of NAWES was Winston "Win" Abbington. Win had recently focused the organization on water and the corporations that bought up and leased water sources and aquifers. He was also seeking to control the dwindling resource as it flowed from rivers and dams. When the corporation had been formed to represent the industry, Win had been elected as its president & CEO. Its headquarters was at the foot of Manhattan atop a high rise with a sensational view of the Narrows.

Mort called and asked for Abbington. After identifying himself and being passed through several other callers in the chain of command, he was directed to the chief financial officer, Ezekiel "Zeke" Shannon. Going through the retinue of callers reminded Mort of the procedures of his cable company when he called to seek a solution to a technical issue.

A crisp, abrupt voice came on the line. "Zeke Shannon here. What can I do for you, Mr. Abrams?"

"It's Ahrens, Mort Ahrens, with the *Washington Post.*"

"And?"

"I'm covering the disappearance of Justice Richter of the Supreme Court, and since your organization has probably the biggest case left on the Court's agenda, I'd like to interview your president, Mr. Abbington."

"Actually, we just heard about this a short time ago. But what has it got to do with us?"

"The case is monumental, and your organization is the lead plaintiff. It's a hotly contested issue, and Justice Richter was the deciding vote in the fracking case a few years back, so we'd like a short interview."

"Let me correct you," Shannon said. "We are no longer the plaintiff. We are the respondent, having won both times in the courts below. It's the government who's appealing. An oxymoron, by the way. And we have every expectation of winning this one in the Supreme Court as well. That old buzzard's presence or absence is of no moment to us."

"I stand corrected," Mort said. "But a short interview with your president would be appropriate."

"He's a very busy man," Shannon said. "I don't think he has the time."

Mort decided to use the same tactic he used with the Supreme Court press officer.

"That's fine," Mort said. "So I'll just quote you that the old buzzard's presence or absence is of no moment to you because you expect to win the case in any event. That should read well."

There was a brief pause, then Shannon said, "Interview on the phone, Zoom or in person?"

"I can hop the shuttle and be there tomorrow afternoon," Mort said.

"Four o'clock," Shannon replied before hanging up.

Eleven

Even with rush hour traffic, Danni got to Travis's office in Gaithersburg around four-thirty. The Montgomery County Police had moved into a new, state-of-the-art building a few years earlier. It enabled them to have the latest, fully-equipped forensics lab and much more. Travis was so proud of the facility that one Saturday, Danni and her mother, along with J.J. and Mort, all went to Gaithersburg to take the fifty-cent tour of Professional Accountability, Field Services, Investigative Services, Patrol Services, and finally the Office of the Chief. Travis had a habit of trying to know every officer—not an easy task with a force of almost 1300—and relished introducing J.J. as they walked around.

Travis's office was not only spacious but decorated by his wife, Michele, in pastel hues. It exuded executive comfort rather than the usual bland governmental utilitarianism. His large oak desk faced a cushioned sofa and three comfortable chairs. The walls were adorned with photos of him in military gear, one with a squad of soldiers, and in the middle a framed Congressional Medal of Honor. On the desk was a photo of blonde, blue-eyed Michele and two maple-sugar-skinned children around twelve and fifteen. Behind the desk, so he could swing his chair right to them, were two laptops with screens up.

Chief Deputy Jim Steves, Travis's admin LeAnne and Dan Harrington, the uniformed head of the dignitary protection unit of the Supreme Court Police were already gathered, along with three officers from Travis's command staff. They were deep into discussion about the triple murder.

Travis did the intros and asked, "J.J. still among the missing, then?"

Danni got right to the point. "I've been thinking about it driving over here, and I think he was kidnapped," she said.

"Kidnapped?" Steves said in amazement. "Who would kidnap a Supreme Court judge? And why?"

"He's a justice, not a judge," Danni said. "The term is winding down, there are only a couple of weeks left and only a few cases are undecided. The biggest case still on the docket is National Association of Water & Environmental Security versus the EPA. It's about water rights and the ability of the federal government to restrict private water use, to restrict or control corporations from polluting the rivers and from leasing all the groundwater that farmers need. The case is about the biggest challenge the world will face in this century—the use of our water."

"Water?" Steves was puzzled. "I didn't realize we had that big a problem."

"Tell that to the farmers whose aquifers and groundwater are getting polluted," she said. "Or to the downstream cities whose river water is full of waste and chemicals. Tell it to the fishermen who are finding their catch full of chemicals, to cities all over the country that are finding lead in the water from ancient pipes. Oh, and also, the aquifers are drying up. Without federal involvement, that will be a complete ecological disaster. Water is what the next world war will be fought over. And that's without getting into the problems caused by the drought."

"I guess I'm a little slow," LeAnne said, "but how would that lead to the kidnapping of a judge?"

"He's a justice," Danni said again. "He's the senior associate justice, and as I assess the court without J.J., it's divided 4–4. No doubt J.J. would vote with the progressives, which would mean the corporations and the industries would be subject to controls and measures that could cost them billions, even trillions."

"A trial judge might have enemies who would stoop to a kidnapping," Travis said. "But a Supreme Court justice? More likely a snatch for ransom, a mental case or someone out to settle a grudge. That's if you're right about a kidnapping, Danni, and that's also a stretch at this point."

"No," Danni said, "it's a mathematical certainty to me. As I look at the case, I see the court as 5-4 in favor of sustaining the ban on private use of water and the aquifers and implementing a bunch of well-needed controls. With J.J. out of the way, it's a tied vote."

"And?" said LeAnne.

"With the vote tied, the opinion of the circuit court prevails, and both the circuit court and the district court have held for the energy companies, lobbyists, the big money, industry—the vultures. That would mean they'd win, short of a reversal by the Supremes. There's only weeks left to the term, and it's the biggest decision remaining. One of the biggest in years. Maybe decades, based on its magnitude. This decision will impact our entire economy, the stock markets around the world, climate change... the works. I'm even debating it tomorrow night on CNN."

"Excuse my stupidity," Jim Steves said, "but what are you two talking about? We talking a court case or a kidnapping, or a disappearance, or what?"

"We're talking politics—and the law," Danni said. "The industry lost the fracking case 5-4 because of J.J.'s vote. But they recognized that the fight over water and water rights is the wave of our future, and they're in it with both feet. Follow the money."

"Fracking? I've seen a TV special on it," LeAnne said, "and there was that movie with that cute actor... what's his name?"

"*Promised Land*," Danni said. "Matt Damon."

"That's it." LeAnne said. "It was all about that."

Looking at Danni, Dan Harrington said, "Well, that leaves little doubt as to what side you'd be on, and you probably know J.J.'s feelings as well as anyone, but I'd never second-guess him." Harrington, in uniform with his Glock on his hip, towered over Danni. She was surprised to see him at Travis's office, but he had come knowing of the close relationship between Travis and J.J.

"I'd never second-guess him either," Danni said, "but I'd bet money on this one."

"And?" Jim said.

LeAnne said, "If the case is not decided, why don't they just adjourn?"

"Tradition," Danni countered. "The court has a tradition of deciding all the cases on the docket by the end of the term. Another reason, unfortunately, is politics. The chief judge, who controls the calendar, has an ultra-conservative background. The senate majority leader lives for corporate donations or anything that will line the pockets of one of the shell corporations that his family controls. The president is to the right of Genghis Khan. So where does that leave us? Gentlemen, two plus two equals four."

"And if a justice is missing?" Dan asked.

"The decision of the circuit court, the next highest court, prevails. And they've already decided for the industry, as did the lower district court," Danni said.

"Can't they substitute another judge if the case is tied?" LeAnne asked.

"Not that simple," Danni continued. "You can't do that in the Supreme Court. It has to be a presidential appointment confirmed by the senate, and that usually takes months. Remember the kerfuffle over Kavanaugh? Also, they can only name a new justice if there's a vacancy. Not because one justice is unavailable. I believe J.J. is the missing link, and that's why I think he's been kidnapped. Follow the money—as always."

They were interrupted by a knock on Travis's office door. LeAnne was in the office with them; there was no one at her desk.

"What?" Travis said, impatiently.

The door opened. There is a certain look that FBI agents have, as if it's in their DNA. Led by Tim Richardson, three crisp-looking men entered the room. They were stereotypes from central casting—dark-blue suits, conservative almost matching ties, dark shoes shined to a patent leather sheen. All three were dark-haired, thirtyish, around six feet tall with an air of authority and confidence bordering on smugness.

"FBI," was all Richardson said.

Travis turned to Danni and said, "I called them in. Patrol saw some weird stuff at the house."

Danni looked shocked.

Richardson stepped forward, and Travis rose from his desk, reached out and leaned over to shake his hand. "Tim Richardson, special agent in charge." He introduced the other two. "Special Agent Royce Malone and Special Agent Buzz Bergdahl."

"So, what have you got so far on Richter's disappearance?" Richardson asked.

"Nothing but curiosity, and Danni's suspicions that he might be kidnapped," Travis said. "Not much at this point. J.J. left for work but never showed up in court. There was a road cone near the entrance to his property."

"Well, before you get in too deep," Richardson said, "we'd like everything you've got, and we'll take it from here and run with it. Witnesses, forensics, whatever. I'll get a team out to inspect his property."

"I was just surmising," Danni said, "that with the end of the court's term only weeks away someone wanted J.J. out of the way for those final weeks. It's unlikely a grudge—that would be rare with an appellate justice, and it certainly wasn't random."

"Thanks, detective, and we'll certainly pursue that theory... among others," Richardson said.

"I'm not a detective."

"Then who are you?"

"Danni Rose, assistant professor at American University Law."

"Danni is very close with J.J. Like family," Travis said.

"All well and good," Richardson said, "and I'll certainly want to talk with her and anyone else close to the judge."

"Justice," Danni said impatiently. "He's an associate justice."

"Whatever," Richardson said. "We may have a serious federal crime here. You don't go around kidnapping a Supreme Court judge... sorry, justice."

They talked for a few more minutes, one of the agents took some notes and then Richardson said to Travis, "I'll want you to give us some background as well. But we'll get out of your hair now. I understand you're working a triple murder."

With that, Richardson handed his card to each of them and left with his agents.

Twelve

At Chickie's suggestion, she, Danni and Lupe were seated for dinner at J.J.'s home on the first evening of J.J.'s disappearance.

"I think that's Mort just pulling in," Danni said. "He was supposed to meet me at Travis's office but had to go back to his office. Must have been really important. I left a message for him to meet us here for dinner."

When Mort had met the unassuming Danni, he didn't know that she was the only daughter of a wealthy communications family. Chickie was now the president/CEO of Rosen-Billings and one of the most spirited and capable people Mort had ever met. Chickie was widowed when her late husband fell off an exercise machine one evening while they were vacationing in Puerto Bahia, Mexico. He'd bled to death, alone in the deserted workout room. So much for exercising at night. *Or exercising period*, was Mort's attitude.

Chickie had stepped in, taking over the company that operated TV stations all over the country and a bunch of radio outlets as well. The stock plunged the minute she stepped in but was now worth three times as much. She had guided it to become even more of a powerhouse in the media world. Mort had turned down the opportunity to step into that media world after he and Danni had drifted apart for a time, intent on a career in journalism.

When he and Danni got together in Washington, Mort hit it off immediately with Chickie, who accepted him—a pudgy, medium-height, non-athlete from a middle-class background—without question. The parents of all the previous women in his life had thought their "princesses" deserved a handsome All-American, or a doctor, at least. Not someone whose ambition in life was just to be a reporter. Not so with Chickie, though, who judged people based on her personal assessments. Even before he and Danni were engaged (without a ring), Chickie used to refer to Mort as her "friend-in-law," which made the process of pursuing Danni so much easier.

J.J. had been missing for almost fifteen hours by the time Mort bustled into the dining room with the apology, "Sorry I'm late."

"Did you find out anything?" Danni asked.

He nodded. "I found out I've been assigned to J.J.'s story by none other than the managing editor, if there is a story."

Chickie smiled approvingly. "Wow. Tells us what the importance of a missing justice is. And Mort, what a feather in your cap. Now all you have to do is find him—before the FBI does. I agree with Danni that J.J.'s been kidnapped."

"If Danni's theory is right," Mort said while sitting down in an empty chair, "there will be a ransom demand, and we'll have to meet it somehow. The president has this 'we don't pay ransom' policy. We'll get J.J. back, Chickie."

The president, who was no fan of J.J.'s liberal leanings, was probably just as happy as the right-wing media that J.J. was missing. J.J.'s untiring leadership of the court's progressive wing had been a pain in his ass more than once. There was no question he would refuse to pay ransom for the release of J.J. even though he had paid hackers for ransomware relief when some of the government departments had been hacked.

After dinner, the small group was flipping through the cable channels in search of breaking news when they stopped on Fox News. Its leading voice, Sean Tucker, who was everything in journalism that Mort detested, was comparing J.J.'s disappearance to that of Justice Joseph Crater in New York.

"Crater was a New York Supreme Court judge," Tucker said, "who disappeared in 1930 after dinner in a New York restaurant. Walked out the door and was never heard from again. He was rumored to be involved in a political scandal. I wonder what Justice Richter's story is."

"Bastard!" Chickie said, angrily switching off the TV. "But that's Fox."

"Consider the source," Mort said.

Without the distraction of TV, they began discussing all possible scenarios for uncovering the truth of what had happened, even ones including FBI involvement. Danni said she'd canvas the court, and Mort revealed that he had an appointment with the chief justice at eight thirty tomorrow morning.

Danni was miffed. "How did you manage that?"

Mort said, "Well, it's my story now. That's what good reporters do."

Chickie leaned forward and asked, "Have we thought about NAWES and the possibility that it might have had something to do with J.J. disappearing? I know, it's pretty hard to imagine they'd do anything that stupid."

"Stupid?" Danni said. "Stupid can be worth trillions. But I agree—it's hard to imagine that a corporation representing the entire industry would be involved in a kidnapping."

"I know Win Abbington," Chickie said. "He's even had some time on our stations. He's a sharp cookie. Mort, you might give it a thought."

"I've got a four o'clock with him tomorrow in New York."

"Good for you. Sounds like Sherlock is on the case," Chickie said.

Danni smiled and shook her head in astonishment. "Jesus, Mort! You touched a lot of bases in a very short time."

Chickie turned to Danni and asked, "You still leaving for England at the end of the week?"

"I'm not going anywhere right now."

Danni had accepted an offer to teach US First Amendment law for six weeks at the London School of Economics, which was a real coup for a young assistant professor, especially one whose bona fides at the law school were in environmental law. She figured that her two years as a law clerk to J.J. probably sealed the deal. She and Mort had already planned some trips around her schedule, with Mort taking a personal week off and then ferrying back and forth—"over the pond," as they say—for two weekends. But now with J.J. missing everything had changed.

Danni sighed and said, "I don't even want to go through with that CNN debate until we know J.J. is safe."

"No," Mort said. "Don't back out of the debate. It's the opportunity of a lifetime. You know J.J. and what he'd say if you didn't go through with it. You can't help him by bailing."

"Mort is right," Chickie said. "You should do the debate."

"Well, at least Travis said he'd make himself available as soon as possible to help find J.J.," Danni said. "And we'll have his brain to pick as well, which is probably better than having the FBI on the case."

Lupe needed company, so Chickie decided to spend the night with her at J.J.'s. Danni and Mort separately headed back to Georgetown.

As he was driving home, Mort's thoughts drifted back to Danni describing her first meeting with J.J. Richter in his chambers and the unusual clerkship year that followed, a year that had cemented their relationship. That seemed like ages ago, not just a few years.

Thirteen

After law school, Danni had clerked in the District of Columbia Circuit Court of Appeals for Simon Grover. At the end of her clerkship, she drummed up the courage to ask him for a Supreme Court reference.

"Where did you go to law school?" Grover asked, even though he knew the answer.

"Syracuse," Danni replied.

"And you're going to compete with the Yalies and the boys from Haaavaad?" he asked, dragging out the pronunciation of Harvard and then smiling. He was a graduate of Michigan Law and had made a similar challenge to the Ivies.

"I want to clerk for J.J. Richter," Danni replied.

Grover's thick eyebrows raised in surprise. "Might as well shoot for the top," he said. "Well, if there's one justice who's not 'class' conscious, you picked the right one. I'll be happy to do what I can."

A month later, she had fidgeted in the waiting room of Richter's chambers waiting for her interview. When at last she was ushered into J.J.'s office, she was surprised. The place was a mess of books and files strewn haphazardly—or so it seemed. Piles of odds and ends everywhere and a flannel jacket thrown over an arm of the couch. J.J. was lounging behind his desk in a western shirt, jeans and boots. He had already read Danni's recommendations.

"Syracuse, eh?" J.J. said. "Don't know that we've ever had a clerk from Syracuse."

"Well, we can boast about All-American Jim Brown, and the law school boasts about Joe Biden and a lot of great federal judges, but I'm ready to trade orange for brown and gold," Danni said. She was referring to the school colors of Syracuse and Wyoming, Richter's home state, where he'd attended both college and law school.

"Done a little research as well, I see." J.J. smiled. "Impressive."

"I'll even sing 'Ragtime Cowboy Joe' if you can stand it," Danni said, referring to the Wyoming school song.

"Please, no," J.J. said. "I'd be tempted to join you, and they'd escort us both out of the building." He switched gears. "What did you think of the decision in Plessey v. Ferguson?"

"Fortunately, it wouldn't fly today," Danni said. "Justice Harlan nailed it in his dissent—'The Constitution is color blind, and neither knows or tolerates classes among its citizens.'"

J.J. nodded and said, "I don't think I could have quoted that. But I'm not certain some of my peers in this court would agree with that statement."

Supreme Court clerkship interviews can take several hours. Danni had been in J.J.'s chambers about twenty minutes when J.J. said, "A couple of things you should know. In chambers, I'm J.J. and not any of this fancy 'Your Honor' crap. And second, if you touch any of these books or files without checking with me first, I'll have you tarred and feathered. You're hired, young lady." He thrust out his hand.

One, two, three—simple. But that was J.J.

"I understand you're a basketball player of note," J.J. had said, his eyes sparkling. "I play a little basketball myself. Think you could take me on?"

"I'd certainly give it a shot…" she said, "to coin a phrase."

"No dogging it," J.J. replied. "I want your best effort. We play right here in this building." He glanced upward and pointed at the ceiling.

"There's a basketball court here?" Danni said, with surprise.

"Highest court in the land," J.J. chuckled. "Top floor, right above the courtroom."

The "highest court in the land" had been an all-male domain when J.J. had joined the Supreme Court, but as women had also joined the court, it had been renovated, workout equipment had been modified and a second men's restroom had been converted to a women's locker room.

"Haven't found the woman who could beat me," J.J. said. "O'Connor wasn't a basketball player, but Sotomayer gave me a good run for my money. A lot of elbows. Learned on the playgrounds of Queens, she said."

"Well, that's where I learned," Danni said, "so we'll see about your perfect record."

Danni started her clerkship that August, but it was probably J.J.'s torn knee ligament that had contributed the most to their growing relationship.

The injury occurred on the basketball court one late afternoon while Danni and J.J. were playing one-on-one. J.J. lost his balance and crashed to the floor in pain, clutching his right knee. After a visit by the EMTs, he left the hospital two hours later with a medial collateral knee ligament tear and a cumbersome brace.

"I'll drive you home," Danni said. "You can't handle the accelerator and brake with that leg."

"You'll do no such thing," J.J. said. "And besides, I rode in on my Harley."

"No problem, do you have an extra helmet?"

"Don't tell me you can ride a bike too?"

"Okay, I won't tell you."

She stayed for dinner after getting J.J. safely home. "I can drive you to court every day until the knee is better," she suggested, as Lupe set another plate, eyeing the young woman suspiciously. The distrust lasted only until Danni offered to clear the table and help with the dishes.

"Don't you live in DC?" J.J. asked.

"Georgetown. No big deal."

"*Very* big deal," J.J. said. "But I'll take you up on that offer only if you move in for a few weeks until I'm back on my feet. I don't want you making double trips a day."

Danni moved into the spare room. For six weeks, J.J. enjoyed what he only imagined was the joy of a father whose adult child was still living at home, the joy that he and Meg had never experienced. Danni and J.J. would often discuss cases and court gossip, and sometimes personal issues too.

Finally, in his seventies, J.J. had become a father.

Fourteen

The president was sitting in his private office next to the Oval when Chad Kennedy, his chief of staff, entered after knocking. The president was watching Fox News and smiling. Apparently, one of the hosts had thrown a compliment to him or his administration.

He looked up. "Chad," he said, "what's the word?"

Chad Kennedy had been the president's chief of staff during his campaigns, and before that, when the president was governor of Indiana. Now in his fifties, Chad had made a fortune as an investment banker, and his holdings still included a substantial portfolio in the energy industry. He had always envisioned himself as the person sitting in the Oval Office, but the vagaries of politics had given the nomination and election to Sinclair Chester, who was a war hero, a farmer, and the current darling of the party's emergent right wing.

President Chester was seventy-two, trended toward obesity and was not the brightest bulb in the box, which suited Kennedy just fine. He envisioned himself as president *de facto*, and ultimately *de jure* somewhere down the line. In his mind, he was the impressionable president's brain.

"Blessing is here," he said. George Blessing had been director of the FBI for several months. He didn't have a law enforcement background, but he did have receipts for the two million he had donated to the president's last campaign.

"Show him in," the president said, then stood up and walked into the Oval.

An obviously flustered Blessing entered. His expensive suit looked as if he had slept in it. His tie was askew, and he was sweating.

"So," the president said, "what's the story on Richter?"

"Nothing so far," Mr. President, "but we've got fifty agents on it, and we're scouring every possibility."

Kennedy spoke up. "Fifteen hours and you have nothing… with fifty agents? Seems to me that an old codger in his seventies shouldn't be that hard to trace, especially with all the toys you've got at your disposal."

Blessing turned to Kennedy red-faced and said, "Well, if you've got any ideas, Kennedy, instead of your snotty inferences, I'd be happy to know them. The guy just up and vanished." He turned to face the president. "It's like an old-fashioned missing person's case. Not a clue so far except a road cone—and who knows if that's anything? No cell phone GPS. No motorcycle. No *nothing*."

The president held up his hand. "Let's not squabble. What's this about a motorcycle?"

"Richter's from Wyoming. Damn fool rides a Harley to the court half the time. Drives the other justices bonkers," Kennedy said.

"A motorcycle? He *is* an old fool. Must be close to eighty," the president said. "He'll turn up—somewhere. He's too feisty to be dead. But I bet it's a hell of a story. Ransom demand?"

"Nothing yet," Blessing said. "But if it's a kidnapping, it should have come by now."

"Maybe he just croaked in some sleazy hotel," the president said. "Maybe he just decided he'd had enough."

"Not a chance—not Richter," Kennedy said. He got in Blessing's face and said, "Put another fifty agents on it… a hundred. Whatever it takes."

"In the meantime," the president said, "it takes the attention off the stock market. Another bad day! Maybe he should stay missing."

Blessing nodded, glared at Kennedy and left without another word.

"What a buffoon," Kennedy said. "You should have made him an ambassador to some god-forsaken spot. He's way over his head. With all their resources, the FBI is shoveling shit against the wind."

The president sat down behind the Resolute desk and sighed. "I needed him in the election. At least I needed his money. And he wanted a plum. Doesn't the FBI have all kinds of electronic gear that we budget a fortune for?" the president asked.

"I take it they tried all that. And they're still without a clue. Whoever pulled this off knew all the tricks," Kennedy said.

"Well, maybe that old fart just took off with some chippie."

"Not likely," Chad said. "Especially not before the end of the term. No, it's a kidnapping. You can bet money on that."

"So where's the ransom demand? Makes no sense."

"Keep watching," Kennedy said. "We'll hear something soon, but either way you're going to come out a winner."

"How so?"

"The way I see it, if he's been killed—although I wouldn't shed any tears—you get to appoint a new associate justice, and we've got a slew of good conservative people salivating for that appointment—which, by the way, would definitely be the balance of power on the court. With Congress in tow, that means our agenda is safe. No sweating it out like we're doing in this water rights case. That one could turn the economy around."

"Even in my wildest dreams, I never imagined the water case had a chance. We shouldn't be taking government control of water or water rights. Leave it to the states, or private enterprise. Isn't that what the do-gooder lefties always want?" the president said. "When did everything get so mixed up?"

"You know the lawsuit and that legislation is left over from the last Congress," Kennedy said, "and we won it in the lower courts. But even if we lost that case, you'd be a hero because it would thrill all the environmentalists. If Richter is dead—even though I'm certain he's still alive—you get to make that next appointment. If he stays kidnapped for a couple of weeks, the Court will be tied four-four, according to what I hear. And then the lower court decision prevails. The chief judge will insist that the case gets heard this term."

"You know that?"

"Trust me. I know her well enough to know that."

"What about ransom?" the president asked. "Strange that there's been no demand if it's legitimately a kidnapping."

"I think there will be a ransom demand," Chad said.

"And?"

"We don't bargain with terrorists and kidnappers."

"Not even for a Supreme Court justice?" the president asked.

"That's your policy," Kennedy said, "and that policy pre-dates you. We follow precedent, Mr. *Prescedent*. Even for J.J. Richter." He smiled at his own remark.

"Not unless something fucks it up," the president said.

"Nothing's gonna' fuck this up. You're a winner, no matter how the coin flips."

Fifteen

In West Virginia, Mateos and Brian sat at a card table in the dining room above J.J., a meal from Angus and Ale spread out before them next to a burner phone.

"See how simple that was?" Brian said. "I just shoot food through the cutout in the door, and he slides the tray back. No muss, no fuss. And he's secure."

"Secure without his meds. He dies on us, there goes the money," Mateos said.

The burner phone gave a distinctive ring. Mateos picked it up, listened, and then said, "A ransom? How the hell am I supposed to do that without fingers pointing at us?"

Brian could hear shouting on the phone as Mateos pulled it away from his ear.

"All right, all right!" Mateos said. "We'll get it done. Somehow."

The "piece of cake" job promised by Mateos suddenly had some recipe problems. Now they had to figure out how to get a ransom demand publicized without drawing attention to themselves. They also had to get J.J.'s "experimental" medicine from his home. Ten million for each of them hung in the balance.

"I'll take care of the ransom demand," Mateos said. "You can get the medicine."

"Thanks a lot," Brian replied. "How 'bout we just switch that scenario?"

"No, you've got the layout down at the judge's place. I'll figure out the ransom demand."

"What am I supposed to do about the housekeeper?" Brian asked. "And the dog? And what if the cops or the FBI has the place staked out?"

"I doubt there's security. They know he's not there, and we know there's no surveillance cameras. For sure, the phones are tapped, but you can use the same method we did on the judge... and the dog, for that matter. It's only a housekeeper. Use propofol. If the dog is a problem, kill it."

"I'm not killin' no dog."

"You won't kill no dog, but you just killed those three young hoods? Jesus! Grow up, man. Just get it done."

"And who stays with the judge?"

"He'll keep for a few hours. He can't go anywhere. Stake his place out tomorrow, just in case," Mateos said.

Sixteen

Travis was at the Gaithersburg headquarters by eight on the morning of day two of J.J.'s disappearance. Jim Steves, the chief deputy, entered his office.

"Chief, you look like you didn't sleep."

"A triple homicide and a Supreme Court justice missing didn't make for a restful night."

"The FBI is on the Richter case, so let's just focus on that triple killing."

"Yeah, let's go over what we've got so far."

"You got to the scene, right?"

Travis nodded and said, "Here's what we know. Three gunshot victims, two got it in the head and one in the back. All dead when our officers got there. Three young guys."

"Who called it in?"

"Couple passing by in a car. They're clear. The woman was pretty shook up."

"Witnesses?"

"As of last night, none that we know of. The area's being canvassed now. Only building around was Pineview Senior Home, and most of them were asleep already."

"The senior home is the only inhabited spot?"

"Yep. A shopping center is just now going up."

"Night watchman?"

"Negative. Shack was empty." Travis scratched his chin. "I checked with the crime lab. They think the shooter was a pro, assuming it's only one shooter. Two were nailed right between the eyes, and the third one got two in the back just a couple inches apart. The shooter was good."

"Anything else?"

"They found a blood spot on the sidewalk away from the bodies. Took a scraping to see what they can make of it. And some feces, probably a dog, seemingly pretty fresh. Took a scraping, just in case. The guys found one shell casing, looks like a .357 hollow point. Other than that, just three dead young men."

"Just one casing? Sounds like the killer tried to clean up."

"Joe Driscoll of CID is out there now with some of his people. We'll see what they can come up with. Crime Scene took the wallets of the three young men, who appeared to be dark-skinned Caucasians. A quick search showed all three had minor records—petty theft, burglary, DUIs—nothing more serious. One had a warrant out for failure to show up in court on a traffic case. Between them, they had eighty-seven dollars in their wallets and a few credit cards. They all had cell phones, and we're working those now to see if there's anything there. We brought the car in, and forensics is going over it."

"Could be they were thinking about hitting the construction shack, or planning for something in the future."

"If so, they were too early to burgle and too late to live. Bad judgment all around. But somebody was sure pissed at them."

* * *

Travis was still in his office two hours later, when Lt. Joe Driscoll came in.

"I think we might have an eyewitness, Chief," Driscoll said.

"*That* would be refreshing," Travis said. "What's the story?"

"Old guy from the home claims he was an eyewitness, out walking his dog on the deserted street. Says the three victims were trying to rob him when a Good Samaritan shows up, pulls a gun and offs all three of them. Says the shooter was African American, driving a van, and got out when the old guy was being hassled. Then he shot all three, told the old man this was his lucky day and to go home and say nothing. Got back in his van and drove off."

"Jesus," Travis said, "that's quite a story. And the killer just drove away?"

"That's what the old guy says. Anyway, I brought the guy in to see if he can ID anyone from our mug books. The rest of my guys are out there interviewing residents. The manager of the senior home viewed our photos of the bodies... almost passed out but didn't recognize any of them."

"Where's the witness?"

"In the waiting room with LeAnne. Nervous as hell."

"Bring him in and let's have a listen."

"He also had a knife with what looked like dried blood on the blade. He had the good sense to wrap it up in plastic and said he hadn't touched the blade. I dropped it off at forensics on the way here."

Driscoll walked out and returned with a diminutive Black man with a cane, probably in his sixties. He was wearing jeans and a yellow polo shirt. Two uniformed officers stood nearby. The man fidgeted and shrank back when he saw Travis, eyes as wide as serving bowls.

"Chief, this is Mikey Washington," Driscoll said. "He's the maintenance man at the home and lives in a basement apartment."

The old man, pulling himself up to his full height, blurted out, "Where were you last evening?"

Travis said, "Excuse me?"

"The shooter," Washington said. "He looked just like you, but he wasn't in uniform."

"I'm the chief of police," Travis said, smiling, "and I have an alibi."

"Well, he sure looked a lot like you," Washington said. "I was taking Matilda for her evening walk. The residents can't have dogs, but I can have one. Everybody loves her."

"I'm sure," Travis said, rolling his eyes.

"There's never anyone around at night, and they—those three punks—were driving by and then stopped. They were trying to rob me. Wanted my wallet and cell phone. I don't even have a cell phone! I took a swing at the big one with my cane, and all of a sudden you... I mean the guy who looked like you, pulls up in a van, jumps out and grabs the big one. The other one stuck him—the driver— with his knife. And the brother pulls a pistol and bam, bam, shoots all of 'em, even the third one, by their car."

Travis saw the old man's hands trembling as he relived the event.

Washington continued. "He checks to see if I'm okay, then tells me to forget the whole thing. Just like that. Told me not even to report it. 'Just go home,' he says. Somebody will find the bodies. Said he was just a Good Samaritan, my guardian angel, and if anyone ever found out, to say that he was the one being robbed, and he shot them. That way I wasn't involved, except as a witness. The guy with the knife dropped it when he was shot, and I picked it up and took it home. I put it in a poop bag," he said. "Rolled it in there with my cane. To preserve the evidence, like I seen on TV, and... he saved my life. That driver did. The big guy stabbed him before he was shot, but this Samaritan guy said it was nothing. Lifted up his shirt and showed me. Probably saved Matilda's life too."

Confused, Travis asked, "Matilda?"

"The dog," Driscoll said. "I questioned her, and she backed up the story."

Washington looked at him like he was crazy. Driscoll couldn't suppress a smile.

Travis ignored Driscoll and looked at the witness. "You didn't call 911?"

Washington looked down at the floor, embarrassed. "No. I was afraid I'd get in trouble, so I did like the brother said. Besides, I was so scared I didn't clean up Matilda's poop. I don't know who called, but later I saw all the cop cars."

"I understand," Travis said, "and you've done us a great service."

Travis turned to Driscoll. "If this checks out, we're looking for a dark-skinned African-American over six feet tall who has a pistol."

Travis opened his tunic and lifted up his shirt so Washington could see he had no stab wound.

Washington smiled and shook his head. "Boy, he sure looked like you."

Travis said, "And don't worry. You won't get in trouble for not picking up Matilda's poop. You might even be in line for a citizen citation."

Washington beamed.

"What kind of pistol, if you know?"

"I watch a lot of TV. It wasn't a revolver. It was one of them automatics."

Seventeen

Mort was at the Supreme Court before eight, but even at that early hour several protestors with placards were marching back and forth in front of the building. Mort looked up at the legend chiseled over the eight marble pillars above the long stairway: "Equal Justice Under Law." To Mort, it represented more than a building. It was the embodiment of the Constitution and of democracy itself.

Stanchions were embedded in the sidewalk as a deterrent to terrorists, and visitors could no longer gain entrance through the giant doors at the top of the stairs. He walked around to the east entrance, had his credentials checked by the female Supreme Court Police officer at the door, checked his laptop, got a receipt and proceeded to the second floor.

He was looking for the office of Brendan Braddock, marshal of the Supreme Court Police, the chief security officer whose unit of 145 officers were charged with protection of the justices and the court building. Braddock's office was tucked away on the second floor. Mort had met him on several occasions when he was with Danni.

Braddock was uniformed, about five-ten, and looked younger than his sixty years. After shaking hands with the marshal, Mort got the feeling that the man was nervous, upset. Maybe everyone was, with J.J. missing.

"J.J., he's the best of the bunch," Braddock said. "This has gone too far."

"Too far?"

"I mean, you can't go around kidnapping a supreme. They're the untouchables."

"I managed to get a few minutes with the CJ," Mort said.

"I heard. Figured you'd stop here first." Danni had been a favorite of Braddock's when she clerked for J.J., and she had probably called him.

"Surprised that the CJ has time for anybody, this being so close to the end of the term and with the FBI all over the place because of J.J.," Braddock said.

"Power of the press."

Constance Treller, the chief justice, was serving her sixth year. She was not only the first woman CJ but also the most openly-avowed conservative to be selected for that position. There had been, and were, other conservative justices, but none who served as chief justice. Even John Roberts had been more moderate.

As Mort and Braddock walked to Treller's chambers, Braddock disclosed he was leaving the court at the end of the term.

"Retiring?" Mort asked.

"Not voluntarily," Brendan replied. "I hit the mandatory goodbye age. Already had one bump to get me to sixty. God knows what I'll do after this, with the expenses I have. One daughter is in rehab at an expensive facility, and the other has spina bifida. Wife passed."

"That's more than anyone should have on their plate," Mort said. "Can't you continue the medical coverage?"

"Oh, sure," Brendan said. "FEHB is good until sixty-five, but it'll be coming out of my pension, and then I'll be thrown onto Medicaid or Medicare or whatever. The drug costs alone will kill me."

They were ushered in to a somber-faced Constance Treller, who pointed to the chairs facing the desk in her massive office. "Mort," she said, "so nice to see you. But not under these circumstances. Give my best to Danni. How is she holding up?"

"You know Danni. Tough outside. Inside she's a wreck."

"All of us are. How could he just disappear like that? By the way, wish her good luck in her TV debut tonight. She's up against a very accomplished opponent."

"CJ," as J.J. invariably called Treller, was a handsome woman—tall, angular, with soft hazel eyes. She looked like she would be comfortable in the saddle, which, given her background and former life in Arizona, was not far from the truth. Her hardscrabble family had toiled on a small ranch until a smelly, black liquid had bubbled up on the range one day. They became, in less than a decade, one of the wealthiest and most politically powerful families in the state. The American success story.

Treller was a woman who rode a horse, became a crack shot with a rifle, enjoyed hunting, possessed a keen sense of the political winds, yet retained her femininity. She had married the governor's son while both were in law school and rapidly showed her skills—in law, in controlling her husband's life and in politics. Good fortune and good planning had been key factors in Treller's life. She ruled the court with a strong and steady hand.

The chief was wearing beige slacks and a raspberry cashmere sweater, her silvering auburn hair pulled back into a bun. From a thin gold chain around her neck hung a pendant of justice, blindfolded.

It was Mort's turn to speak. "I'd just like a few minutes to question the other members of the court, and particularly staff, for the *Post*... to see if anyone can shed any light on J.J.'s disappearance."

"Out of the question, I'm afraid," Treller said with a thin smile. "The FBI has already been here twice, with a flotilla of agents. They already did that. And they were very specific about not granting interviews. I'm afraid I can't give you permission. There is no one who has more respect for J.J. than I do, as you know. He's been both a friend and a mentor to me."

"And if he's not found by the end of the term?"

"We've decided many cases with eight justices... where one member was not voting or incapacitated. We can't let one event stand in the way of the court doing its business. I hate to say it, but the structure of the court is more important than any one justice, even Justice Richter. I'm certain, knowing J.J., that he would concur."

"But what if one of those remaining cases might turn on his vote?" Mort asked.

Mort could see Treller's cheeks reddening almost to the color of her raspberry sweater.

Treller snapped, "No one, myself included, knows how the final votes will go. The decisions of the court and its internal procedures, as you well know, are sacrosanct. We had one incident recently with a leaked draft opinion, and it became a national outrage. We *cannot* speculate," and she emphasized *not*, "and we *will not*. That is not a matter of discussion. In any event, I'm certain the FBI will solve this mystery."

The conversation quickly ended. After Mort and Braddock were ushered out, they headed back toward Braddock's office.

"The wheels of justice," Mort said, "don't even slow down for a senior justice who suddenly disappeared. That's bullshit. Pardon my French."

"Mort, she's also a good politician, otherwise she wouldn't have insisted to the other justices when they met yesterday that the court calendar will be cleared by the end of the term, with or without J.J."

Mort's eyes widened at that remark.

Braddock stopped walking, then leaned closer to him, whispering. "She never thought Justice Everson would side with J.J., but that was the 5-4 J.J. needed in the water rights case."

"Are you saying, Brendan, that with J.J. unavailable, not present, the NAWES case is locked at 4-4?"

Brendan looked embarrassed, glancing around. "I'm saying… that I've already said too much and should learn to keep my mouth shut. Please don't repeat that or put it in your story. That was off the cuff. Just my speculation."

* * *

Mort left the Supreme Court before nine and tried to piece together the previous conversation with Brendan Braddock. He wasn't due in New York until four that afternoon, so he headed toward Reagan International, spotted a diner and called Danni from a booth while he ordered breakfast.

Danni was still in Georgetown preparing for her TV debate when she took his call. "You certainly couldn't have been at the court very long," Danni said.

"Long enough to get a good quote from the CJ, which I don't think she realized making. The FBI put a lid on the court, so I couldn't see anyone else. But I'm very curious about a couple of Brendan's statements. For one thing, he said the court was tied on the NAWES vote until Everson adopted J.J.'s reasoning and made it 5-4. And he said Treller had met with the court yesterday afternoon and said that they were going to clear the docket with or without J.J."

Danni reacted angrily. "There's no way he could know either of those things! Not even the clerks know what goes on inside the Black Box."

"Black Box?"

"The conference room. The inner sanctum where the justices meet to go over the cases, fortify their positions, argue the law. No one is in there with them—no clerks, no laptops, no staff. Just the nine justices."

"Maybe someone has a loose tongue," Mort said. "One of the law clerks or such."

"There's no way," Danni said. "They're in the dark. You know they have a code of honor, a wall of silence, a *steel* wall. There's no way Brendan could have known."

"Well, he got embarrassed and backtracked, said he was just speculating."

"I certainly hope so," Danni said. "That is very disturbing talk. He couldn't possibly know those things."

"Anyway, Treller wished you good luck at the debate. If I'm not back from New York, I'll catch it later. Love you."

Eighteen

Before heading to New York for his next interview, Mort researched NAWES and Win Abbington. He learned that the corporation was an amalgam of giant companies interested in locking up control of water and water rights not only in the United States, but eventually throughout the world. NAWES recognized that diminishing supplies of water, drought, the melting of glaciers and global warming were not only a burgeoning problem but the challenge of the future. This meant that water rights and distribution was the future's growth industry.

The US government, for one, saw the monopolization of water rights as a danger to society and antagonistic to its Constitution. Win Abbington had been prescient in that regard, studying the likely future and closely following the water supply and its diminution.

Abbington had waged a battle to increase fracking rights, which his company had lost in the Supreme Court. He then had turned his eyes toward the next likely source of energy—wind and solar power— and was very successful. Companies around the world recognized his ability to see the next problem and be the first to attack it.

His next move was to control water and water rights. He accurately predicted that this was the next challenge. He established NAWES and successfully recruited membership from the leading energy companies, which readily participated and contributed huge sums of money to corner the market. The Environmental Protection Agency and several other governmental agencies implemented rules and regulations to not only protect environmental needs but individual rights. To combat this, NAWES sued the US Government. The lawsuit had wound its way through the courts and ultimately arrived at the Supreme Court.

The government claimed it was within its rights to implement regulations, since groundwater, flowing water and rivers were not only essential to the people, but also crossed and intersected state lines. The government contended that the Commerce Clause of the Constitution was the controlling instrument. The NAWES position was that under the Tenth Amendment to the Constitution the matter should be controlled by individual states and not the federal government. NAWES prevailed in both the US district court and the circuit court of appeals, where its claims were sustained by a split decision. Now the case was before the US Supreme Court.

Whatever the decision, it would be one of the most monumental ones in years involving trillions of dollars. It would impact economies for generations.

* * *

Mort caught the United shuttle from Reagan International to Newark Liberty International, and on the short flight he perused the material he had printed out on NAWES and their CEO, Winston "Win" Abbington.

Under NAWES, hundreds of companies were involved with buying up rights, leasing, or otherwise controlling aquifers and river flow. Hundreds. Under Abbington's leadership, NAWES had gobbled up many of the little guys and was in a position to play a major role in controlling how water was not only distributed, but to whom. All this in a time of shrinking glaciers and expanding world-wide droughts.

Mort was awed at Abbington's financial wizardry. But he also concluded that Abbington was too smart to have any hand in J.J.'s disappearance.

When Mort arrived in Newark, he took the Air Train to lower Manhattan. He had time to pick up several of the New York dailies. Even the *Times* and *The Wall Street Journal* had prominent stories about J.J.'s disappearance and its long-term ramifications. Was he kidnapped for ransom, the victim of a hit, or was there a nefarious reason in his personal life that prompted him to disappear, as Fox News had suggested?

The FBI reluctantly held a press conference in the early afternoon. "We are following up every lead, interviewing witnesses and investigating every piece of evidence," its formal statement read. Translation—they didn't have a clue and were treading water.

The NAWES offices were on the twenty-third floor overlooking the Narrows. After being ushered in by an admin, Mort could see across the water to New Jersey, and in another direction, the Verrazano Bridge and the Atlantic. The Statue of Liberty was visible in the distance.

Abbington's office was gigantic but stark, almost sterile. The gleaming desk was bereft of clutter, but some files rested on a Perigold pedestal conference table with eight chairs. Mirrors reflected the Hudson. On a huge globe, red pins marked the corporation's partners. The only continent devoid of pins was Antarctica. Only one picture hung on the wall. Mort recognized it as Marc Chagall's *Blue Circus,* its bright and dazzling colors a vibrant contrast with the office décor.

Abbington was a striking six-foot-two with a patch over his left eye. He had lost his eye in a traffic accident in Great Britain, in which his fiancée had died. He was wearing a bespoke pin-striped Zegna striped suit over a white French-cuffed and monogrammed linen shirt, a dashing Pangborn tie and patent leather black boots. Mort felt like Cinderella at the ball.

Abbington thrust out his hand and gave Mort a firm handshake.

Mort said, "I appreciate your seeing me on such short notice."

"Don't give it a thought," Abbington said. "The disappearance of one of the SCOTUS pack is inconceivable, though I don't think we can be of any help to you."

"Just wanted to touch all the bases and to see if you had a statement, since you've got that big case still pending before the court."

"I better call in my consigliere," Abbington said, "to make certain I don't say anything untoward." With that, he walked to his desk and pressed a button on the side of his desk. Then, he pressed it twice.

A rumpled man around forty, whose appearance Mort immediately related to, entered the room without knocking. He was clutching a piece of paper.

"This is Boris Rosenthal," Abbington said, "or as some would say, my brain. Boris, this is Mort... I'm terrible on last names... from the *Washington Post*."

"Ahrens," Mort said.

"Lonsman?" Boris asked after giving Mort a good looking-over.

"I plead guilty," Mort said, somewhat surprised.

Abbington looked on, mystified. Boris turned to him.

"A term of endearment," Boris said, "between members of the tribe."

With that, a third man entered the room. He reminded Mort of the FBI agents he had met during his career—tall, neat, polished, with a certain smugness about him. He smelled of too much after shave and had eyes like the slits of a gun turret. Ezekiel "Zeke" Shannon was the corporation CFO. He had a Navy Seal Team 6 emblem in the lapel of his grey suit.

"We talked yesterday," Shannon said curtly. "You really wasted a day coming here. As I told you yesterday, we have nothing to hide about that judge's disappearance. I can guarantee you he's not in our vault."

"As I told Mr. Abbington, I just like to touch all the bases," Mort said.

"It's just Win," Abbington said.

"Well, on this one, you struck out," Shannon said. "We have nothing to say, other than that we have no knowledge."

"Not quite," said Boris, handing over the paper in his hand to Mort. "Just a short statement from Win about how upsetting this disappearance is and an offer to render any assistance that we can."

"Unnecessary," Zeke snapped. "We should just keep our name out of it altogether. The FBI will find an answer, one way or another. They even showed up here yesterday—God knows why —and we told them the same thing."

"Zeke is our enforcer," Win said, trying to lighten up the conversation. "He did the whole Iraq and Afghanistan thing. Check out his office, and you'll see an awesome display of medals. From sharpshooter to Silver Star. He is really a genius with the books, in addition."

"Just lacking a sense of humor," Boris said, shooting a look at Zeke.

Zeke retorted, "I hope Boris said we win this case hands down in that statement of his. No question about that, according to the boy genius. With or without the famous J.J. Richter. And he's always right. Except, of course, when he's wrong, like in the *fracking* case."

Mort thanked them for their time and decided it was time to leave. The tension between Boris Rosenthal and Ezekiel Shannon was palpable.

Nineteen

When Mort got back to Reagan National, he headed straight for his office. In less than an hour he had completed his article, but now he had to run it by Steve Ginsberg. Mort had quoted Chief Justice Treller, described the somber mood at the court and had a colorful description of his time in New York bolstered by the prepared statement from Boris Rosenthal and the clueless FBI press conference.

"Good stuff," Ginsberg said, "but there's got to be a clue out there somewhere. And still no ransom demand. Do you think whoever grabbed him possibly killed him?"

"And face the death penalty? I don't think so. Danni, my fiancée, who knows the situation as well as anyone, thinks it has to do with one of the few remaining decisions at Scotus. Probably the water regulation case."

"Well," Ginsberg said, "work that angle, and let's hope tomorrow is a better day."

Mort and Danni were staying at J.J.'s to give Chickie a break, so he headed to Travilah to watch Danni's debate on CNN, which was quite a feather in Danni's cap. To have it moderated by Wolf Blitzer was something else. Danni was an assistant professor at American University Law specializing in ecological issues. The debater on the other side was a full professor, Cecil Barker, from Georgetown Law.

Blitzer did the usual intros and then explained the debate and the ground rules. "The biggest case still pending before the Supreme Court," he said, "is the National Association of Water and

Environmental Security—known by the acronym NAWES—versus The Environmental Protection Agency and others. The Supreme Court traditionally holds the decisions on its biggest cases until the end of the term, which is only a few weeks off.

"We're all aware of the environmental problems the nation has been facing—devastating fires in the West and Midwest, with incredible rains and flooding in the South and East. On top of that, drought has ravaged large areas. The thirst for water, if I can use that phrase, has become critical. And it's a condition that's becoming worldwide.

"On the one hand the government, through the EPA several years ago, and with the participation of the Department of the Interior, implemented regulations governing the use of water and its distribution throughout the nation. The industry—the water industry—brought a lawsuit contesting the right of the government to do this, stating that it had overreached its authority, and that any rules or regulations should be left to the states where the water is found, including rivers flowing through those states. The United States District Court in Utah upheld that argument by the plaintiffs, NAWES. That lower court decision was ultimately upheld in a divided decision in the United States Circuit Court of Appeals, Tenth Circuit, in Salt Lake City, and now, several years later, the final decision is pending before the US Supreme Court.

"Professor Rose, who clerked for Senior Associate Justice J.J. Richter in the Supreme Court, who unfortunately has been mysteriously missing for several days, will argue the position of the government. Professor Barker, who clerked some years ago for Associate Justice Anthony Battaglia of the Supreme Court, will argue the position of the respondents, who were the original plaintiffs—the industry that was successful in the courts below.

"Of course, the disappearance of Justice Richter, the senior associate on the court, is another factor to be considered in this important case. And so, immediately following the debate, we have scheduled a special half-hour program on all the ramifications to be considered if one of the justices is unable to participate. It will be led by Neal Katyal, former assistant solicitor general of the United States, and a panel of experts. So stay tuned following the debate. By coin toss, Professor Rose will go first, for three minutes, and then Professor Barker will respond. After each question, the rotation will switch. If there is nothing further, Professor Rose..."

Danni dove right in.

"There is no environmental issue facing us as important as our need for water—in every phase of life—to live, to grow crops, to manage the environment. We cannot exist without water, and I predict that, God forbid we ever fight another world war, it will be over water and water rights. That said, the control of our nation's waters, our aquifers, our rivers, is a national problem, especially in a time of climate change. Water is truly an international problem, as we share numerous waterways with other nations, such as Canada and Mexico.

"The Department of the Interior, which controls our government lands, wisely banned some of the water extraction procedures on those lands. But corporations, like the respondent NAWES in this case— which represents a consortium of large corporations seeking to control the use of water for profit—have leased lands from farmers, ranchers and even in some urban areas, and it had paid handsome sums for the drilling rights to the water under those lands. They have also sought to divert water from our rivers for profit.

"The Environmental Protection Agency responsibly got involved, with the cooperation of the Department of the Interior and the Bureau of Reclamation, which is an agency of the department. They issued rules and regulations to level the playing field and control this drilling and water-diverting practice—both on land, on our rivers and in the aquifers far beneath the surface. The EPA imposed tight standards to stop this practice and protect us all. They did so under the Commerce Clause of the Constitution, which controls the right to regulate commerce between the states, and of course these agencies and the EPA are an arm of government—*ipso facto*, of Congress, which has an unquestioned authority to step in in matters of environmental emergency, such as the diversion and utilization of water between the states.

"As we speak tonight, the drought-plagued Colorado River has forced water cutbacks and rationing to farmers in Arizona, leaving crops unplanted and bleak future prospects. The Great Salt Lake is shrinking, threatening disastrous consequences, and California has been forced to ration water usage. Lake Mead is at its lowest level in history."

At this point Blitzer rang a gong and raised his hand to signal time was up.

Cecil Barker was a beefy, well-known champion of conservative causes, and he was ready to do battle. His grey eyes sparkled over fleshy cheeks, and he pointed fiercely at Danni as he began his attack with derision.

"*Assistant* Professor Rose," he said, positioning Danni, a decade his junior, in the position of David to his Goliath, "suffers from the vibrant energy of youth but neglects to place any emphasis on the fact that *two* federal courts have already found her arguments untenable. And as to the Commerce Clause, its relevance to disputes involving the states primarily focuses on navigable waterways, *not* on the rights of farmers and landowners to control their own lands.

"Indeed, the Tenth Amendment to the Constitution clearly states that 'powers not delegated to the United States are reserved to the states respectively, or to the people,' and I believe I quoted it verbatim. But nowhere does that revered document state that the government, or its agencies such as the EPA or the Department of the Interior, have the right to intervene, or interfere with, a citizen's or a state's use of its water rights.

"While the progressives may not like that concept—although they profess to be the champions of the individual—that is the long-settled law. The government has overstepped its authority here, and the Supreme Court should do—dare I say *must* do—what the learned courts below have already decreed and find for the respondents here."

Danni couldn't contain herself any longer, and said, "I may be younger than you, Professor, but I would never have the gall—the chutzpah—to tell the Supreme Court what it *must* do."

At this point Blitzer intervened and asked the next question to Barker, and so it went for an hour, back and forth, with neither debater giving an inch. Danni scored points by raising the Colorado River

Compact of 1922, which governs water rights for the seven states affected by the compact, and which really controls irrigation not only in the Southwest but as far as the river delta in Mexico.

Barker countered that it was an archaic document that was no longer relevant in modern society. He pointed out that efforts were ongoing to amend or replace it. They battled over the Klamath Project, the rights of Indian tribes—whose treaty guarantees to fish and hunt were being decimated by water scarcity—over an article in the *New York Times* in which a fifth-generation farmer said it was better business to sell his water than grow his crops (which Barker described as anecdotal), and they differed over the reasons that Corcoran, California, is suffering from subsistence, or sinking, at an alarming rate.

In their summations, Barker went first. Both reiterated their positions and the importance of the upcoming Supreme Court decision. Danni closed with, "So under your concept, Professor, it's perfectly OK for a state like Arizona to go to Minnesota and attempt to buy five hundred million gallons of water from an aquifer as though they were making a purchase in a supermarket. Fortunately, they were stopped legislatively. No, water rights are a national problem, and the only way we can deal with those rights equitably is with federal intervention so we will not be in a position where corporate robber barons can drain our lifeblood—our water."

* * *

Mort and Danni watched the replay while sitting up in bed. "Dynamite finish," Mort said. "You scorched his ass."

She gave him a sideways glance. "I love it when you're so articulate."

"What's true is true."

"You just want the favors of my body," she said, "and you'd say anything for it."

He leaned over and kissed her—a long, soft kiss. Then she reached back and switched off the light.

Twenty

On the morning of day three, Mateos Panopoulos answered the burner phone by yelling, "What?"

The response was harsh. "Who the hell are you barking at?"

Mateos immediately softened his tone. "Oh, I thought it was Brian again calling from the location. They have a cop stationed there. Which raises another problem."

"Listen, I think we made a big mistake in not making a ransom demand right away. That would have made it look more like just a kidnapping."

"*We* made a mistake? You're the one calling the shots."

"Well, the problem is yours as well. Your pot of gold is at the end of this rainbow."

"Yeah, I'll just snap my fingers."

"I already told you once. I don't want to have to tell you again. Figure it out! Just get a demand out there. Big bucks. Now, what's the other problem?"

"Apparently the old man has some experimental heart drug that he needs every day, and two other prescriptions."

"So?"

"So the only place we can get the experimental drug is from his home."

"Tell Brian to make it happen. There's only the housekeeper. Deal with it."

"That's *all*?"

"Time to earn your money. Get that ransom demand out there right away. Ask for fifty million—that should open a few eyes. Get it to the FBI, the media. I sure as hell can't do it. Get it done. And switch burners!"

The line went dead. Mateos stared at the phone and said to no one, "Thanks. I couldn't have figured that out." This was getting far more complicated.

Mateos Panopoulos and Brian Abernathy had the world by the tail. Until the world got away. They had been two of the top officers in the presidential detail of the Secret Service.

Mateos, a former tennis pro and a handsome six-foot-three, and Brian, an inch shorter and a former college football star a hundred pounds heavier, lived the good life. Their Secret Service brethren derisively called them the "Oreo Brothers."

Posted to the presidential protection division, they were charged with arranging security and almost every other aspect of presidential trips, especially those out of the country. They had become inseparable friends and were regaled after they broke up a forgery ring run by a crime family. In a spectacular shoot-out, Mateos saved the life of an agent who had been shot in the throat by stemming the wound with his hand and a plastic cup until a medical team arrived.

But after that, something bad happened. The president had an international meeting in Cartagena, Colombia, and the Oreo Brothers led the advance team, securing the airport, hotel and scheduled locations. Afterward, they finally got to relax for a night out. Having picked up some feminine companionship in a local bistro, Brian, who had fallen asleep after too much tequila, refused to pay his new lady friend for services rendered because, he claimed, no services had been rendered. She had a screaming fit, the police arrived and the two agents were quickly cashiered from the service for causing an international incident. The media had a field day.

After they'd returned to DC, being too young to access their pensions, they partnered in a detective agency, but pickings were slim. They were living an ongoing financial struggle until they were solicited for a job which could put ten million dollars each into offshore accounts in the Cook Islands. All they had to do was kidnap a Supreme Court justice and hold him captive for a week or ten days until the court session ended. Then, after being set for life, they would release their prisoner and disappear.

When they were approached for the job, Mateos suspected either a setup or some jokester pulling their chain. Though risky, it sounded too good to be true. "Why us?" Mateo wanted to know.

The answer was, "You come well recommended. I've got friends in high places, very high places. I'm willing to meet with you—*only* you—and my good faith will be demonstrated in greenbacks."

The Oreo Brothers decided to have Mateos meet the contact at night in the parking lot of a hotel in Baltimore. The man was tall and muscular. A pulled-down hat and a Covid-type mask obscured his identity.

While Mateos couldn't make out most of the man's features, he had no trouble savoring the cash that he was handed. One hundred thousand dollars.

"Seed money," the man said, "and nobody gets hurt. That's a requirement." With that he handed Mateos a bag of burner phones and disappeared into the night.

Mateos was all in, but Brian wasn't buying it.

"Kidnapping? A Supreme Court judge? That's nuts. It's also twenty years in stir. And if something goes wrong and the judge dies, it's the death penalty. This is insane! Besides, you don't even know who this guy is talking about. I'm definitely not in if the judge is a woman, and I don't think I'm in on this anyway. Period."

"Ten million for ten days. A piece of cake. We snatch and babysit and have no worries for the rest of our lives. No stress, no mess. We'll find out who the black robe is before the snatch in time to set it up and do some surveillance. It's not a woman. He said so," Mateos lied.

"You're an idiot, Mateos."

"You want to struggle for the next twenty years? Bullshit. We can do this. We're having a hard enough time meeting the rent, for Chrissake. And if you're out, I guarantee I'll find someone else. No problem."

"You'd do that?"

"Hell, Brian—if you want to play detective for the rest of your life and worry about where the next case will come from, be my guest. This sort of thing comes along just once in a lifetime. It's something we can handle without raising a sweat."

Mateos picked up the stack of fifties, cut it in half and handed Brian fifty thousand.

Brian took the money. "How are you so sure you can trust this guy? You don't even know who the hell he is."

"We're meeting again in a few days," Mateos said. "He's going to have everything down on paper. Proof. Untraceable bank accounts in the Cook Islands. Payable upon delivery. We'll have the access code to the accounts. Obviously, whatever is going down is worth billions to him. And it's worth ten million for each of us. It sounds too easy because it is."

At the next meeting, Mateos learned that the victim would be Justice Richter, seventy-eight years old. Mateos spent a few days in Travilah checking the roads and the Richter home, looking for any security devices, formulating a plan and using the surveillance and investigative skills he had learned in the Secret Service. Simultaneously, Brian looked for a suitable furnished house in a quiet area that they could rent for a few months to hold Richter. They decided that grabbing the justice first thing in the morning, when he left early for court, would make the most sense.

A few days later, Brian announced that he had found the perfect house. "In Great Capcapon, West Virginia," he explained. "Town has almost no population, but it's in a touristy area so coming and going won't stand out. Used to be a railroad town, but the world moved away. Near a state park and forest area. Belonged to a widow, family wants to sell or rent. Long or short term. Big piece of property. Restaurants nearby to feed us all."

"What did you tell the realtor?"

"I rented a big corporate-looking Audi and hinted that we might be an advance team for a big corporation that might be scouting for a resort. Guy almost came in his pants. And there will be nothing to tie this place to us. We'll drop the judge far away when the time comes. And I can button the place up and make it secure in a few days."

"Like I said, piece of cake."

And now, all that was left was to plant a ransom demand and obtain the prescriptions.

Twenty-one

Travis was at his desk when Lt. Deb Raker, head of the crime scenes unit, charged in without knocking. LeAnne trailed her, looking apologetic for the lack of protocol.

Raker was almost shouting as she said, "Chief, the Magic Box gave us a DNA match!"

"You're shitting me," he said, cussing uncharacteristically.

Travis had been skeptical about adding this latest tool to the unit's arsenal. It was a printer-sized machine that could analyze a DNA sample quickly. It was also prohibitively expensive, but Deb was so insistent that she had found one used for ten thousand. "Like new," she had insisted, and now the Magic Box had proved its capability.

Still, she seemed a bit cautious about the result. "Gave us an unlikely CV for the killer, but the guy sure fits the description we have, and the DNA is a perfect match. Only thing on his record was a DUI about eight years ago. He's a Black guy, accountant, VP of a top firm in DC, six-two and 240 pounds, thirty-eight years old. Name's Scott Littlejohn—divorced, two kids living with the ex. He lives in Frederick with a girlfriend."

"What the hell was he doing in North Potomac?" Travis asked Deb.

"Beats me. Maybe he was passing by, saw those three trying to rob the old Black guy..." She paused, giving Travis an embarrassed look. "...*African American*, like the old man said—then got pissed off and took care of the problem."

"A pretty drastic 'take care of,'" Travis said. "He licensed to carry?"

"No record of one, but there's thousands unlicensed out there."

"Copy that," Travis said. "Incredible work, Deb, but we've got to be very cautious. Keep this buttoned up in your department. Not a word—no leaks. I'll run it up the ladder."

* * *

Later that day, Travis brought Raker to a meeting with Flo Nickerson, the county executive for Montgomery County, who was ecstatic upon hearing the news of the DNA match.

"How did you do this so quickly?" she asked.

"New piece of equipment that we weren't budgeted for but Deb insisted would work," Travis said.

Nickerson, who was up for reelection, was already thinking ahead to the headlines. "How can we break this to get the most publicity?" she asked.

Travis raised a hand, giving a stop signal. "No publicity," he said. "If everything checks out, and we make an arrest, the press can be there at the arraignment. Nothing before that. Absolutely nothing."

* * *

An hour later, Travis was in the Rockville office of Randall Cobb, the state's attorney, for the issuance of an arrest and search warrant.

"Great piece of police work," Cobb said, extending his hand. "Triple murder solved in two days. How'd it go down?"

"Great staff, great forensics, and a piece of equipment I didn't want to buy," Travis said, then handed Cobb a piece of paper on which LeAnne had typed all the particulars. "We need to expedite this. Can do?" Travis's questions sounded more like a demand.

"I can get it done before you leave the building," Cobb said. "What else do you need?"

"I'll coordinate the Frederick City Police with people from my tactical unit to make the arrest—but without disclosing the nature of the crime. The less info leaks out, the better."

"When does this happen?"

"I'd like to move as soon as possible. Hopefully early morning. No publicity, no perp walk, just a statement. The press can have a field day at the arraignment. Tomorrow morning then?"

"Done," Cobb said, "and congratulations again. Great piece of work."

When Travis got back to Gaithersburg, five miles away, he called Deb Raker into his office. "This thing better be accurate," he said.

"No worries. I've already sent the DNA readings to Parabon Nono Labs in Reston. They're the gold standard. They'll do another match with their sequencing equipment. By wire. A rush job."

Within an hour, Parabon had confirmed that the blood on the knife was a match with Littlejohn, who was in their database.

Twenty-two

Late the next morning, a frustrated Brendan Braddock placed a call, cursing under his breath as he waited impatiently for the other phone to pick up. When a voice greeted him, Brendan exploded with rage. "What the hell is going on?" he shouted. "A kidnapping? Are you crazy? What have you gotten me into? That was never even mentioned. And Richter—he's the most decent one on the court."

After a pause, the voice on the other end said, "Who's crazy? You're probably calling on your office phone. That's what's crazy."

"I'm on my cell," Brendan said, "and don't change the subject. There was never any mention of a kidnapping. That's twenty years. You said you just needed information."

"You've been paid handsomely for that information. One hundred thousand by my reckoning. Twenty-five grand a month. And nothing is going to happen to your precious Richter. He'll walk out unscathed once the court is done for the summer."

"That's bullshit, and you know it," Braddock said. "Something always goes wrong. There was never *anything* about a kidnapping."

"Well, it's a little late for that now," the voice said. "Shit happens. We'll just sweeten the pot a little, and you'll be a richer boy."

"A little? What do you mean a little?"

"How does another two hundred fifty thou sound? Just keep doing your job. We're over the hump here."

"Sounds like shit. That's how it sounds," Brendan said. "Now I know why you wanted this information for your special case. You needed to know how it was stacking up, how the vote looked. And I found your answers. You're gonna reap millions."

"You're a little low," the voice said sarcastically. "I'm thinking billions."

"Well, you got me into this mess, and you're not getting off that cheap."

"As I recall, you were the architect of this little arrangement. And you've done very well."

"And now I'm going to do a lot better," Brendan said. "This is not a bargaining point. I want ten thousand shares of your stock, and I want it by tonight, or there just might be a little information that the FBI would find very interesting."

"Ten thousand shares? Do you know what that's worth? How the hell am I supposed to do that?"

"If you can't do it, who can? I can read the market as well as you can. And you just told me it would be worth billions. Ten thousand shares gets you off cheap—let's say, by eleven o'clock tonight. Five thousand shares to Anne Marie McCarthy and the rest to Lucinda Carlson, my daughters. Last thing I need when I retire is an inside trading charge. You got those names?"

"How do you think I can get this done so fast?"

"Hey, you can kidnap one of the justices and make him disappear. I'm sure you can get this done. You're the financial genius, right? Your words, not mine. And Richter better not be harmed."

Brendan repeated the names of his daughters so they could be written down, then said, "Eleven o'clock. Deerlick Park in Fairfax County on Braddock Road, route 620. Place it in a large envelope by the deer feeder."

"Braddock Road—isn't that quaint? You've got this all figured out, huh?"

"I do now. Be there, be on time and come alone. I want stock in the names of my daughters."

"I am not a magician," the voice said. "It can't be done in one day. And I have a commitment with my Mr. Big this evening, so forget it. Tomorrow at the earliest."

"Your Mr. Big? You mean somebody else knows about this? Jesus, how many other people are involved?"

"It's way above your pay grade," the voice said, "but I'll see what I can do. Tomorrow night at eleven. With my fingers crossed."

"Okay, tomorrow," Braddock said, "but I'll have backup and protection that you won't see, so just make sure you're alone and that you have the stock."

Twenty-three

The next morning, Mateos, wearing surgical gloves, stopped at a novelty shop to purchase a wig, false moustache and goatee. Wearing dark rain gear and a baseball cap, he cruised Foggy Bottom and then moved on to the NoMa section near the Union Station area where there were several homeless encampments. A steady drizzle moistened the windshield, and the world was turning greyer.

A few blocks from an encampment beneath a bridge, he spotted a disheveled woman in a ragged coat pushing a shopping cart full of odds and ends. He quietly walked up, tapped her on the shoulder and she spun around.

The woman, perhaps forty but looking more like sixty, was one of the ageless victims of society. She immediately took a frightened, defensive posture. "Stuff in here is throwaway," she said. "I can take it just like anyone else."

"Of course, you can," Mateos said in a soothing voice. "I was just wondering if you'd like a quick way to make a hundred bucks?"

"I don't do none of that sex stuff," she practically spat. "Piss off and find someone else."

"No, nothing like that. I just want to play a little trick on the feds. Get them running in circles. They're certainly no friends of yours, or mine."

"What kinda trick?"

"Just make one short phone call."

"For a hundred bucks? You're crazier than me."

Mateos pulled a large wad of bills out of his pocket and held up two crisp fifties. The woman stared at it.

"Two minutes and it's yours," he said.

"What I hafta do?"

"I'll make the call, and when it answers, you just read what's on this paper. That's it—for the hundred bucks. You can read, can't you?"

"Whaddya think I am, a dumb ass?" she said, reaching for the paper, but Mateos held both the phone and the paper away from her.

He punched in a number, waited as the call went through the standard introductory information and then handed it to her. She took the phone, glanced down and read the message aloud.

"If you want Richter back, it'll cost fifty million. We'll get back to you in a day. Let the papers know when you've got the cash, and we'll give you the instruct..."—she stumbled over the language—"orders on what to do."

She handed the phone back and held out her hand for the cash. She grabbed the money, stuffed it into the pocket of her ragged coat and asked, "Why you wearin' those gloves?"

"I've got a skin disorder," he said. "Nothing serious."

"I don't need no sex diseases either, bud," she said, as he turned away.

Mateos had taken only two steps when the homeless woman said, "Not so fast! You think we're dumb and stupid just 'cause we're homeless? We got TV, we hear news. You want that money for the judge who's kidnapped, and it's gonna cost ya. I'll take the rest of that stash you got right now, and don't try nothin' funny." She waved the ransom demand.

Mateos was stunned. "It's nothing like that. I just want to have those bastards running in circles."

As he pulled out his pistol from under his jacket, the woman's cane came down on his wrist once, twice, in quick blows. He yelped as his gun skittered to the wet ground.

"Bastard," she snarled. She raised her cane to strike again, then started screaming. "Help! Help! Robbery!"

Mateos grabbed the cane and twisted it out of her hands, then struck her savagely across the face. She reeled back, blood pouring from her mouth but still screaming. Mateos struck again, and again.

"Worthless bitch," he snarled. The woman fell to the ground, but her cries had attracted attention from the encampment, and Mateos could see people running toward him. He turned, scooped up the gun, fired one shot into her head and ran toward his parked sedan. The cane still dangled in his injured right hand as he dove into the car and pulled away, tires screeching.

Several homeless men reached the fallen woman. As they saw her bloodied head, one gasped and another called 911. By the time the DC police arrived, all they learned was that the killer had driven away in a tan sedan. But the ransom demand was still clutched in the dead woman's hand.

Twenty-four

J.J. stretched, pushed his blanket aside and dropped his legs to the floor. He was now wearing a sweat suit, which he had been given yesterday after yelling through the doggie door, "Hey, body snatcher! I don't know about you, but I like to change my clothes every so often. If you're planning on keeping me here, I need some clean clothes."

J.J. had no way of knowing the time, since his captors had taken his watch, but he was usually awake around five a.m., and since there was no noise from upstairs, he assumed it was probably around that time, and too early for his breakfast.

"Well, what are we going to do today?" he said aloud and then chuckled. "Talking to myself already! Gives me a whole new perspective on those solitary confinement cases."

Thinking about his captivity, J.J. assumed that if it was for a ransom, either the government or some official body was discussing it. "I know the president has a no ransom policy," he said to himself, "but I think there will be a public outcry when a Supreme Court justice is the victim. If not, Chickie will find a way. Lucky to have her in my life." He enjoyed filling the silent room with his voice.

J.J. thought back to when he and Chickie had first met. Danni had invited him to her mother's New Year's Eve party. He fingered the ring which still hung around his neck—a ring Chickie had given him on their fifth anniversary. The kidnappers had not taken it from him.

In those lonely years following Meg's death, he had lived the home life of a recluse except for his time in court and those occasions when Anthony Battaglia, his constant philosophical opponent, had urged J.J. to accompany him to a game or some social event. Anthony had become a close friend, and their battles were restricted to dueling opinions.

Several months after his knee injury had healed, Danni moved back to Georgetown, and the court was preparing for Christmas recess—or as J.J. had described it, "Holiday recess because we're officially religiously neutral around here, or at least we're supposed to be." That's when Danni asked him a question that would turn his life around. "J.J., what are you doing for New Year's Eve, if it's not too presumptuous to ask?"

"New Year's Eve," J.J. mused. "I'll probably have a quiet evening at home, wait for the ball to drop in your Big Apple and wonder whether the world can survive another chaotic year."

"My mother is having a sort-of dinner party, and she asked me—no, begged me—to invite you." J.J. realized that he knew little of Danni's family life other than she had a mother who was a business executive, and her father had died. J.J. realized how little he knew of the lives of any of his law clerks.

"I'm not much for parties and hubbubs," he replied.

"Oh, c'mon J.J. She lives right here in DC now, and she's dying to meet you."

"Dying to meet me? I wouldn't want that on my conscience. Is it one of those fancy black tie affairs?"

"Some people will probably be formal, some casual, so you can take your pick."

"Can I wear a robe?"

"Your court robe?"

"No, the one I wear at home in front of the fireplace."

"Well, that would be different," Danni said.

"Okay, I'll come," J.J. said, "but only for you. And because I don't want her dyin' on my account."

He asked if Chickie would mind if Travis and Michele accompanied him, so at least he'd have some familiar people around.

"I'm sure that will be fine," Danni said, smiling.

* * *

On New Year's Eve, Travis drove with J.J. in the passenger's seat and Michele in the back. Ahead of them, on the Potomac, stood the imposing Kennedy Center for the Performing Arts, and beyond that their destination. "Damn," J.J. said, almost in awe, "she lives in the Watergate."

They parked and rose up in a mirrored elevator as J.J. inspected himself from all angles. The elevator stopped and opened right into Chickie's apartment where they were greeted by an attendant who looked like a bouncer from a disco or a professional wrestler—J.J. couldn't decide.

The apartment had floor to ceiling windows overlooking the Potomac, modern furniture that looked like a display in a design magazine and waiters carrying trays of hors d'oeuvres for the guests, perhaps forty of them, most of whom were elegantly dressed and the women bejeweled. J.J. looked around like a deer in the headlights as a string quartet provided a live soundtrack for the evening.

Danni rushed over to greet them. "I had no idea she lived in the Watergate," J.J. said.

"Part-time," Danni replied. "This is my mother's show place. She still prefers New York."

A radiant woman detached herself from a couple across the room and approached them. Moving with grace, she looked fortyish, not in her late fifties as J.J. knew she must be. A shimmering, sequined, chocolate gown clung to her svelte figure. As she got closer, her intense hazel eyes seemed to sparkle, or so J.J. thought. She wore a large, brown diamond necklace and no other obvious jewelry. She was much taller than Danni, almost as tall as J.J.

"Justice Richter," she said, smiling. "I'm *so* glad you came." With that, she leaned into J.J. and planted a kiss on his cheek, an act of warmth that caught him completely off guard, but not unpleasantly.

J.J.'s hand went to his cheek momentarily, and he said, "Well, if I knew I was getting that sort of a welcome, I would have been here earlier. You're... Danni's sister?"

"Flattery will get you *everywhere*," she quickly responded. "I'm Chickie Rosen, the mother."

"I would never have guessed," J.J. said.

"Hidden under makeup, and wrapped in a Balenciaga gown, anyone can be deceiving, Your Honor."

"Well, consider me deceived." He paused. "By the way, it's just J.J. The justice part is only when I put on a robe."

"And it's only Chickie. Even when I put on *my* robe. I have to circulate, but I'll keep my eye on you. We'll have time to talk later, when some of the others begin to migrate back to their lairs."

Mort arrived as they were circulating and immediately started to assist with introductions. Travis and Michele were in a corner of the room talking to a general in full regalia. J.J.'s glass of Cabernet Sauvignon was constantly refilled by eagle-eyed waiters, and by the time they sat down to dinner—rack of lamb, julienne potatoes, fresh asparagus and freshly baked rolls—he had consumed far more than his daily single glass of wine. Chickie had seated him next to her as the guest of honor, and one guest after another sought a moment of his time.

As the clock had ticked down, the guests stared at a huge television screen watching as the giant ball dropped at Times Square.

Shortly after ringing in the new year, the string quartet packed up their instruments, and guests slowly filtered toward the elevator. J.J.'s wine glass was still being refilled. "It's a good thing I'm not driving," he said.

Chickie came flying across the room, looking only at J.J. "I have no intention of letting you leave. We haven't had time to talk." She turned to Danni, Mort, Travis and Michele, who had now joined them. "I hope you don't mind, but I've heard so much… read so much about this man. I'd like the opportunity to see why my daughter is so infatuated with him."

"No worries," J.J. said. "I'd like that too, and then I can taxi over to chambers and sack out. It wouldn't be the first time I've slept in court after losing track of time."

"You'll do no such thing," Chickie said in her self-assured way. "We have four bedrooms here, so you've got your pick. I'll get you home in the morning." It was a pronouncement, not a question.

Chickie excused herself and reentered shoeless a few minutes later in a soft silk blouse and matching maize slacks.

"Your place is beautiful," J.J. said, still overwhelmed by the opulence.

"Roche Bobois furnishings," Chickie said, "and an expensive decorator. But I feel the same way. Let's go into my sitting room."

A few remaining guests were still lingering, so Chickie said, "Happy New Year all. We'll see you later." Taking the hint, everyone left, and Chickie led J.J. into her sitting room, which was actually a comfortable office.

J.J. started the conversation with a question. "Pardon my asking, but what does Chickie stand for?"

"Chickie stands for the National Anthem, among other things, with my hand over my heart. But sometimes, when appropriate, I can take a knee."

J.J. could not suppress a smile. She was quick. Sharp. His kind of person.

She laughed. "I was born Helene, in a middle-class Jewish family in Forest Hills—Queens County, which is in New York City but is part of Long Island. I have—*had*—two older brothers. One has passed away. Every time they needed a lookout, if they were sneaking a beer or whatever, I got elected. That was before smoking pot was the in thing with kids. So, I had to yell *Chickie* from the time I was eight or nine, and it just stuck."

J.J. smiled to himself. From that moment on, Chickie became a figure in J.J.'s life, together several times a week and always on weekends. He even persuaded her to ride on the Harley, something she swore she'd never do, even though Danni had become a motorcyclist. There they were, the Fortune 500 corporate exec and the senior associate justice of the US Supreme Court.

* * *

J.J. snapped back to the reality of his basement prison. "If all else fails, Chickie will find a way. But in the meantime," he said defiantly to fill the empty space with proof of life, "let's see what I can do to help myself."

He went around the entire room, carefully looking for a possible way out but found nothing. In the bathroom, he removed the towel hanging from the carpenter's nail and gave it a tug. It barely moved. He tried moving it back and forth. A little wiggle.

"If nothing else," he said, this time to himself, "I might be able to pry that sucker loose."

But then what? he wondered.

Twenty-five

Tim Richardson, who was normally happy to be the agent in charge of an investigation, was feeling pressure every hour from the director, George Blessing, to identify a solid lead. But he still had nothing. Agents were scouring the district, and every known contact of J.J. had been interviewed including all family members, even Lupe. He had personally visited J.J.'s home, everyone at the court had been questioned—but he still had squat. Nothing but an orange road cone, which may not even be a clue and a torn piece of uniform fabric that had been analyzed with no helpful results.

The only solid clue was the fact that the motor oil of the 4x4 had been drained in J.J.'s garage, but the Bureau had been unable to tie it to anything else. It pointed to a possible setup for a kidnapping of the justice on his Harley, but where was the motorcycle? Where was Richter? There was no cell phone data, no GPS tracking—nothing.

As usual in high-profile cases, there had been several dozen ransom demands and following them up had led to nothing but crank calls. The latest was a woman who had made a fifty million dollar demand an hour ago. He had listened to the recording several times, but it had offered no more help than the others. The phone was untraceable, but the scientific sleuths were trying to trace the signal through cell towers.

While Richardson was nibbling on a sandwich at his desk and looking through the reports for just one good lead, his office phone lit up and pinged.

"Richardson," he said.

"Agent Richardson, this is Captain Walter Rogers of the DC Police. I think we have something solid on the Richter case."

Richardson almost choked on his sandwich. "What have you got?"

"A murder in the NoMa section near Union Station only an hour or so ago. Victim was a homeless woman near one of those camps. The investigating officers found her clutching a note with a handwritten fifty-million-dollar ransom demand for the judge in your kidnapping case."

Richardson was up on his feet. "Where are you now?"

"Here at the location. Coroner's still here, but I thought I'd give you a heads up."

"I can be there in five," Richardson said.

* * *

At the scene, Captain Rogers stared at the covered body of the woman as Richardson studied the note secured by tweezers in the hand of the medical examiner.

A crowd of onlookers was being held back by the police, most of them people from the homeless encampment. Already, federal agents were circulating among the crowd asking questions.

The medical examiner explained, "She had two new fifties in her coat, and a couple more singles. They've been bagged. You probably want to have them analyzed."

As Richardson nodded, special agent Buzz Bergdahl approached, followed by a disheveled but distinguished-looking Asian man in his sixties.

"Tim, this is Professor Liu," Bergdahl explained. "He lives here in the encampment. Used to teach at Howard."

"We're a pretty tight group," Liu said. "We have some squabbles, but nothing like this. Murder. Unheard of."

"You knew the deceased?" Richardson said.

Lieu nodded and said, "Alice. Just Alice. Eccentric, but a nice enough lady. Used to own a fabric store, she said, until the recession wiped her out."

"Did you see anything that might help us?" Richardson asked.

"We heard her screaming, and people started running toward her. Never heard a gunshot. A guy was running away—jumped into a tan-colored car about a block away and took off."

"Description?"

"Dark clothes is all. She certainly deserved better than this."

"How likely would she've had a couple of fifty-dollar bills on her?"

"Can't say, she was pretty secretive. But I'd guess very unlikely."

"Thanks for your help," Richardson said. "Special agent Bergdahl will take your statement. And I'd like you to listen to a recording that came in to see if you can identify the voice."

* * *

An hour later, Professor Liu listened to the recording and identified the caller as Alice. "No question about it."

Richardson speculated that the kidnapper had offered Alice a hundred dollars to make the call and then killed her. The paper with the ransom demand only had Alice's fingerprints on it. Same for the money. After reporting these results to director Blessing, who then reported to the White House, it was decided to make the ransom demand public.

The investigation was still at zero.

Twenty-six

As Mort was writing a follow-up article about J.J.'s disappearance, he got a call from the city desk that told him, "I think this is for you. There's a three o'clock press conference at FBI headquarters. Something about a ransom demand on the Richter case."

At a quarter past three, an FBI spokeswoman took the lectern in a press room crowded with reporters, television cameras and media people. "As you know, we have received numerous calls and demands purporting to ask for ransom in Justice Richter's disappearance case," she said. "Each has been followed up and checked by our agents for verification, and most have proved to be groundless. But a phone call was received earlier today from within the district demanding fifty million dollars for the release of the justice. We believe it to be legitimate. The person who made the call was apparently murdered immediately afterward, and this event is now the subject of a full investigation."

In the commotion that followed, most of the additional information about the call and the death of Alice-with-no-last-name was forthcoming, so Mort headed back to his office. His story for the next day would now have some teeth in it. Finally, a ransom demand.

From his car, he called Danni and brought her up to date.

"You think it's legit?" she asked.

"The feds seem to think so. The woman who made the call was killed right after making it."

"Oh my god, that sounds legit enough. I'm going to call my mother right away. Speak to you later."

Mort returned to his desk and called Craig Fisher at the FBI to see if he had any further information. Craig was out on a case but answered on his cell phone. He had nothing to add. In fact, he didn't even know about the ransom demand.

Mort next called Steven Ginsberg, WaPo's managing editor, and told him about the demand.

"Fifty million?" Ginsberg said. "Seems to me a SCOTUS member, especially the senior associate, would command at least that much. But who knows? It might be a real demand. See what you can find out from the White House. Will they pay it?"

"That was my next step."

A few minutes later, Danni called back.

"My mother got really excited—thinks it's proof that J.J. was kidnapped and is still alive. She suggested we meet at J.J.'s tonight and talk out our next move."

"The FBI is on it."

"Yeah, but let's put our heads together again. She already called Lupe about dinner."

"I'm on my way to get reaction from the White House," Mort said. "Where are you?"

"In my office at the law school."

"I'll pick you up at five," Mort said. "We don't need two cars. You can ride back in with Chickie in the morning."

* * *

George Blessing was ushered into the Oval Office by Chad Kennedy. Blessing wanted input from the president before proceeding.

To the president, Kennedy said, "I suggest we take the posture, at least for the moment, that the FBI is on the case, and we hope for a swift and successful conclusion."

"What about the ransom demand?" Blessing asked. "If we get a follow-up about delivering the money, how should we proceed? We've handled many cases like this."

"If I may, Mr. President," Kennedy said, "we should release a statement that it's in the hands of the FBI, and we have full confidence in them. Until we hear further from the kidnappers we have no further statement. I don't think we should mention the demand."

"What about our policy of not meeting ransom demands?" the president asked.

"Let's cross that bridge when we come to it," Kennedy said.

* * *

Dinner at J.J.'s found Mort, Danni and Chickie in the dining room, with Lupe acting as server, cook and participant. Lupe was excited at the news. The demand meant the justice was alive. The FBI would definitely want proof before any ransom was paid.

"Or *if* it will be paid," said Chickie. "Remember the president's inflexible no-ransom policy. I think we should come up with a contingency plan, just in case. J.J. is no favorite with this administration."

"I can't believe they'd go *that* far," Mort said.

"It's not outside the realm of possibility," Chickie said. "They can always blame the debacle on the FBI and tell everyone to keep J.J. in their hearts and minds."

"Mom, that's beyond the pale," Danni said.

Twenty-seven

At five thirty on the morning of the abduction's fourth day, a law enforcement task force showed up at Littlejohn's house. Comprised of Montgomery County Police backed up by Frederick City Police, a portable command post, and a tactical unit in riot gear and holding a no-knock arrest and search warrant, the unit smashed in the front door, bypassed a hysterical girlfriend and made the arrest.

"What the hell is this all about?" Littlejohn demanded. He offered no resistance, got no answer and asked for an attorney even before the reading of the Miranda warnings.

The police searched every corner of the house and the garage but found nothing that would connect Littlejohn with the slayings in North Potomac. His Range Rover sat in the garage next to his girlfriend's Audi. There was no white van.

* * *

Travis was impatiently waiting at headquarters. Littlejohn, the managing partner of his large accounting firm, was allowed one phone call and chose to contact the president of his firm, not a lawyer. Travis ordered Littlejohn to stand in a lineup for eyewitness Mikey Washington, who had been routed out of bed and was already at headquarters. Mikey, who was thrilled to be part of the action, immediately picked Littlejohn out of a hastily arranged group of six Black men.

"That's the one," he said at first glance, pointing to Littlejohn. "He's the man who saved my life. Can I thank him?"

"Afraid not," Travis said. "Maybe another time."

Travis authorized the press to be notified. It was too late for the morning newspaper editions but fully covered by TV and radio.

Mort, Danni and Chickie heard the news while having breakfast in Travilah before separating for the day. Each had a different reaction.

"I can't believe Travis and his people solved those killings this fast," Chickie said.

"Great news," Danni said. "Now Travis can focus on searching for J.J."

Racing out the door, Mort said, "I'm going to the arraignment."

* * *

The courtroom in Rockville was packed with reporters, the usual spectators and people awaiting the start of the judicial process in regularly scheduled cases. Several well-dressed men and women from Littlejohn's accounting firm and the company's attorney were also there. A Maryland court rule blocked photographers from the courtroom but allowed reporters, so Mort found a seat and spotted two other WaPo reporters—Alison Powers, whose desk was near his, and a male reporter whom he couldn't name.

The bailiff announced Judge Marcia Finley, everyone stood, and once the judge had taken her seat on the bench the sheriffs brought Littlejohn into the courtroom. The accused man was still dressed in the clothes he was allowed to put on after his arrest. He was secured with leg irons and handcuffs linked to a belt around his waist. He looked totally confused, even with his attorney at his side.

The Bailiff called out, "People of the State of Maryland versus Scott Littlejohn. Three counts of murder in the second degree..." He continued reading a list of lesser charges.

Prosecutor Thaddeus Thayer, a grizzled state attorney and veteran of numerous homicide cases, indicated he was ready to proceed. Littlejohn's firm, Ernst & Ellie, had quickly hired Ron Ciresi to defend Littlejohn. Ciresi was ranked as one of the best defense attorneys in the nation—and one of the most expensive. An imposing sixty-year-old with flowing grey mane and a suit with creases that could probably slice bread, Ciresi was flanked by two younger associates.

Two thoughts went through Mort's head. First, Littlejohn's firm must really have faith in this Ciresi guy. And second, how the hell did they get him to Rockville on such short notice?

Mort noticed that Travis, in his dress blues, was at the prosecution table along with the assistant prosecutors. This underscored the importance of the case. Mort had been at quite a few arraignments and had seen arresting officers and detectives present, but never a chief of police.

As Travis looked around the courtroom, he seemed surprised to find Mort there.

Judge Finley had a reputation for being a calm and fair jurist. She once had been featured in the *Post* as the first Black woman to ascend to the state bench in Maryland out of 219 judges.

Mort turned to Littlejohn who was nervously glancing around the courtroom. Suddenly, the defendant seemed to spot someone—a well-attired Latina woman, probably in her thirties—who blew him a kiss.

Must be the wife, Mort thought, unaware that Littlejohn was divorced and living with a girlfriend.

Thayer, the prosecutor, opened with, "Your Honor, we have the slaughter of three young men here, shot on a quiet street in North Potomac—three unarmed young men, I might add, under circumstances that are still being investigated. We have a DNA match from a weapon recovered at the scene, as we have noted in the prosecuting information. The state strenuously opposes bail in this case."

Ciresi bristled. "Your Honor," he said, "the state is quick to mis-characterize this incident as a slaughter. I'm sure that will look good in the media, but the fact is that we don't have a clue as to the circumstances. Unarmed young men? We heard a few minutes ago that there was a knife or switchblade involved, and we have not even been given the opportunity to see the prosecutor's evidence. They claim to have a DNA match according to the accusatory information, but Mr. Littlejohn, who is the managing partner and a respected vice-president of a nationally known accounting firm—a pillar of his community and father of two—stands before you with an unblemished record of professional, charitable and civic accomplishments."

Mort had expected this kind of counter by the defense attorney, so he settled back in his chair to hear the rest of the oration.

"In over twenty years, Mr. Littlejohn has risen to a position of prominence not only in his firm, but in his profession. This is obviously a case of mistaken identity, as we have read so often in the press these days. This is a rush to judgment, and I am certain Mr. Littlejohn will be vindicated. He doesn't even own a weapon, and probably wouldn't know which end of it is up if he had one. The president of the accounting firm stands here to vouch for him, as well as members of the company's executive committee. We stand ready to meet any bail demand."

The judge paused, then said, "We have a triple homicide here, Mr. Ciresi, and I have to think of that and the safety of the community. At this time, bail is denied."

But Ciresi wasn't finished. "Your Honor, I propose an immediate lie detector test by anyone the prosecution selects. If Mr. Littlejohn passes that test, or tests, his firm is prepared to post bail in any amount you set. Two lie detector tests. Or three, if you wish. That's how certain we are that this is a case of mistaken identity. Mr. Littlejohn is an innocent man who is entitled at least to that much."

Ciresi stepped away from his table and took one step toward the judge.

"Moreover, according to the prosecution's information, the perpetrator of this crime was allegedly stabbed in the side by the knife on which the DNA was found. With the court's permission, I would like to request Mr. Littlejohn to lift up his shirt and display his body to the judge."

The judge motioned her approval. "Mr. Littlejohn, please show us if you have any wounds."

Littlejohn struggled with the handcuffs, and one of the deputy sheriffs pulled up his shirt. Littlejohn turned his body around. No wound.

"This is proof of nothing!" Thayer said, spitting out the words.

"No wound, Your Honor," Ciresi said. "They've got the wrong man, and a prosecution-controlled polygraph will prove it."

The judge turned to the state's attorney as if to ask if there was an objection.

The prosecutor turned to Travis. They whispered back and forth a few times and then the prosecutor shook his head, obviously disagreeing with Travis about something. Finally, he turned to the judge.

"Your Honor," the state's attorney said, "while it is highly unusual, Chief Anderson of the Montgomery County Police has agreed to have a polygraph examination performed at his headquarters later today, but only the defendant can be present with the interrogator, and he must waive his right to have his attorney present."

Ciresi and Littlejohn conferred quickly. "Agreed," Ciresi said.

Mort was astonished at this development.

Mort asked Travis if they could meet somewhere briefly. Travis pointed to a corridor behind the courtroom. Mort watched Travis talking to Ron Ciresi as they exited the courtroom. Ciresi then knocked on a door, and a few seconds later Littlejohn appeared. He was flanked by two deputies and spoke briefly to Ciresi in Travis's presence, heads nodding. Mort was aware of the "no camera in the courtroom" rule, but this was in the corridor, so he quietly lifted his cell phone and took several shots of Littlejohn speaking to his attorney.

Littlejohn was then led back behind the closed door and taken out of the courthouse by a back door to avoid the press and the photographers outside the entrance.

Mort walked over to Travis. "What was that all about?" he asked.

"I can't talk now, but I'll call you later." They parted.

On the way out of the courthouse, Mort spotted Alison Powers and the other reporter. He waved them over.

"You on this case too?" she asked. "Isn't a missing judge enough to fill your days?"

"Stopping by to see a friend," Mort said. "Can I have your cell phone number?"

"I'm involved," she said, "but thanks for asking."

"I'm engaged," Mort said, "but I thought you might like a headshot or two of Littlejohn."

"How the hell did you get that?"

"God works in wondrous ways," Mort said.

Alison gave him her number, and he forwarded two photos.

"I don't know how to thank you," Alison said. "I really owe you one for this."

"All in a day's work," Mort said.

Mort headed to his office and checked out a few alleged leads on J.J.'s disappearance, which proved fruitless. Nothing had come back from the White House.

Later that afternoon, Mort got a call from Travis, one of the few people who had his personal number. "Mort, any chance you can stop by my office?"

Mort was in his car within minutes and called Danni to suggest delaying dinner with her mother until later.

"What does Travis want with you?" she asked.

"Haven't a clue," he said.

Twenty-eight

Travis was in his shirt sleeves when Mort entered his office. "Something just doesn't feel right about this case," he said.

"That why you were in the courtroom?"

"Yes. The biggest case to hit in years. Solved in days. But it just doesn't pass my smell test."

"Are you free to talk about the lie detector test?"

"I'm probably not free to talk about any of this, but I know I can trust you," Travis said. "The test? He aced it. Answered every question truthfully, according to our guy, who's as good as they come."

"He wouldn't be the first guy to beat the box," Mort said. "Anything else you can talk about?"

"Well, there's an eyewitness of sorts. An old man who lived in the nursing home. He picked Littlejohn out of a lineup early this morning, but Ciresi would have a field day with him on cross. The old man originally thought I was the killer when he first saw me."

"No shit!"

"It will definitely come out in the trial. And it's one of the reasons I asked you to stop in. Littlejohn's lawyer spoke to me. He's a pretty straight guy. Said that Littlejohn was willing to give an exclusive interview, and I could pick the reporter. That's how sure they are of his innocence. I couldn't think of a reporter I could trust, so I suggested you."

"Thanks a lot," Mort said, sarcastically. "We've got several good reporters on the case already. They'd do a good job." He didn't mention the two cell phone photos he had taken.

125

"I know it's unheard of, and you're on J.J.'s case," Travis said. "But I've been reading your stuff. Very good, and not slanted, despite the relationship. Anyway, that's how sure Ciresi and the people at the accounting firm are of this guy's innocence. Ciresi said he checked me out and would never make such an offer if he wasn't sure I'm a straight shooter. Whaddya say?"

"The guys at the paper would think I'm butting in."

"An interview's different than a news story, isn't it? It would just be an hour of your time, maybe two, and then a short article. Even with everything on your plate, you can do it. J.J. isn't going to be found any quicker if you agree. Bottom line—I really do trust you. I really couldn't live with myself if an innocent man was convicted here of a triple homicide, and this equation just doesn't add up."

"Would this mean a jail interview?" Mort asked. "I've never done one of those."

"There's something else you should know," Travis said. "After the polygraph, Ciresi got an expedited bail hearing from the judge, and Littlejohn's firm put up a five-million-dollar bail to release him. Thayer screamed like a banshee, but he had agreed to the terms. They put a leg monitor on the guy, and the bail was paid within an hour. Crazy, huh? Even with the DNA and eyewitness. He's either back home or with Ciresi, who said he was moving Littlejohn to a hotel to avoid the press."

This story was guaranteed to be on the front page of the paper. As crazy as it seemed, the first thing Mort thought of was all those parents of the women he had dated who looked down on him because he wanted to be a reporter.

But he had to clear it with the paper. He decided to bypass procedure and called Steve Ginsberg directly from Travis's office.

Ginsberg was almost speechless. "How the hell did you manage that?" he asked. "On second thought, don't tell me. I've got eight hundred reporters available, and Pulitzer Prize winners. You're on the kidnapping case of a Supreme Court justice, and now this defendant's lawyer wants you to interview a triple-killing suspect? I'm tempted to fire everyone else and just let you have the front page."

126

Mort was holding the phone away from his ear, and Travis heard the conversation.

Travis reached for the phone.

"Mister, uh… I'm sorry, I don't know who I'm speaking to."

"Steve Ginsberg. I used to be managing editor here until Ahrens took over the paper."

"This is Travis Anderson, the Montgomery County Chief of Police. Defense attorney Ciresi will only let his client be interviewed by a reporter who I trust—God knows why—and I'm close to Mort, and Justice Richter, for that matter. I can say without reservation that I trust Mort's integrity implicitly. We're talking about an hour or two of Mort's time—and, of course, an exclusive interview for the *Post*."

"This thing is getting incestuous," Ginsberg said, "but I'll let Ahrens run with it."

And so, instead of being on his way to London with Danni, Mort was the lead on the kidnapping case and was going to do an exclusive interview with the accused triple killer. A lot of reporters were going to have their noses out of joint, especially Alison Powers.

Twenty-nine

By dinnertime, J.J. had figured out the daily schedule for meals, the times when two men were present upstairs instead of one, and when he could sneak into the bathroom to work on loosening the nail. He also did some yoga, which relaxed him, and decided to become more cantankerous. Not that he was ever submissive.

He spent a lot of time in the bathroom free from the surveillance cameras. Using the towel to protect his hands, he pried the nail back and forth, and it gradually loosened. It was the only thing even close to a weapon.

When the doggie door opened with the evening meal, he stood at the bottom of the stairs and shouted, "Where are my pills? I don't know how long my heart can hold out."

A voice yelled back, "Check your meal tray!"

He checked and found two pills set out on the napkin. He could recognize them on sight—Valsartan and Simvastatin.

He ate and had to admit the food was well-prepared and satisfying. The routine had now become juice, coffee and a pastry for breakfast, a sandwich for lunch and a full meal at dinner with a main course that varied day to day, vegetables and even a dessert.

It was clear they needed him alive.

When he was finished with dinner, he set the tray by the doggie door as usual. When the door snapped open to retrieve the tray, he said, "My Diogensamine—the heart medicine. That's the one I need the most. I could also use a shower, for God's sake, and some sunshine."

"We're working on it," a voice said. "Probably tomorrow. As for the shower and the sunshine, you'll have to be patient. We don't like this any more than you do."

"Like I believe that!" J.J. shouted back.

The door snapped shut.

J.J. smiled to himself and went back to the bathroom where the nail was very loose.

Thirty

Danni had accompanied her mother to the offices of Rosen-Billings, the media conglomerate where Chickie was CEO. Nothing was pending for her at the law school. She was supposed to be in London with Mort. But J.J.'s disappearance had foiled that plan.

Rosen-Billings was located in an upscale area of Arlington. The firm owned television and radio stations throughout the country. Mort often teased Danni that it was just his luck—to be a journalist engaged to a woman whose family was in TV and radio.

Chickie and Danni started a conference call with Mort. "Anything new on J.J.?" Chickie asked.

"Nothing at all," Mort replied. "If the ransom demand was valid, nothing has happened—no directions on where or how to leave money, use of cryptocurrency, nothing."

"And the White House?" Danni asked.

"Another big nothing," Mort said. "Of course, as long as the FBI is clueless, they don't have to make any further statements about the ransom."

"Do you think it's really a demand from the kidnappers?" Chickie asked. "Because the more I think about it, the less I think so. It was too open-ended. Had no proof that they have J.J. And you know how many nuts are running around."

"I'm inclined to agree," Danni said. "I still believe this whole disappearance is a subterfuge to cancel out J.J.'s vote on the NAWES case. I think we don't wait any longer. The president will jerk this thing around, taking his time while his pollsters test the waters, trying to avoid making a decision on the ransom. No, we need to take this into our own hands."

"How do we do that?" Chickie asked.

"We set up a GoFundMe account to raise money from people all over the country. J.J. is the most well-known and probably the most respected justice in the country, even now, when public opinion of the court is falling dramatically. We'll make it personal, and that way it doesn't step on the toes of the FBI—and might even embarrass the president at the same time."

"Do we need a corporation or something like that to do it?" Chickie asked.

"No, all we need is a bank account, a way to get the word out, maybe some graphics and it's a done deal," Danni said. "We can do it in my name, which is a natural because of my long association with J.J."

"How long would it take?" Chickie asked. "What would it cost?"

"Cost is minimal, less than 2 percent of what we raise," Danni explained. "And it's perfectly safe. But we can act immediately—make the announcement in advance and ask people to pledge a donation. Let's arrange a press conference—today maybe."

"That's the easy part," Chickie said.

* * *

At four o'clock that afternoon, perfect timing for exposure on the evening newscasts, Danni stepped to a lectern set up in the PR center of Rosen-Billings. The media had been told that this conference would announce a major development in the kidnapping case. Photos of J.J. appeared on a backdrop behind Danni.

As the event began, Danni said, "My name is Dannielle Rose. I am an assistant professor of law at American University Law School and was formerly a law clerk to Associate Justice J.J. Richter, the senior associate justice of the United States Supreme Court. As the nation is aware, Justice Richter disappeared mysteriously four days ago, and we now know that that disappearance is the result of a kidnapping. A ransom has been demanded—an outrageous fifty million dollars.

"We know that the policy of our current administration is to refuse to pay ransoms. While we have not yet heard from the White House whether they will adhere to this policy, I am going forward as an individual—and I ask for your help as fellow Americans to raise the ransom from our own pockets to rescue this American patriot, this lion of the Supreme Court and protector of the Constitution of this United States. We have had far too many incidents that challenge our freedoms over the past few years, to say nothing of the pandemic and crimes that have killed hundreds of thousands of our friends, neighbors and loved ones. Here is our opportunity to rescue this seventy-eight-year-old icon of our democracy. Please call the number on the screen and pledge any amount you can afford. By doing this, you will show once again that tyranny has no place in our society. Thank you."

The video of the event was shown on every network's evening news and all but the Fox News Channel on cable. By ten o'clock that evening, forty million dollars had been pledged.

Thirty-one

At eleven o'clock, a man in dark clothing walked to the deer feeder. The area was lit only by a distant park light on a pole. He looked around, put down an envelope and walked away in total silence. A few minutes later, a Phantom 4 V2.0 quadcopter drone equipped with low noise propellers moved into the park and hovered about forty feet above the feeder. It was equipped with a robotic origami claw and a DJI Mavic 2 LED searchlight.

The searchlight went on, its bright light illuminating the bird feeder as it dropped down, it hovered, and the claw scooped up the envelope before heading for the far side of the park near an outcropping of trees. Hidden by the trees, Brendan Braddock maneuvered the drone to the ground next to a metal informational sign about the park. Braddock had been preparing for something like this since J.J. had disappeared. He was glad he hadn't trusted the other man.

He plied the envelope from the drone's claw, turned and prepared to walk away, but the envelope slipped from his hands.

"Damn!" He said, stooping to pick it up.

A rifle in the distance fired, almost unheard. The round clanged against the metal sign, startling Braddock, who turned to run.

Another muffled shot rang out. Braddock staggered and then crumpled to the ground.

A hundred yards away, a figure in fatigues and military boots stepped out of the trees. He wore a stocking cap with GPNVG-18 night-vision goggles pulled down over his eyes and was holding a

Steyr SSG-69 Austrian sniper's rifle fitted with a sound suppressor. He searched the ground and retrieved the casings as he watched Braddock. After another thirty seconds, Braddock had not moved.

The sniper gingerly walked to the body and picked up the envelope. "Not quite as smart as you thought you were," he said to the dead man. "Reminds me of the old days." He pushed the goggles back from his eyes. "Good enough for Bin Laden—it was no contest with a schmuck like you." He stooped, picked up the drone and the remote controller and walked out of the park.

A jogger found the body at five the next morning, called the Fairfax County Police, and within minutes three patrol cars and a sergeant were on the scene. Braddock was lying face down.

The sergeant came up with Braddock's billfold and looked through it. "Jesus Christ," he said to the other officers. "This guy has ID from the Supreme Court. Better get the FBI on this."

Within an hour, Special Agent Tim Richardson was standing over Braddock's body. "This has got to be tied to the kidnapping," he said to the agent next to him. "Too coincidental to be coincidental."

He turned to the Fairfax County Police sergeant. "We'll take jurisdiction from this point on. And we want to question the jogger who found the body."

"You'll want this," the sergeant said, handing Richardson the bullet that had hit the sign.

Thirty-two

Danny, Chickie and Mort had decided to spend another night in Travilah, not only to help Lupe's nerves, but on the outside chance that if J.J. was able to get word to them, or to get away from his kidnappers, he'd head for his home base. Chickie stayed in the master bedroom, where she and J.J. normally slept, Danni and Mort in the guest bedroom.

On this morning of the fifth day of J.J.'s disappearance, Chickie and Danni had an early breakfast at J.J.'s and then left for Rosen-Billings in Arlington. Mort headed for his interview with Littlejohn at Ron Ciresi's office. They parted company before nine o'clock.

* * *

At NAWES headquarters, Win called his two lieutenants, Boris and Zeke, into his office as soon as they arrived. "I think we should pledge five million to that ransom fund," he said. "Will make us look good. And it's the decent thing to do."

Boris said, "No can do. Legally an offer to contribute to the ransom can't be done because it would create a conflict of interest."

Zeke's reaction was somewhat different. "Are you nuts? With Richter missing, that's our guarantee to win this case. We're in like Flynn. You can't do it."

"Well, it seems like the right thing to do," Win said, "especially if he was kidnapped because of our case, like Danni Rose believes. I'm going to make the offer anyway. We look good either way."

"You're out of your fucking mind," Zeke said, then stomped out of the room.

"He never did take his losses too well, did he?" Boris said. "And I wish I could be as sure as he is on the outcome of the case. I think we'll win, but with Richter out of the way, it's already a done deal."

Win contacted the members of the board, and they agreed. Even if it wasn't possible, publicity about the offer to donate would look good to the public.

* * *

The reaction at the White House was somewhat different. "Jesus," the president said. "This grandstanding by raising the ransom with donations is going to make us look like fools. She's gonna get sympathy and probably raise enough to pay the damned ransom. And we're sitting here with our thumbs up our asses."

Chad Kennedy wasn't upset. "I don't see it that way," he said. "We issue a statement that we were waiting for verification from the FBI about the veracity of the demand—which we still haven't received—and say that we stand ready to meet it once we have proof he's alive. But since the phone call, there's been no proof, so we win either way."

"Except the thing that really counts in this world," the president said, "is PR. A private citizen raises money, and the government sits silent. These wars are won and lost on public relations. And that woman just scored a hole-in-one."

* * *

Chickie got a call from Win Abbington less than an hour later. "I saw the news last night. This ransom demand is outrageous. I spoke to my board, and we've agreed to pledge five million toward the ransom."

Chickie almost dropped the phone. She covered the mouthpiece and whispered to Danni, "Win says NAWES will pledge five million."

Without hesitation, Danni whispered back, "You can't take it. Thank him and turn it down."

"Why?" Chickie asked.

Danni took the phone from her mother and said, "Mr. Abbington, this is Danni Rose, and that's a very generous offer. Which has to be refused, unfortunately."

Win said, "Because?"

"Because you have a really big case pending before the Supreme Court, and a pledge from your organization would compromise the entire court. Clearly a conflict of interest."

"Damn, that's what Boris said," Win replied. "But it seemed like the right thing to do. Some things are more important than a lawsuit."

"It's incredibly generous, but the rules of ethics prevail."

"Well, short of that," Win said, "if there's anything I can do…"

"Maybe put out a statement calling for J.J.'s release, or something like that. Your PR folks can wrap it in the flag and have a ball with it."

"Done," Win replied.

"Anyway," Danni said, "the calls have tied up the phone lines. Eighty million in pledges are already in."

* * *

J.J. was also busy that morning. After breakfast, he went into the bathroom to continue prying the nail loose. After about ten minutes, it pulled free. Now, what was his next step?

* * *

J.J.'s mechanic determined that the problem with the 4x4 was not mechanical. The oil had simply been drained. Mort replaced the oil and volunteered to take Connie, the golden retriever, to the veterinarian in Potomac on his way to the interview and pick her up in the afternoon.

"You've been hankering to drive that truck anyway," Danni said.

"Just trying to be helpful," Mort said, knowing she was right. Connie seemed perfectly normal to Mort, but Lupe was worried about her severe lethargy since the day of J.J.'s disappearance. *Probably just lonesome for J.J.*, Mort thought.

As he drove, Mort thought over what they knew so far. A few things had started to fall into place. First, if the kidnappers knew J.J.'s schedule, they knew that he left for court early, usually the first of the court's brethren to arrive. Second, it would be easier to waylay him if he was on the Harley rather than driving the truck. Draining the oil would ensure that he was on his bike. These steps required some careful planning. Mort was also certain the FBI had already reached these same conclusions even though they hadn't led to anything useful yet.

* * *

Brian Abernathy was about a quarter mile down the access road from J.J.'s property, where he could see the entrance to the driveway. He had tried to convince his partner, Mateos, that he should stay with J.J. while Mateos retrieved the heart drug that J.J. needed so badly. As usual, it was a short argument that he had lost. Mateos had kept silent about his role in killing Alice-with-no-last-name.

Brian observed for a half-hour and noted that a squad car periodically drove by the premises, but there was no constant police presence and no FBI—probably just wiretaps on the phone and the occasional drive-by. Still, there were others in the house with the housekeeper. His rental car was parked farther down the road in a secluded area leading to a traffic department storage facility. He felt reasonably safe but was apprehensive about how to obtain the medication with at least two civilians and a maid in the house.

Suddenly, good fortune smiled upon him. A car with two women drove by followed a couple minutes later by the 4x4 with a dog standing in the bed of the truck. He couldn't see the driver but assumed it must be the housekeeper. He figured this meant the house was now deserted. He didn't know how long these people would be gone, but he would be in and out within minutes. All he had to do was find the drug and split.

Thirty-three

Mort was only fifteen minutes into his trip when his phone sounded the distinctive ringtone when it was Danni. He pulled over and answered.

"Brendan Braddock is dead," Danni said.

"What?"

"Shot in the head. They found his body in a park in Virginia."

"Jesus!" Mort said. "Who would want to kill Braddock unless it was some kind of an accident? He was clearly upset because of his retirement. You think maybe suicide?"

"Too much of a coincidence," Danni said. "The kidnapping, the court term ending, and now Braddock's dead. No weapon by his body, they said. That weird conversation you had with him has been bugging me."

"I know," Mort said. "You told me he seemed to know more than he should about the court. Maybe it was just a hunting accident."

"Morton," she said, and he knew he was in trouble. She only used his full name when she was pissed. "Hunting season is in the fall. Somebody was hunting *him*."

"But what was he doing in a Virginia park? Let me roll this around in my head while I drive to the interview. This is so weird."

"Get a copy of the *Post*," Danni said. "The ransom demand is on the front page with Brendan's death there as well."

Things were swirling out of control. Mort dropped Connie off at the vet and stopped to pick up a paper. Both articles were featured on the front page as Danni had said. He'd read it later.

Mort's phone rang, and he pulled over again.

It wasn't Danni—it was Mort's mother calling from home in Harrisburg. "Morton," she said, "where are you?"

"I'm on the other end of the phone, Ma."

"Don't be a smarty pants. Are you in the country?"

Mort had asked his mother a thousand—no, a million times—not to call him Morton, his given name. That was reserved for Danni when she was pissed off. "I'm in Maryland after driving the dog to the vet."

"You have a dog? You didn't tell me you had a dog. You seeee, I'm like a foreigner to you." A pause. "What kind of dog?"

"It's Justice Richter's dog."

"Oh, thank God. They found him?"

"No, Ma, they didn't. Danni and I are staying at his place while we search for him."

"You're searching? That's what the FBI is for. You'll get hurt. And your friend Danni as well."

"Ma, you know that Danni is my fiancée."

They had been down this road many times as well. If you're engaged, your fiancée has a ring. Otherwise she's your friend, your girlfriend, whatever. Mort's mother even offered to send him money for a ring, but money wasn't the issue.

After ten minutes he finally got his mother off the phone. While continuing to drive to Ron Ciresi's office, he had an epiphany. Danni was troubled because Braddock seemed to know too much about what was going on inside the Black Box, the inner sanctum of the justices. But maybe the room was bugged. That was something he'd have to discuss with Danni, Chickie and Travis.

Thirty-four

Mort arrived fifteen minutes early for his interview with Littlejohn. From the nameplate on the door, Mort saw that Ciresi had several associates and had even posted the names of his paralegals. The office was not in the "showy" area of the Capital—Ciresi had nothing to prove.

Seated on a sofa, Mort found a copy of the *Post* and checked out the stories on the ransom demand and Brendan Braddock's death. The receptionist, a young woman in her twenties, asked if she could get him anything. He settled for water, and she returned in a moment with a large pitcher of water and a glass filled with ice. She never gave Mort a second glance. Women rarely did.

The inside door opened, and Ron Ciresi, in shirtsleeves, greeted Mort. He wore colorful suspenders with various legal scenes on them. Mort made a mental note—it was time to get rid of his shopworn belts.

"Mr. Ahrens," Ciresi said, thrusting out his hand, "good of you to come. Mr. Littlejohn is waiting in my office." Ciresi was taller than he had seemed at the arraignment and built solidly.

"Happy to have the opportunity," Mort said, taking his hand. "Please, just call me Mort."

"Fair enough, and I'm Ron."

With introductions out of the way, they proceeded into Ciresi's office. Scott Littlejohn, the accused, was standing up, and his handshake was warm and firm. He didn't seem to be at all nervous, unlike his appearance at the arraignment.

If I stood accused of a triple murder, Mort thought, *I'd be traveling with an extra pair of Jockey shorts.*

Littlejohn towered over Mort with an ebony complexion and in a paisley, short-sleeved polo that exposed strong forearms. His cuticles looked carefully manicured. Everyone sat down. Mort pulled a chair close to Ciresi's oak desk and opened his laptop.

"I'll record the interview rather than take notes, if that's okay," he said.

"No problem," Ciresi replied, "but I'll stay in here just in case the questions wander into something that could factor into the defense—beyond the fact that the police have the wrong guy."

"I have no intention of stepping on the legalities," Mort said.

"I obviously checked you out," Ciresi said, "and you were recommended by Chief Anderson. Unusual. A newspaperman who is actually liked by the police and graduated the Newhouse School with honors, which is quite an accomplishment. Shall we get to it?"

Even before being asked a question, Littlejohn blurted out, "I'm innocent. I didn't do it. They've got the wrong guy, DNA or not."

Mort nodded sympathetically and started with the usual questions, learning that Littlejohn had been adopted as an infant by an upper middle-class White couple and had privileges that most Black men were denied—private school, stable homelife and several older White siblings. His adopted parents—he referred to them as "my parents," or "my folks"—had been unable to have a third child and decided to adopt.

In high school, Littlejohn had been a basketball player of note and then attended MIT, having had the luxury of declining a basketball scholarship to Pittsburgh to study mathematics. Nice to be supported by a family that could afford passing up a free ride. His mother was a teacher and his father the owner of a well-known haberdashery. Scott, however, had wanted to work in the financial world since his teenage years.

Following college, he had gone on for his Masters and then a PhD, picking up a wife along the way, a White woman he had met as an undergraduate. They'd had two children before they realized they were "going in different directions." They still maintained a good relationship, and they alternated custody with the children every other month. His ex-wife had remarried and with her new husband chose to live in Frederick, where Scott lived, so the children could have a stable home life and a good education.

Ciresi interjected that the ex was very supportive and absolutely did not believe that Littlejohn was capable of violence. "In fact," Ciresi said, "she jokingly told a story about having to be the one who killed a mouse, which had gotten into their home, because Scott couldn't do it."

Littlejohn had been hired by a medium-sized accounting firm after completing his schooling and then had moved on to his present firm, one of the top ten accounting firms in the country, where he was now a vice-president and the managing partner.

All in all, Scott Littlejohn seemed like the least likely triple murderer anyone could think of. He claimed to be totally ignorant of North Potomac. After about an hour, Mort thanked them and said he would write the article after he had picked up Connie, the retriever, from the vet.

Like Travis, Mort was pretty well convinced that there had to be a mistake in this accusation.

Thirty-five

J.J. stared at the carpenter's nail in his hand. It was not much, but it was all the weaponry he had. The next step was to figure out what to do with it.

If he could hide at the top of the stairs, when a hand pushed a food tray onto the top step, he could impale the hand with his nail. Then, with the hand inoperable, maybe he could bargain his way out. He was certain they didn't want to kill him.

He knew this plan would only work if only one of the captors was present at the time. So, he listened for footsteps and any other telltale signs that would signal only one of his captors was in the house. He had no idea of his location, but it had to be somewhere near DC. If he could get free, he could flag down a car or find a neighbor. Or the police.

* * *

With Brian in Travilah attempting to obtain the mythical prescription, Mateos was alone upstairs at the kidnap site in Great Capcapon. As J.J. was listening attentively for clues that a sole captor was present, Mateos was thinking about the ten million dollars that lay at the end of this kidnapping rainbow. He decided that instead of picking up lunches at the Angus and Ale Restaurant, he would have the meals delivered so he could watch television instead.

He ordered and then turned on the news. The lead story was the ransom demand. Great! Just as he had planned it. And no mention of the murder of the homeless woman. Apparently, the police or investigators hadn't connected the dots yet. Probably, the death of a homeless woman wouldn't lead to a very thorough investigation.

* * *

After watching the 4x4 leave J.J.'s house, Brian believed it was empty and decided to move quickly. Staying in the trees and shrubbery where possible, Brian made his way toward the Richter property. He was angry with Mateos and himself, realizing now that he would be much more visible as a tall Black man than Mateos would have been. And a Black man would raise far more curiosity than a White man in lily-white Travilah.

There was no movement at the house and no police car cruising by—at least right now. He silently moved down the driveway and into the garage. Inside, he saw the housekeeper's car and another one, a Subaru—whose car was that? Then he recalled seeing the two women leave earlier in one car. The Subaru must belong to one of them.

Brian headed to the back door, which was locked. Prepared, he pulled out a lock pick. Just in case, he also had two syringes filled with Propofol and the Glock in a holster strapped behind his back. He prayed he would not have to use either of them.

The lock pick worked, and the door opened with a creak. He froze, listening for any sound. Nothing. He entered the mud room and slipped in. His leg hit a cane resting against the wall and sent it crashing to the floor. Shit! Why not just open a cabinet in the kitchen and throw all the dishes against the wall to advertise his arrival? Again, he waited, but heard nothing. His armpits were drenched with sweat.

* * *

Once the breakfast dishes were washed, Lupe had gone into her attached two-room apartment to lay down for a few minutes. These last few days had been very traumatic. Now, J.J. was missing and Chickie, Danni and Mort had taken up residence, at least in the evenings. They were good to have around, but... She kicked off her sandals, laid back and within seconds had dozed off.

* * *

Barely a minute later, Lupe awoke to a noise. Connie was not in the house—she was with Mort—so Lupe got up to investigate barefoot.

Another louder noise startled her as J.J.'s cane crashed to the floor in the mud room.

Attentive now, Lupe heard footsteps moving through the house from the kitchen into J.J.'s bathroom. She slipped out of her room and padded into the kitchen, picking up her large, cast-iron frying pan. She took up a position just outside the bathroom door.

She heard the contents of the medicine chest being dumped into the sink. She stood there poised with the frying pan raised like a baseball bat.

A large Black man appeared in the doorway. He spotted Lupe at the same time the frying pan smashed into his already-bandaged face. He went down instantly and remained motionless.

Lupe looked down, then stooped over the man. He was large, but she grabbed his unconscious form and managed to drag it into the kitchen. He was still motionless. She rummaged in a kitchen drawer and pulled out a roll of duct tape. She wrapped the unconscious man's arms tightly to his sides. As he began to stir, she quickly removed the pistol from its holster. Then she picked up the frying pan and hit him again. Hard. He stopped moving.

Lupe found his wallet, rolled him over and saw the syringes in his shirt pocket. She removed them, then wrapped him from head to foot in the gray tape. Only then did she go to the kitchen, look up Travis's cell phone number and place the call.

"Mista Travis, come quick!" she shouted. "I got a bugglar in the judge's house!"

Thirty-six

J.J. was beginning to think he had made a huge mistake. His bones ached from being crouched by the door for so long. Breakfast had been a long time ago, and he had to urinate. The nail clutched so tightly in his hand was causing his fingers to tingle. If he descended the stairs to go to the bathroom, he might be heard. Earlier, the television upstairs had been on but had been quiet for quite a while.

At last, he heard movement, although the footsteps seemed to be fading, moving away from what he thought was the kitchen. If he had been wrong, sore muscles would be all he'd have to show for his efforts.

Then the footsteps returned, moving closer. The bolts on the doggie door unsnapped. Suddenly, he was filled with apprehension. What if the hand did not appear? What if the tray was slid in rather than pushed in as before? Suddenly, he heard several loud knocks on the door. Too late to change the plan now.

He waited, nail in hand, ready to plunge it into flesh and leverage his weight with his other hand.

The bolts on the door snapped open, and the tray slid in, pushed by a hand—a White man's hand—and J.J. struck. With all his strength, he jammed the nail down on the back of the captor's hand, using his other arm to push down harder. He felt the nail go all the way through the hand into the tray.

The scream was even louder than he had imagined it would be.

Thirty-seven

Mort pulled into J.J.'s driveway. As he was dropping the tailgate on the 4x4, two police cars with flashing lights tore into the yard and screeched to a stop. Two cops jumped out, one from each car, with guns drawn.

Connie didn't wait for the tailgate. She jumped to the driveway, running toward the police and barking.

"Hold it right there," the younger officer shouted. He looked nervous.

So was Mort, with the pistol pointed at him.

"Drop it," the older officer said, pointing to Mort's laptop.

Sarcastically, Mort said, "My laptop? Drop my laptop? It's not loaded."

The younger officer waved his pistol.

Mort bent and placed the laptop on the ground, then raised his hands.

The name on the officer's uniform shirt said "Young," which seemed appropriate.

"Who are you?" asked the older officer with a nametag that read "Fleming." The officer lowered his pistol to his side.

Mort had the presence of mind to say, "What's going on? I live here."

Connie was barking loudly, but not charging.

"Connie, stop," he commanded.

Connie obeyed, which seemed to calm the cops.

"We've got a 459, burglary in progress," Fleming said into his radio.

Those words shot terror into Mort as he suddenly knew the police had been sent to the scene of a burglary, which meant someone may still be inside the house. Without waiting, Mort wheeled and sprinted up the stairs into the house. Connie followed with the two officers behind her.

Mort found Lupe seated in the kitchen with a heavy, cast-iron frying pan on the table in front of her. On the floor, mummified with duct tape, lay a large, semi-conscious Black man. Squatting to look at this man's face, Mort was astonished. It was Scott Littlejohn with a bandage over his nose.

"Littlejohn!" Mort said. "What the hell is going on?"

Mort turned to the two officers. "I left this man less than an hour ago. I interviewed him for the *Washington Post.*"

The semi-conscious man looked at them through half-open eyes and incoherently muttered something.

One of the cops said, "You know him?"

Confused, Mort turned to Lupe, who had defensively lifted the frying pan again and was now towering over the man.

"Lupe," Mort said, "What happened here?"

"Mista Mort," she said, "he trying to rob us, and I catch him and hit with the pan. Then I tie him up and call Mista Travis, and he called 911... I think. This man try to rob the judge's drugs. Mista Travis on his way."

Confused, the younger officer said, "The judge's drugs?"

"The chief's on his way," Officer Fleming said, "and this is judge Richter's house, right? The kidnapped judge?"

"*Justice* Richter. You got it," Mort said. "Just calm down, Lupe, and tell us what happened." It seemed natural for Mort to take charge, and the two officers didn't object. Officer Fleming bent and inspected the duct tape, then stood up, holstered his weapon and indicated for the younger officer to so the same.

"I in my room," Lupe said, "and I hear noise in the house. In the judge's bathroom. I know that Connie is with you, so I sneak around and see him in the judge's medicine closet." She took a deep breath. "I tippy-toe into the kitchen and get my frying pan, and when he walk out the door, I smash him hard in face."

"You knocked him out?" said the younger officer.

"Knock out good, but he a big man," Lupe said. "But I strong, too, so I drag him here, tie up with tape, call and wait for Mista' Travis. Then you show up, Mista Mort, with these cops."

The taped man was shaking his head, trying to clear away the cobwebs.

"Littlejohn, how the hell did you get here? And why?" Mort asked.

"Who's Littlejohn?" the burglar stammered.

"His gun and stuff on counter," Lupe said. Fleming saw an automatic pistol there with syringes and a wallet. Mort picked up the wallet. Brian Abernathy was the name on the driver's license.

And then, in a flash, it hit him. In his interview, Littlejohn said he had been adopted. But he didn't say that he was a twin. Maybe he didn't even know. Whoever this guy was—Brian Abernathy or someone else—he certainly wasn't Scott Littlejohn.

Another police car screeched to a halt in the driveway. Travis jumped out and raced up the steps.

"Travis," Mort said, "have I got a surprise for you."

Thirty-eight

Another squad car raced into the driveway, and a fourth officer entered the house.

Travis looked at his three officers, at Mort, and at Lupe, who was still brandishing the frying pan. He moved around to the front of the burglar and had the same reaction as Mort.

"Littlejohn! What the hell?"

Mort interrupted. "He's not Littlejohn, but I'd bet money that his DNA is the same. I think they're identical twins."

"I'll be damned!" was all Travis could muster.

The other officers looked completely confused.

"Who are you, and what are you doing here?" Travis asked.

"I got no twin. My name's Brian Abernathy," the burglar said, "and I want a lawyer."

"You're going to need one," Mort said, "if your DNA matches the triple killer's. In fact, you're going to need a magician."

"I only shot those punks because they were trying to rob the old man," Brian said. "I saved that old guy's life too. He'll tell you. I know the law."

Travis held up his hands. "Whoa," he said, turning to Officer Fleming. "Read him his rights before I hear another word out of anybody."

"You have the right to remain silent, you have the right to an attorney, anything you say can…" At this point, Brian interrupted the officer.

157

"I know my goddamned rights," he said. "I was a federal officer. I never wanted to get involved in this fucking thing. I'm an asshole." At this point, he sniffled and started to choke up.

"What thing?" Mort asked.

"This thing with the judge. And his prescriptions. I knew it wouldn't work."

"You know where Justice Richter is?" Mort asked.

"I know a lot," Brian said, "but I want a deal before I say another word."

They didn't have time for "a deal," which would require carting this guy to jail, getting a prosecutor, assigning a lawyer and then negotiating some sort of arrangement. Brian didn't know who Mort was but apparently thought he was law enforcement since he was there with the police.

"Look, I'll get you a deal," Mort lied, then turned to silently implore Travis to go along with him. Turning back to Brian, he said, "If you really killed those three in the middle of a robbery, that can go away. But kidnapping a Supreme Court justice, that's twenty years hard time. Come clean and maybe you'll save your ass. Is Justice Richter okay?"

Travis and the three officers were watching Mort as if in a trance. Lupe was still in her aggressive position with the frying pan.

Tears suddenly were running down Brian's face, and Mort assumed they meant Richter had died.

"He's okay," Brian said, stammering as he choked through his tears. "High and dry. We didn't hurt him. First, I want something in writing."

"No problem," Mort said.

Mort looked at Travis.

"Don't let me stop you now," Travis said.

Mort asked Lupe to get him paper and a pen—and a knife to slice through some of the tape to free Brian's writing hand. She was reluctant to leave this stunning melodrama but did as she was told.

"Okay," Mort said to Brian, "now where is the justice?"

"First, you write down that because of me is the only reason you know where he is," Brian said.

Mort scribbled on the pad. He had Brian give his full name and address, and then wrote, "Without the assistance of Brian Abernathy, the whereabouts of Justice Richter would be unknown." Then he cut through some of the tape, freeing Brian's right arm so he could write.

"Sign it," Brian said.

Mort signed. "The guy's in West Virginia," he said. "Some burg called Great Capcapon about ninety miles away from here—a good hour and fifteen minutes. Straight up I-270 north." He gave specific directions. "It's a rented house with a barn where we keep the cars... and the motorcycle."

Travis was already on his phone, getting GPS coordinates. He asked Brian, "How many men are guarding the justice?"

"Just the two of us. Mateos is at the house, and I'm here. This whole fucking thing just blew up."

"Fleming," Travis said to the older officer, "this guy looks ready for a FedEx pickup, but let's unwrap him and slap the cuffs on. Take him to HQ and book him. He turned to the fourth officer. "Boswith, you go with him." To the last officer, he said, "Young, you're coming with me. We're alerting the FBI and going to get J.J."

Travis turned to Lupe. "You did great." He looked at Mort. "You did great too."

"What about me coming along?" Mort said.

"You've done more than enough. This is what we're paid for. Stay here with Lupe. It'll take the feds a little time to organize. With luck, we can be there and get J.J. out safely by the time they get there. They'll probably arrive with bells on, but I want to make sure the old guy is safe."

"I call Miss Chickie," Lupe said.

Travis looked at Young and said, "Let's do it. Let's rescue an American hero."

"I wanna see that paper," Brian said as he was being de-mummified.

Mort held it up for him to read and then handed it to Fleming.

"What's WaPo?" Brian asked.

"The *Washington Post*," Mort replied.

"Wait, aren't you a lawyer?"
"No, but my fiancée is. Without a ring."

Thirty- nine

The sandwiches were delivered to Mateos as requested.

"Cheap bastard," the delivery boy, Caleb Azar, muttered as he walked out the door. He was delivering food to make some extra money. When the tourist season got into full swing by July, things would be much better. The delivery had come to $18.85, and a twenty-dollar bill had been thrust into his hand with a sarcastic "Keep the change."

As Caleb was getting back into his idling Ford, he heard the scream and headed back to the house where he hesitated, then slowly pushed the door open. He could see straight through to the kitchen. Mateos was on the floor with his hand inside a doggie door at the bottom of the door leading to the basement. Caleb saw what looked like a holster strapped to his belt in back.

"Are you okay?" Caleb asked, nervously.

Mateos twisted his head and spotted Caleb.

"He's got my fucking hand pinned, and it hurts like hell. Help me," Mateos pleaded.

"Who?"

"Just help me get my hand free," Mateos said. "A hundred bucks."

A hundred dollars would go a long way.

On the other side of the door, J.J. heard the plea for help, and then a second voice. He kept his hands pressed down on the nail and shouted, "Help me! They kidnapped me. Help me! "

Caleb took one step forward and stopped. "What's going on?" he asked.

Mateos was sweating from the pain. "He's just a crazy old man," he said. "We had to lock him in the cellar. Just fuckin' help me!" He commanded.

"I'm a justice of the Supreme Court!" J.J. shouted.

Thoroughly confused, Caleb spun around and said, "I don't know what's going on, but I'm calling the cops." He started for the front door.

"No!" Mateos shouted. "We've come too far!"

Caleb was almost to the front door when Mateos reached behind his back with his left hand and managed to pull his pistol from the holster. "Stop!" he shouted.

Caleb was opening the door when Mateos fired with his left hand. Once. Twice.

Caleb spun, took a staggered step or two back inside the house and fell.

Mateos screamed at the cellar door. "You see what you made me do, you old bastard!" He fired twice at the cellar door.

J.J. had been leaning over when Mateos fired.

A bullet creased his skull. He released his grip, raised his hands to his head as he tried to stand, but lost his balance and tumbled down the stairs.

Mateos pushed the basement door open, holding his right hand to his chest. It was bloodied and already turning purple. "Motherfucker!" he yelled as he looked down the stairs. "Oh, Jesus!" he screamed.

Moving cautiously down the steps, gun in hand, he looked down at J.J., who was unconscious with blood seeping out of one ear and from his forehead. Mateos turned and fled up the stairs, past the body of Caleb Azar, not even stopping to look. He had to get out of there, to get as far away as possible, to save his skin.

He remembered a gas can in the garage. He would torch the house and the garage and then get away in the van. Evidence burned, nothing to tie him to this fucked up crime.

He ran to the garage.

Forty

Brian Abernathy had said that the trip to the West Virginia house would take about an hour and fifteen minutes. Obviously, he hadn't considered Travis doing over a hundred miles per hour up I-70 and then cutting over to West Virginia 9 in his drug-forfeiture Lexus LS.

"This thing really moves," Officer Young said, nervously looking out the window. "How come you didn't wait for the FBI to coordinate with us? Or the locals?" he asked.

"The last thing we need," Travis replied, "is helicopters, swat teams and flashing lights. And I don't know if the locals are pros or yahoos. If the kidnapper panics, J.J. will get hurt. Or worse, we'd wind up in a hostage situation. With just us, we'll have the element of surprise."

They arrived in Great Capcapon in just over forty minutes. Travis slowed and cruised down Capcapon Road, two lanes of black asphalt divided by a double yellow line. The houses on both sides were vintage 1920s. Going the legal twenty mph, he continued through town, all two blocks of it. The rented house where J.J. was being held was outside town with no other houses nearby, according to Brian. The homes here seemed to be built on slabs, but Abernathyhad said that J.J. was locked in the basement. Basements and slab construction were mutually exclusive.

Before long, they spotted the house, a white clapboard two-story home with a front porch and back deck. The house sat at the rear of a property that looked to be at least several acres. There was a barn with its door open about one hundred feet from the house and an old Ford sitting on the driveway, its door open and the engine idling, Travis concluded, based on wisps of smoke coming from the tailpipe.

"Uh oh," Travis said. "Has our guy got company?"

He parked the Lexus several hundred feet from the house, just past a copse of cedars. Travis popped the trunk, which contained flares, road cones and other emergency equipment, and an AR-15—standard issue for all Montgomery police vehicles. There was also a Remington 870 Field Master shotgun. He looked at Young and pointed to the AR-15.

"You ever been involved in anything like this?" Travis asked.

"No sir, except in training. I know how to use the AR-15 though." Travis handed the weapon to Young.

"Work your way around to the rear of the house as best you can. Stay low and cover the back in case he makes a run for it. Don't hesitate. Shoot if you have to." Travis headed for the front door, the Glock in his left hand, the shotgun dangling in the other.

* * *

With his reporter's mentality, Mort was not about to let this situation pass him by. He had memorized the address that Brian had provided, and after Travis and Young had left J.J.'s house, he had run to his car to follow Travis. From the front porch, he shouted to Lupe, "Tell Danni I'm following Travis to get J.J."

He arrived in Great Capcapon just minutes behind Travis. When he arrived at the kidnapper's house, he spotted Travis's Lexus and pulled in behind it. He started toward the house but then turned around, walked back to his Subaru and popped the trunk. He carefully slid his Winchester skeet-shooting rifle out of its case along with a box of pellets. He loaded the rifle, put another two shells in his pants pocket and cradled the gun under his arm as he moved toward the house.

After a few steps, Mort turned back toward his Subaru with second thoughts. *What am I thinking? I'm a lousy shot, and this is a job for the pros.* He returned the Winchester to the trunk and started toward the house again, slowing down at the edge of the property.

He could see Travis cautiously approaching the house. Young was nowhere in sight. The screen door was open about six inches, and the front door was wide open. Travis stepped in, then was suddenly back on the porch, shouting, "Young! Here!"

Mateos, who was in the garage, looked out and saw Travis, a uniformed police officer, at the front door. Travis suddenly jumped from the porch and stood by the idling pizza-delivery Ford in the driveway.

Mateos looked at the van in the garage. His only thought now was getting away. But first, he had to dispose of the cop in the driveway. He jumped into the van and sped out of the barn, heading straight for Travis. Travis spun around, saw the van coming toward him, raised his pistol and fired once. The van continued straight for him, closing rapidly.

Travis started to raise the shotgun, but the van was practically on him. At the last second, he jumped to the side. The van clipped him, and he went flying, landing in a heap. The shotgun flew out of his hands. The Glock fell to the ground at his side.

Having heard the noise, Officer Young came running from the back of the house and glanced at Travis on the ground and then at the van. He started to raise the AR-15 when two shots rang out from the van as it turned toward the roadway. Young clutched his chest and went down.

Mort's first thought was of Travis. He ran toward his friend and bent over him.

Mateos spun the van around and headed straight for Mort.

Mort dove to the ground, landing next to Travis's shotgun. While lying prone on the ground, he reached out and grabbed the shotgun, instinctively raised the weapon and fired both barrels at the van.

The vehicle's windshield shattered, the van swerved and then it smashed into the idling Ford, turning it sideways before coming to a stop. Mort ran back to the spot where Travis was lying.

The chief's arm was at a peculiar angle, but he was conscious. He lifted his head and said, "J.J.—get J.J. inside." He then slumped to the ground again. Mort picked up the Glock and cautiously approached the van. He held the Glock with both hands, as he had seen in many TV shows. There was no movement inside the van, but there was blood everywhere. The remains of the driver's face were plastered all over the cab.

Young was on the ground, unconscious. Mort rolled him over and saw the young officer was wearing his protective vest. The slugs had knocked him out, but Young was otherwise not injured.

Mort ran to the house, pushed the screen door open and cautiously entered. Just inside he found a man's body face down with blood seeping from his back. At first, he thought it was J.J.

As he approached the body, he noticed that the body was taller than J.J. With his foot, Mort carefully flipped the body over. It was a young man, probably late teens or twenties with an Angus and Ale uniform shirt on. Blood stained the front of his uniform shirt in an expanding circle.

He called out, "J.J.? Are you here? Where are you?"

No response.

There was no one else on the main floor. He didn't head upstairs for two reasons. First, he was uncomfortably holding a Glock, which was totally unfamiliar to him. Second, Brian Abernathy had said J.J. was being held in the basement by his partner, who was alone. Brian's partner must have been the driver of the van.

In the kitchen, Mort saw the open door that led to a basement and what appeared to be a paper bag on the floor. The bag had "Angus and Ale" printed on it. He approached the stairs and looked down. At the bottom, he saw J.J. lying motionless.

Mort flew down the stairs. J.J.'s eyes were closed, and there was a bleeding wound on his skull. Blood was seeping out of one ear. Mort felt for the carotid artery and nearly cried when he found a weak pulse. He knew that moving J.J. could cause more injury, so he raced up the stairs to get help.

Forty-one

Mort ran to Travis, who was still on the ground. His shoulder looked misshaped, and a bone was sticking out of his upper arm, but he was conscious.

"J.J.?" Travis asked him.

"Alive but unconscious. Hurt bad," Mort said.

As Mort looked at Travis's distorted arm, his mind flashed to the dead man in the van who was missing half his face, Young still lying on the ground conscious but moaning, a dead man in the house and J.J. lying at the bottom of the stairs. Suddenly, he lost it and threw up.

Travis grunted, "Trauma. But you've got to get on the horn and call for help."

Mort didn't have to call. He could already hear sirens.

Within fifteen minutes, there were more local, state and other law enforcement officials at the site than there were people in Great Capcapon. Roadblocks had been set up in both directions. It was just the kind of chaos Travis had predicted and wanted to avoid.

Mort puked twice more as police arrived from all over—Morgan County Sheriffs, the Bath police from Berkeley Springs, the West Virginia State Police, the Jefferson County Sheriffs, ambulances and EMTs.

Young was conscious, in a lot of pain and having trouble breathing, but his vest had saved him.

Travis was in severe pain but functioning like the leader he was.

Then the helicopters started arriving. The feds were here in force. A Medivac chopper landed, and two EMTs rushed into the house at the direction of someone. The next chopper landed with several FBI officials whom Mort didn't recognize and Dan Harrington from the Supreme Court, whom he did recognize, plus two doctors who immediately made their way into the house.

Another helicopter landed. It was a good thing this was a large property. The last chopper disgorged a swat team in full riot gear. *You're a little too late,* Mort thought. *What the hell did we need a swat team for after the fact?*

A team was bringing J.J. out and heading for the Medivac. Mort tried to get close and called out to one of the doctors, "How is he?"

The doctor looked back at Mort, probably wondering who he was, and said, "We'll know more when we get to Walter Reed." With that, the chopper lifted off with a doctor and the EMTs accompanying J.J. Mort figured that they'd be at Walter Reed in less than a half hour.

More grabbed his phone and called Chickie.

Nothing had hit the TV news yet, so Chickie asked, "Mort, what's going on?"

"J.J. is alive, injured pretty badly. He's on his way to Walter Reed in a chopper. And Travis got hit by the kidnapper's van. They're working on him and an injured cop who was saved by his vest. And—I… I killed a guy."

"You killed someone?" Chickie said, shocked. "Who?"

"One of the kidnappers, I think. At least I hope it was. He was trying to run me down. This place is a circus at the moment."

"Danni is here with me listening in," Chickie said, "so you don't have to call her. Are you OK?"

"Yeah, but I puked all over West Virginia."

"You guys are heroes," Chickie said. "I'm heading to Walter Reed to be with J.J. Here's Danni."

Danni started talking, her voice trembling. "Are you sure you're OK?"

Mort was embarrassed to explain that he seemed to be the only one who was unscathed.

"Did I hear you say you killed one of them? How?"

"Not sure. With a shotgun," Mort said. And he left it at that.

"What? Never mind. When will you be back? Jesus, we raised almost a hundred million on GoFundMe. What are we going to do with that?"

Mort was amazed at Danni's practical mind.

"Mort," Danni said, choking up, "I'm so proud of you. I love you. Take care of yourself."

Mort felt dizzy. Was it the trauma, or Danni's words? She had never spoken like that.

An ambulance made it to the house, and Travis was placed on a gurney. Young was getting into the back of the ambulance and holding his chest.

It was at that point that Mort saw Dan Harrington and some of the FBI men heading toward Travis. Mort had met Harrington on several occasions, including at J.J.'s summer barbecues. He liked Harrington. With these men was Special Agent Tim Richardson, who had been leading the team assigned to find J.J.

Travis raised his head and saw them. "Oh, shit," he groaned. "Here's where it hits the fan."

Forty-two

Harrington led the small contingent straight to Travis. "You guys are heroes, you know that?" Harrington said.

"Not so fast," said a portly man in his fifties. He was wearing a blue dress shirt with a tie that was askew. Harrington introduced him as George Blessing, director of the FBI.

At this point, Special Agent Richardson said to Travis, "You were *specifically* instructed to stay away from this case. It was in our hands. You're going to have to answer for this."

Blessing reached out and put his hand on Richardson's arm as if to restrain him.

Mort interjected, "How about we let this man get to the hospital to get his arm looked at?"

"And you are?" asked Director Blessing.

"Mort Ahrens, *Washington Post.*"

"Jesus, the press is here already. How did you get through the street closure?" he asked.

As he was being loaded into the back of the ambulance, Travis answered, "Mort's the one who killed the kidnapper in the van."

Blessing seemed thoroughly confused. "A reporter killed a kidnapper? I don't think I understand. What's your connection here?"

Mort was shaking with the after-effects of the trauma. He couldn't think of an answer, so he simply said, "My fiancée is sort of Richter's adopted daughter."

"I didn't know that Justice Richter had any children."

171

"Oh, he didn't adopt her," Mort said. "She adopted him."

Blessing shook his head and turned to Richardson. "You're going to have to get statements from everyone so we can put this thing together. Richter—when and if he's able, of course. But I'm talking about the rest of them."

Richardson just nodded.

Mort said, "I feel sick. I think I need to go to the hospital too."

Officer Young climbed into the back of the ambulance with Travis, nodding to Mort. They left.

"Where are they heading?" Mort asked.

Blessing looked to Richardson, who had no idea either. Richardson walked to the closest sheriff.

"The War Memorial Hospital in Berkeley Springs," the sheriff said. "Close by. They should be there in minutes."

Mort said, "I think I can drive, but can someone get Travis's car back to Maryland?" At that point, he threw up again.

Blessing spun away and said, "Go. We'll take care of it."

"I'm free to go?"

"Go. Go now," Blessing said. "But we're going to have to sort all of this out. As quickly as possible." He looked at Richardson and said, "Give him your card."

Richardson handed Mort his card. "As soon as possible," Richardson said.

"If it's okay, I'll go with him," Harrington said, gesturing toward Mort. No one objected. "I'll take the chief's car, then I can return it to Montgomery County. The cars aren't evidence, I assume." He turned to Mort. "Can you drive?"

"I'll follow you, and I hope I won't heave again."

"I'll keep my eyes on the rearview," Harrington said.

Forty-three

Mort realized that his front-page exclusive interview with Scott Littlejohn had just been shot down. Littlejohn was no longer an accused triple murderer. He was, in fact, exactly what he appeared to be—a respected accountant. There would certainly be a follow-up story, and Mort was sure that refining the DNA analysis would show that he and Brian Abernathy were identical twins.

As often happens, Mort had been pre-empted by late-breaking news— the rescue of a kidnapped Supreme Court associate justice and the apprehension of his kidnappers. And because Mort was now part of the story, someone else would be writing it.

He realized, though, that no one else would have the news yet, so as he drove to the hospital, he called his managing editor, Steve Ginsberg.

"Steve, it's Mort Ahrens."

"Why is it that I get nervous every time I hear your voice?" Ginsberg asked.

"We got Justice Richter, and he's on his way to Walter Reed. But he's unconscious. I don't know how serious it is," Mort said.

"Jesus Christ!" Ginsberg shouted. "Incredible. Let me get someone on the line so we can start writing. Wait—what do you mean, *we*?"

"I was with Chief Anderson. He's hurt. We're in West Virginia. That's where they were holding him. I killed one of the kidnappers. It's kind of a convoluted story."

"Good God! You killed a kidnapper? How?"

"Shot him with Travis's shotgun. Like I said, it's convoluted. It started when Lupe knocked out the other kidnapper with her frying pan."

"Lupe? Who the hell is Lupe? What frying pan? Are you okay? You're not making any sense."

"I'm on my way to the War Memorial Hospital in Berkeley Springs, West Virginia. I'm OK, but I puked a lot."

"Stay right there at the hospital," Ginsberg said. "I'm going to get someone on this right away. Was the FBI involved?"

"They showed up after the fireworks. Justice Richter is in their chopper on the way to Walter Reed."

"Ahrens, I can't believe this. Are you sure you're OK?"

"No problem, Steve. Oh, and Littlejohn is not a killer. One of the kidnappers is his identical twin I think," Mort said.

Ginsberg shouted, "Stop! We've got to get on this immediately. Stay at the hospital until our people arrive."

* * *

Harrington and Mort entered the hospital through the Emergency doors and were told to wait. About ten minutes later, Officer Young entered.

"Young," Mort said, as though they were longtime buddies. "Are you all right? What's the story with Travis?"

"I'm just bruised up. And I never got a shot off. You were the real hero. The chief is in the operating room where they're working on his arm." Young appeared a little unsteady.

During the interminable wait for a doctor, Mort said to Harrington, "Is it possible the inner sanctum where the justices meet is bugged?"

"Almost impossible," Harrington said. "That place is locked up tighter than a drum."

"Well, while I was speaking to Brendan Braddock a couple of days ago, he seemed to know everything that was going on in there. Danni thought it was suspicious. He knew too much."

"Wow!" Harrington said. "And Braddock is dead now. I don't see how that's realistic, though. Probably just good guesses on Braddock's part. But I'll certainly get the FBI on it, along with our own security. If you're right, the chief justice will have apoplexy."

After another fifteen minutes, a doctor finally arrived. He was in his scrubs, balding and serious. "Chief Anderson has a severely broken arm, shoulder and collar bone," he informed Mort and Harrington. "Snapped his humerus right in half. He's going to need further surgery. We want to admit him, but he refuses to be held overnight."

A few moments later, Travis walked through the door with a nurse at his side. He looked like hell.

"He refused to get into a wheelchair," the nurse said.

"We've got to get to Walter Reed and see how J.J. is," Travis said. "I've got to find out."

"I'll take Officer Young back to Travilah," Harrington said to Mort, "and if you're OK, you can drive the chief to Walter Reed. I know that's where you're headed."

They split up. Travis was on painkillers and sprawled across half the back seat, but Mort could see him wincing in the rearview mirror. There was little or no conversation, and with Travis's eyes closed Mort couldn't tell if he was awake or asleep.

Mort called Steve Ginsberg and told him of the change in plans. The new destination was Walter Reed.

* * *

As soon as George Blessing arrived back in DC, he headed to the White House. He had been summoned while the chopper was in the air. The president was waiting for him in the Oval Office with Chad Kennedy, his chief of staff.

"OK, George—what's the story?" the president asked. "I'm told that Richter has been rescued, but he's injured. How badly?"

"We don't know, Mr. President," Blessing said, "but apparently quite badly. Head injury, unconscious, flown to Walter Reed where neurosurgeons are waiting as we speak."

"Brain injury? Concussion? Bleeding?" Chad Kennedy asked.

"We don't know yet."

"And the kidnappers?" the president asked.

"We're not certain. Two dead at the scene, and they told me that a third is in lockup in Gaithersburg."

"Three? You're sure there were three?" Kennedy asked.

"That's what I understand," Blessing replied. "Our people are all over the place at the moment."

"Why Gaithersburg? Isn't the captured one in your custody?"

"It's a confusing tale at this point," Blessing said, "but the Montgomery County Police seemed to make the arrest of the one kidnapper, and they were first on the scene in West Virginia. We're still sorting it out."

The president turned to Chief of Staff Kennedy. "We don't want this one to get away. We're too late for the early news, but issue a special report, or bulletin, or whatever, that Richter has been rescued and the FBI was on the scene and blah blah blah. That sort of bullshit."

"Done," said Kennedy as he left the room.

The president turned to Blessing. "How the hell did that local cop preempt you?"

"We've still got a lot to sort out," Mr. President.

"Well, the last thing I need is to be accused of favoritism. When Chad comes back, I'm going to direct that Richter be cared for in the Presidential Suite at Walter Reed."

* * *

Within an hour, regular television and radio programming was interrupted on stations throughout the nation. "We have a special report from the White House," numerous announcers read. "US Supreme Court Associate Justice J.J. Richter, who was kidnapped and held for ransom four days ago, has been rescued and is presently undergoing evaluation at Walter Reed National Military Medical Center in Bethesda, Maryland, where his condition is unknown. The report from George Blessing, Director of the FBI, states that the operation and heroic rescue was part of a coordinated law enforcement effort. The justice was being held at a private house in West Virginia, and preliminary reports are that at least one and possibly two of the alleged kidnappers were killed while another is in custody. No ransom was paid, and no public monies were involved in the rescue. There is no danger to the public."

Forty-four

Using his GPS, Mort took I-70E and cut over to I-270 South to Walter Reed, which took a little over an hour. J.J. had been whisked right into the operating room. Chickie and Danni arrived within minutes of Travis's wife, Michele. Mort and Travis had a hard time talking their way past security, but Travis, in uniform, with his arm in a sling, got them in. They joined the others in an executive waiting room where they all viewed the special report on TV.

Mort couldn't believe it. "Coordinated effort, my ass," he complained. "That's bureaucratic bullshit!"

Steve Ginsberg had already dispatched two reporters and a photographer to Walter Reed. Mort thought a photo of Travis looking like hell would make him appear even more heroic.

After about a half-hour, an Asian doctor somberly walked into the room. He looked at the assembled gathering, a little confused, then introduced himself as Dr. Choupatka. "Who is who here?" he asked.

Chickie made introductions, then asked, "How is he?"

"In critical condition," Choupatka said. "His skull is fractured— an epidural hematoma, we call it, as in three-quarters of skull fractures. An artery gets torn inside the skull from a trauma. We had to go into the skull to relieve the swelling—a craniotomy. We removed blood and placed him in an induced coma. We are also lowering the body temperature to reduce swelling on the brain."

"Is he going to make it?" Chickie asked, her voice practically a whisper.

"He has endured a tremendous trauma to the skull. His age and recuperative powers are certainly a factor. Right now, we watch and wait."

"Why did you have to go into his skull?" Danni asked.

"This has become a common procedure in serious head trauma," Choupatka said. "The skull is an enclosed space, and a traumatic brain injury causes swelling in the damaged area. The brain collides with the skull. We need to release the blood that accumulates in the skull, then try to reduce the blood flow and pressure to allow a healing process to begin."

"My God," Chickie said, "that's the same thing that they had to do to my husband when he fell and fractured his skull in Mexico years ago. And he *died.*"

"Fortunately," Choupatka said, "this is *not* Mexico. And you are in the hands of the best professionals in the world. A lot has been learned from head wounds received in battle. Our procedures are far advanced today. We induced what we call a hyperammonemic coma with a controlled amount of drugs to relieve intracranial pressure, to reduce swelling, as I said, and lower the body temperature—therapeutic hypothermia—which provides the maximum chance for recovery."

"How long will he be in a coma?" Chickie asked.

"There's no gauge," Choupatka said. "Perhaps twenty-four to forty-eight hours. I know who he is, and he has my greatest respect. He's a true patriot, and we will do everything possible to restore him to good health. A lot depends on his responses. And God."

Chickie clutched the doctor's arm. "Can I stay in the room with him?"

"I'll arrange it. But no visitors. Absolute rest is imperative."

As the doctor got ready to leave, Mort said, "Doctor, I'm the one who found him at the bottom of the stairs. He also seemed to have a wound on his forehead."

"We've treated that already," Choupatka said. "Something creased his skull from what I understand, but no internal damage. Our biggest concern, though, is the fracture. Do you know how it was sustained?"

"As I said, I found him at the bottom of the stairs, and I assume he was either pushed by the kidnappers or fell."

Choupatka nodded. "A fall down a flight of stairs would certainly explain the fracture."

* * *

Chickie, as usual, had quickly gathered her wits and directed Danni to go to the Watergate and bring her some clean clothes and toiletries, and her laptop.

Danni turned to Mort. "I hope there won't be any brain damage."

"It's out of our hands, but you know what a tough old bird he is."

Except for Chickie, they all prepared to leave. Chickie reached out and hugged Danni, who kissed her. Mort had never before seen any outward affection between them. Then, to his great surprise, Chickie kissed him and said, "You were really brave. And you saved J.J."

Mort reached up and touched his cheek in disbelief.

Forty-five

After leaving the waiting room, Mort and Danni discovered two people from the *Post* waiting for them in the Walter Reed lobby—a photographer and Alison Powers, the reporter Mort had spoken to at the arraignment. They had been allowed inside—rather than kept outside with the rest of the media circus—by explaining that they had an appointment to see Mort.

Mort told Danni he'd see her back at Travilah after conferring with his colleagues. "We've got to bring Lupe up to date," he said. "We owe her that."

"I called to tell her J.J. was rescued," she said. "But she's full of questions."

Travis was fading fast. Michele was going to drive him straight to Adventist Health Care Hospital in Gaithersburg.

"Why don't you let them take care of you right here at Walter Reed?" Mort asked.

"Not close to home. Not close to the office," Travis said.

Michele just shook her head. "Not worth arguing with his stubbornness," she said.

The photographer took pictures of Travis with his cast on and of Travis and Mort and then left.

Mort took Alison into the hospital cafeteria, and they sipped coffees while he related the whole tale. Alison took notes on her laptop at a frantic pace. At the end of his dissertation, he realized he was absolutely drained, but she still had questions.

"Why didn't Captain Anderson wait for the FBI?" she asked.

"He thought the best chance to rescue J.J. was without the arrival of an overwhelming force. We had no idea he was unconscious at the bottom of the stairs."

"We? It sounds as though it's a good thing you followed him."

"As fast as I could. Got there just in time."

She said she'd stay at Walter Reed and write the story on her laptop, then send it in and head back to the *Post* to review comments from editorial.

Forty-six

On the morning of the sixth day since J.J. had disappeared, the story created a fire storm. The banner headline in the *Washington Post* read: "Justice Richter Rescued: Two Die in Shootout."

The subhead gave Mort the front-page recognition he had always sought, but not as a journalist: "*Post* Reporter Instrumental in Chaotic Events." The byline was "Alison Powers."

Mort and Danni read the story online in Travilah. Over breakfast, Lupe said, "Mista Mort, you save the judge." She still insisted on referring to him as the "judge," as did most people, oblivious of the distinction between "judge" and "justice."

Danni's cell phone rang, and she looked at the screen. "It's Chickie," she said, switching to speaker.

"How is he?" Danni asked her mother.

"About the same. If you come to visit, you'll have to clear security. We're now in Ward 71... marshals are guarding the floor."

"What's Ward 71?" Mort asked.

"The Presidential Suite. POTUS apparently directed the move and sent the marshals for extra protection."

"Fancy place, I'll bet."

"You wouldn't believe. You'll see when you get here."

"Mort has to go into DC and give his statement to the FBI," Danni said. "It will probably just be me."

"No visitors allowed, in any event," Chickie said, "so you'll be relegated to one of the lounges."

183

"Lounges?"

"Like I said, you wouldn't believe this place."

* * *

Mort parked in his space at the *Post* and walked the short distance to the FBI field office on 4th St. NW. It was a sunny day, not yet oppressively hot as DC can be in June. Even with his distaste for exercise, the short walk felt good after yesterday's adventure. Walking was clearly a wise choice. The district was already crowded with weekend tourists.

At the field office, he showed his ID and was led to Tim Richardson's office, where the agent was waiting for him with special agents Malone and Bergdahl.

"We met at Chief Anderson's?" Richardson said.

"No, I wasn't there the day of the kidnapping. You met my fiancée, I believe."

"Oh, that's right," Richardson said. "Do you want to have an attorney present?"

"Do I need one?" Mort asked. "I thought I was just giving a statement."

They spent the next half-hour going through preliminary matter—Mort's background and history from Harrisburg to the *Post*. Occasionally, Richardson jotted down a note on his pad. The other two agents said and noted nothing.

"Why were you in Great Capcapon yesterday?" Richardson asked.

"Hoping to get a story and find Justice Richter."

"Did Chief Anderson invite you to that location?"

"No. He told me not to go there. I went on my own."

"How did you know where to go?"

"I was at Justice Richter's home when the first kidnapper, Brian Abernathy, was captured."

"And?"

"And I overheard the address he gave for where the justice was being held."

"Why did Chief Anderson take off for that location before the federal authorities were in position?"

"That's a question you'll have to ask him. But I recall him notifying someone before he left."

"Why were you carrying a weapon?"

"I wasn't carrying a weapon. I grabbed the chief's shotgun when the guy in the van was trying to kill me. I dove to the ground and acted... guess you could say instinctively."

"You're experienced with weapons?"

"I'm a reporter. I didn't know what to expect, but it was the only thing I could do."

"Have you ever killed a man before?"

"Never before, and I hope never again. Have you?"

"That's irrelevant. But you fired at the deceased?"

"I fired at a van that was trying to run me down. The driver had already hit Travis and shot Officer Young. It was a defensive reflex, and it's the only reason I'm here today—to give a statement. I puked all over West Virginia, couldn't sleep last night, and hope never to relive that scene once we've debriefed here."

"We'd like your statement in writing."

"Longhand or on a laptop?"

Half an hour later, Mort gave his statement to Richardson, who printed it. Mort signed the printout, received a perfunctory thank you from Richardson and was on his way with the agent's card.

Mort had assumed they would ask questions about Brendan Braddock, but that topic never came up, so he didn't mention it.

* * *

Win Abbington was still asleep at six thirty when he was awakened by the ring of his phone. It was Zeke Shannon, the corporate CFO, who sounded elated.

"They got Richter rescued in a shootout, and both kidnappers are dead," he said. "Richter is apparently in pretty bad shape. They're tight about his condition, but he was medevaced to Walter Reed in Bethesda."

"Whoa," Win said, shaking his head to wake up. "Not so fast. Run this by me again."

Suddenly, caller ID indicated another caller on the line. Win put Zeke on hold. This time it was Boris, the company's corporate counsel.

Win put them on conference call and said, "Okay, Zeke—now start from the beginning."

"Are you alone?" Zeke asked.

"Yes, I'm alone," Win said, impatiently, "not that it's any of your concern. Boris is on the line as well."

"I've got great news," Zeke said, "but I don't want it to get out of the loop."

"Boris," Win said, "are you there?"

"All ears," Boris said, "although I'm not sure I'm in Zeke's loop."

Zeke said, "That boy reporter and a couple of Maryland cops somehow ended up in West Virginia at the house where Richter was being held. There was a shootout, and the two bad guys are dead. Plus, Richter's seriously injured. He'll probably have to miss the last week of court."

"How recent is your information?" Boris asked.

"Got a confidential call at six," Zeke said, "and I turned on the news. Confirmed."

"And how do you know this is the last week of court?" Boris asked.

"Well, Mr. Bright-boy-know-it-all, I have impeccable sources. I also know that the court is tied 4–4 in our case, so if Richter's out, then we win based on the lower court's opinions."

"Excuse me," Win interrupted, "but if you girls can quit squabbling with each other, I'd like to know how serious the justice's injuries are? That's really most important."

"He's in a coma, is what my information is," Zeke said. "And they're not even sure he's going to make it."

"Shit!" Win said. "If he dies, it will be because of our case and the kidnapping. We'll really buy a ton of bad press and hostility. Plus, the guy's like a legend."

"I had a feeling this would happen," Zeke said. "It didn't come out of thin air."

"Like a premonition, huh?" Boris said. "Well, here's another update for you. One of the dead guys at the scene is a deliveryman, and one of the kidnappers is apparently in jail in Maryland."

"Where the hell did you hear that?" Zeke asked, flustered.

"*My* confidential source," Boris said. "Name is ABC News. By the way, Zeke, where do you get all *your* confidential information?"

"Three?" Zeke said. "And one in jail? There were only *two*, goddammit."

"Only two what?" Win asked.

"I've got to check my source," Zeke said and hung up.

"I don't understand how he could know some of that stuff," Boris said.

Win shook his head. "There's a lot I don't understand."

Forty-seven

Back at the *Post*, most desks were empty—it was Saturday—but of those who were in the bullpen, several came rushing over to congratulate Mort.

"Deadeye Mort," one of the reporters said.

"Are you always armed with a rifle on your stories?" asked another.

Where he had previously been barely noticed—at least from his point-of-view—he was suddenly a celebrity.

He sought out Alison Powers, who was at her desk. "Terrific story," Mort said.

"Thanks to you."

"Did you have to put in the part about me puking?"

"Thorough reporting," she said, smiling.

"You're in early for a Saturday."

"Are you kidding? I've been here all night."

"There are some other angles to this that we've—or I—have got to pursue," Mort said. "There must be a connection between everything that just happened and Brendan Braddock's shooting. It's just too coincidental."

"I'm with you," Alison said. "From what I can gather, so is the FBI."

At his desk, Mort checked his voicemail and was shocked to find inquiries from producers with *Meet the Press*, *This Week* and *Good Morning America* inviting him to appear as a guest and a host of other congratulatory calls. *My fifteen minutes of fame*, Mort thought.

He decided to go to Bethesda before doing anything else because that was what he had told Danni he would do. Then he would decide his next move.

* * *

On his way to Bethesda, Mort called Dan Harrington. Dan had already contacted the FBI about Danni's suspicions concerning Brendan Braddock's uncanny knowledge of the inner secrets of the court. The FBI was already on it.

"Dan, what's the latest?" he asked when Dan answered.

"Can't talk at the moment."

"Are you at SCOTUS?"

"Yes, and not alone. I'll speak to you later."

* * *

Several minutes later, Mort got a call. He assumed it was Dan Harrington calling back with an update about what was going on in the Supreme Court, unusual for a Saturday morning. He was wrong.

"Morton, my God. Are you all right?" his mother said, alternating between sobbing and screaming. "Are you meshugah? Shooting guns? What do you know about guns? Vey iz mir, I won't sleep for a week."

Mort noticed that his mother had said nothing about her son being featured as a hero for his bravery. Still, he simply replied, "Mom, it was just one of those things. And lucky that I was there. We got J.J., and I'm on my way to the hospital." He honestly felt that circumstances had placed him in a situation where he had just reacted instinctively.

His mother said, "I have to find out about what happened early in the morning with a phone call from my sister, Aunt Jenny in Hackensack. How do you think that made me feel?"

Still not a word of congratulations, or pride.

That was when his father took the phone and said, "You did real good, Son. And remember how you used to complain when we would go and shoot those skeets? How's the judge?"

"*Justice* Richter," Mort said, "and he's in pretty serious shape. I told Mom I'm on my way to the hospital now."

In the background, he heard his mother say, "Harry, ask him when he's going to come and visit with us. And bring his lady friend."

"Your mother wants you to come and visit," his father said, "and your fiancée as well."

Fiancée? At least he had gotten through to one of his parents.

"Soon," Mort said. "As soon as life calms down a little. I promise."

Forty-eight

Dan Harrington was in uniform outside the Black Box, the conference room where no one except the nine justices of the court was allowed in, and neither were any electronic devices, even for the court members. Geoffrey Taylor, a portly man in his late fifties, was with him. Taylor, as marshal of the court, served as timekeeper during arguments before the court and was technically in charge of building security. Harrington, with a Glock holstered on his right side, was head of the dignitary protection unit. Over the years, Dan Harrington had become a favorite of J.J.'s, and they would often swap stories of their Midwestern roots and love of fishing. It had been a long time since J.J. had indulged in fishing.

Inside the conference room, two FBI forensic specialists wearing latex gloves and holding detection equipment, were carefully scrutinizing the room. FBI Special Agent Tim Richardson, who had been in charge of the search for J.J., watched from the doorway.

"We've got a hit," one of the specialists said. Richardson entered the room as an agent exited, went to the equipment that was stacked in the hallway, unzipped a plastic bag and took out a Nikon camera.

"We're going to need a tall ladder," the agent said to Harrington and Taylor.

In the conference room, an agent pointed a handheld instrument at the overhead chandelier. It blinked green.

"We've got to report this to Treller immediately," Richardson said.

Hanging by the open door, Harrington and Taylor could clearly hear the conversation.

"Jesus," Harrington said. "Looks like suspicions about a bug are right."

Taylor shook his head and said, "Shit, this could be my ass. I'm in charge of building security. But that room is always locked tight—only the justices are allowed in. Even when the cleaning people enter, one of us observes what they do."

It was another half-hour before the FBI agents exited the room with their equipment.

"The chief justice is in her chambers," Richardson said.

"On Saturday—that's a first," Taylor said. "Follow us."

Constance Treller was her usual, impeccable self, clad in a mauve pants suit with a multi-colored silk blouse. She was seated behind her massive desk facing three armchairs and walnut shelves lined neatly with law books. Richardson and one of the forensic specialists were facing her.

"I'd like the marshal and Chief Harrington in here," she said.

"Not advisable," Richardson said. "The room is now a crime scene, and basically no one is eliminated as a suspect. We found a mini-camera with microphone in the overhead chandelier and another microphone in a wall socket. Our people will want to go over the room more thoroughly and close it to any traffic. What we found were the transmitters. Now we've got to find the receivers."

"This is terribly distressing," Treller said, "but based on the circumstances of this week, I suggest that you start with Brendan Braddock's office."

"As soon as I get a warrant," Richardson said.

Treller bristled. "Agent," she said firmly, "this is *my* building. Do what you have to do under my authority."

"Yes, ma'am."

Taylor and Harrington led the FBI agents to Braddock's office. For some unknown reason, they had not yet searched it. Taylor unlocked the door, and they all went in. After searching the desk, the agents tried to get into the closet, but it was locked. Taylor opened it.

"Nothing in there either," the forensic specialist said.

"Check the bookcase." Harrington suggested.

Ten minutes later, they were looking at a mini-receiver and recording equipment that had been stashed behind some books on the deep shelves.

"We'll take it from here," Richardson said. "Please—not a word of this to anyone... except the chief justice."

* * *

By the time Mort arrived on J.J.'s floor at Walter Reed, he felt he had been put through the ringer.

"First I went through security," Mort said to Danni, "and then they checked my ID, and then they called upstairs to the federal marshals. I didn't know the marshals were on guard."

Danni interrupted. "The president's idea. I'm sure he did it for PR value and not because J.J. needed protection up here."

"Give him the benefit of the doubt," Mort said. "But 'up here' is incredible. When I heard he was in Ward 71, I didn't expect the Taj Mahal."

"It's the Presidential Suite," Danni said. "The entire floor with six patient rooms. They even have a separate room for the first lady—assuming most presidents have one, I guess. The floor has waiting rooms, sitting rooms with sofas and easy chairs, offices, a conference room, even a kitchen and private examination room."

Mort and Danni took seats in one of the sitting rooms. "All on the people's dime," Mort said.

"Hear anything about J.J.?"

"It hasn't even been a day yet. Chickie is in there with him. No one else allowed in."

"Well, in any event, I've got news for you," Mort said. "You were right."

"About what?"

"About most things—but specifically about Brendan. Dan called—he can't talk about it, but he said tell Danni that she must be clairvoyant."

"The conference room was bugged?" Danni said.

"That's my take," Mort said. "Which explains some of the weird things Braddock said, or things he shouldn't have known about."

"Hard to believe. Where do we go from here?"

"Well, the FBI is all over it, but I've got a few ideas of my own."

"Yeah, and your ideas almost got you killed. Travis too. Have you spoken to him? How's he doing?"

"That's my next stop."

"Just promise that you'll be careful."

"That almost sounds as if you cared."

"Don't get carried away," Danni said, giving him a peck on the cheek and squeezing his hand.

Forty-nine

Mort called Travis's home from the car and his wife, Michele, answered, saying Travis was asleep. "That arm is pretty messed up, and he's going to need another operation, but he claims he'll be in the office this week. By the way, Mort—I really owe you... my husband's life."

"Just in the wrong place at the right time," Mort said.

Back at the office, he sat down to figure out how to write a story about the Supreme Court being bugged without disclosing information he wasn't supposed to have. Temporarily stumped, he read Alison's article about the rescue again. She had done her research, and it was clear that Caleb Azar, the delivery person from Angus and Ale, had been caught up in something no one could explain. He had been shot, apparently by Mateos Panopoulos, who had the only pistol the FBI had found on the scene. The pistol had four rounds missing. But with two dead and J.J. in a coma, there was no one who could explain what had happened.

Mort found his story about Littlejohn on an inside page. No longer a suspect in a dramatic triple homicide, the accountant was now just the subject of a human interest story. The article had been updated and edited by the city desk.

Mort's desk phone started flashing, and he picked up.

"Ron Ciresi here," the caller said. Mort assumed he was calling to comment about the short article on Scott Littlejohn. He was partially right.

"Good article," Ciresi said, "and needless to say, Scott is thrilled not to be under arrest. The thing is, he never knew he had a sibling. Crazy as it seems, he wants to do whatever he can to help his brother out."

Mort sat back in his chair and said, "I think, other than visitation, he's going to have a long wait."

"That's another reason why I'm calling. I've got some ideas in that regard. Would it be possible for you to come to my office tomorrow… Sunday? Scott can be here, and we'd like you to have the story."

"I can do that," Mort said. They fixed a time to meet.

Mort called Danni at Walter Reed. "Any change?" he asked.

"Status quo, but the doctor has been in several times. He thinks J.J. could come out of the coma any time now."

"How about I head over there and take you to dinner at Chef Tony's? It's only minutes from Walter Reed."

* * *

At dinner, Mort and Danni shared a small table near the back corner. The soft-yellow walls were decorated with numerous scenes of Italy, and a bottle of Chardonnay iced in a bucket sat beside the table.

"Would your mother like one of us to relieve her?" Mort asked. "I'm sure she's not getting much sleep."

"I doubt that she's slept at all, but you know Chickie. As you saw, the kitchen is right in the suite—but if she wants anything, the marshal gets it for her."

"So what did Doctor Chou… whatever his name is, have to say?"

"Choupatka… it's Indian. He's a class act, Mort," she said. "Visits several times a day, and he's really going out of his way. He says J.J.'s vitals are good, and the cranial pressure is going down. They put two of what they call burr holes in his skull, and when the pressure's down enough, they'll start easing him off the meds."

"What about brain function or damage?"

"Too early to know, but let's not even consider the possibilities right now. J.J. is J.J. When he's ready—when his body tells him it's time—he'll wake up. Sanjai—that's what Chickie calls Doctor Choupatka, like they're old buds— he says that they see full recoveries all the time. And they deal with lots of really serious battlefield injuries."

"What does she do there all day?" Mort asked.

"Holds his hand, talks to him—about the kidnapping, about current events, about whatever she can think of to talk about. She says sometimes he squeezes her hand, so she believes he knows she's there. She intends to be the first person he sees when he opens his eyes."

"And if he's not back in court to close out the term?"

"She just wants him back with us. And so do I. But I also want him back on that bench using his judgment and influence for the good of the country. Starting with the NAWES case."

Fifty

Sunday morning. Chickie was by J.J.'s bedside when his eyes momentarily flickered open.

"Did you see that?" she shouted to the nurse, who was just entering the room.

Within minutes, Chickie was out in the hallway, and J.J. was surrounded by a medical team.

A nurse came out and told Chickie, "We've notified Dr. Choupatka, and he's on his way in."

Peering through the doorway, Chickie could see J.J. move his head, as if scanning the room, and then he made several unintelligible sounds.

Shortly after Choupatka arrived, he told Chickie in the hall, "It's a very good sign that he opened both eyes. The next twenty-four hours are critical. I know you've been by his bedside, holding his hand and talking to him. This is very good. Sometimes people come out of comas aware of everything that had been going on—even what was being said to them. So, we're going to remove the breathing tube now. Anything else?"

"Well, I brought a portable CD player to the room," Chickie said, "and I've been playing a song over and over—Crystal Gayle singing 'When I Dream.' It was a favorite of J.J.'s and his late wife."

Choutpatka smiled. "Crystal Gayle? Over and over? I'm not sure I like his taste in music, but that was a very good idea. If his progress continues, we'll examine his responses on the Glasgow Coma Scale."

201

"Which is?" Chickie asked.

"We measure three categories—motor responses, verbal responses, and eye reactions. He opened both eyes, an excellent sign. He tried to speak, though he was not yet intelligible, but he seems to be curious about his surroundings. Not surprising."

Later that morning, Choupatka told Chickie, "I gave him some commands—to squeeze my hand and move his eyes. He did these things, which is very encouraging. On a score of one to fifteen, he was nearly fifteen. Amazing, after what he's been through. He tried to speak, but it was still mostly unintelligible."

Tears came to Chickie's eyes.

The doctor continued explaining. "We have to monitor him very closely now, remembering he is seventy-eight, which factors in. Fortunately, he's in good shape, which is probably what saved him."

"He's a tough Wyomingite," Chickie said. "Tough but gentle. If all continues to go well, how long will he be here in the hospital?"

"My best guess is maybe five days or so," Choupatka said, "depending on his recovery, of course."

As the day progressed, J.J. emerged from the coma quicker than anticipated. Weak and tired, he was nonetheless alert and anxious to know where he was.

Chickie was at his side. "You're at Walter Reed Hospital in Bethesda," she replied.

J.J. looked around the room. "Thought it might be the Plaza in New York. How'd I get here?" His speech was slurred and hard to understand.

"What was that?" Chickie asked. "Could you say it again?"

"Hurts," he said, pointing to his throat. "Pad?"

Chickie went to the door and asked the marshal to get a pad and pen. A few minutes later, the marshal returned with something even better—an Etch A Sketch.

"Where did you find this?" Chickie asked the marshal.

"I think it belonged to the last president," he said, smiling.

Chickie handed the device to J.J., who slowly wrote, "How get here?"

"We have a lot to talk about," Chickie said. "But it's important for you to rest and get your strength back." He nodded, then closed his eyes and dozed.

When Dr. Choupatka stopped in later, Chickie said, "He's slurring his words pretty badly. Is that something that will improve?"

"In someone his age, dysarthria, or slurring, is rather common. It generally will clear up with the passage of time. If not, there's very effective treatment."

"I hope it gets better," Chickie said. "He's so headstrong... he won't tolerate it."

* * *

When Mort arrived at Ciresi's office later that morning, he was greeted by the same pretty receptionist who had mostly ignored him several days earlier. Mort was impressed that she was in on a Sunday, though dressed in a sweater and jeans.

"Mr. Ahrens," she said, "you were really something. A gun battle and killing that kidnapper. That was some experience."

"Something I never want to live through again," Mort said. He wondered where this kind of recognition had been all his life. A few days ago, he was just a pudgy reporter. Today, he was greeted as a hero. How times had changed.

The inner door opened, and Ron Ciresi beckoned him into his office, putting his arm around Mort's shoulder. "What's the latest word on Justice Richter?" Ciresi asked.

"He might be coming out of the coma. I'll be on my way there after we're done here."

In his office, Scott Littlejohn, in a colorful striped polo shirt, sharply creased jeans and sockless loafers, rose and pumped Mort's hand. Behind him was a very attractive brunette introduced as Stephanie, Littlejohn's significant other. She was the woman Mort had seen at the arraignment.

"Let's get right to it," Ciresi said, "especially after that good news about the justice."

He motioned for them all to be seated.

Littlejohn spoke first. "This DNA mix-up—and I'm sure that's what the science will prove—brought an entirely new aspect into my life. As you know, I had these great parents who adopted me, but I never knew I was a twin. Now, suddenly, I have a twin brother, and it's opened up a new world for me. I can't wait to meet him, but at the moment it's not possible, as you know."

"The point is," Ciresi said, "Scott wants to do everything he can to help his brother. And he's ready to do just that. We want you to write the story, not only because of the human interest, but because you were so instrumental in where we are today."

Mort had mentally prepared for this topic to come up, but now that it had, he wasn't sure what to say, so he just started talking. "Your brother—and I have no doubt that you're right about him being your twin—is charged with a triple murder in North Potomac, plus the kidnapping of a Supreme Court justice. I'm very happy that you have been exonerated, Scott, but your brother is going to need a miracle worker, not a lawyer—as I told Brian when he was captured."

"The other side of the coin," Ciresi said, "is that we have in Brian an expert marksman who had an exemplary career in the secret service, and who was decorated for bravery several times, including breaking up a forgery ring run by a crime family. We have a man who was a college athlete of note and who served his country with honor, and who had only one blemish in his career."

"Are we talking about the same guy?" Mort asked. "This model citizen you describe also just happens to be one of the kidnappers of a Supreme Court justice, and then holds him hostage for ransom. I will be happy to write the human interest article—it will certainly get attention—but good luck recommending him for sainthood."

The room fell uncomfortably silent.

Mort looked at the other faces in the room, which were all avoiding his eyes. Finally, he said, "I will say one thing, though—we've got to find out who was behind this kidnapping. I'm certain the murder of Brendan Braddock factors in. Anything we can learn in that regard would be priceless—to me, and the FBI. If Brian could help solve this mystery, it would probably help him out."

Fifty-one

~~⟋⟍~~

Danni was alone in a Ward 71 lounge when a marshal poked his head in and announced, "Visitor."

Since no visitors were allowed, she assumed it was Mort, so she was shocked when Associate Justice Anthony Battaglia entered the room. He carried a large bouquet of yellow roses, sunflowers and tulips in one hand and held a cane in the other. Battaglia was pale and moved slowly. He handed Danni the bouquet.

"Justice Battaglia," Danni said, "How did…?"

"I just had to come," Battaglia said, "although getting admitted to this place is harder than being admitted to the White House. Federal marshals? J.J. and I aren't the type who wants US marshals hovering over us."

"The president insisted," Danni said. "I certainly didn't expect to see anyone from the court. Still no visitors."

"I had to come and see for myself. J.J. and I have been down too many roads together. In different lanes, I'm afraid, but on the same road."

Danni smiled. J.J. was the court's progressive leader, Battaglia an entrenched conservative. Despite their close personal friendship, they had frequently crossed philosophic swords over twenty-five years of deciding cases. Battaglia had announced his upcoming retirement as he battled pancreatic cancer. Justices usually announced their retirement on the last day of the term, but Battaglia recently learned that he also had an early case of Parkinson's Disease and felt duty-bound to publicize his decision "in fairness to the court."

"How are you feeling, Your Honor?" Danni asked.

"One day at a time, which is all we can ask for. I'm not as brave as RBG was, I guess. There are still a few things left on my bucket list, and I want to take what time I have left to enjoy my family. Things have changed radically just this week in that regard. With Gracie gone these past years—losing our wives is another thing J.J. and I have in common—they are my legacy."

"I'm not sure I understand," Danni said.

"Well, you are partly at fault."

"Me?"

"It's a little disjointed, but I'm scheduled for treatments at the Mayo Clinic in Minnesota once the term ends and then I was heading to Arizona to spend time with my daughter, son-in-law, and my only granddaughter. Two days ago, my daughter called, and I learned that they had just escaped a fire that not only consumed their beautiful home but also the entire community where they lived. You must have read about it. And they thought they were in paradise.

"In any event, they barely escaped with the family dog in one of their cars. But they lost everything else. They've been in a hotel dealing with the insurance and necessaries. The fire couldn't be contained—even with those fire-fighting planes dropping retardant—because there wasn't enough water to fight the flames. A sad commentary, wouldn't you say? So, I talked them into moving East to live with me, at least for the time being. My son-in-law works from home. It's incredible how life can change in a few weeks, days… or even minutes. And then there was you in that debate a few days ago. You did a great job."

"How is all this affected by the NAWES case?"

"You know I can't discuss a pending decision with you, but I've been thinking about a lot of things, like what's important in life. What legacy we leave behind. What people will say fifty years from now. So, you in that debate are responsible, if nothing else, for my doing a lot of reading."

"You know," Danni said, "the world is ever-changing, and we have to change with it. Especially when it strikes so close to home. If you went to Israel, you'd find that the Dead Sea is drying up, just like the Great Salk Lake in Utah, and these can release all sorts of dangerous toxins into the atmosphere. It's not just Arizona that's burning up."

"Your debate is over, my dear," Battaglia said. "The case is argued, and you've made your point."

"Yogi Berra said, 'It ain't over until it's over.'"

Battaglia smiled. "Can you find something I can put these flowers in?"

Uncomfortable with the conversation, Danni suggested that Chickie would want to see Battaglia, so she went to the door of J.J.'s room and motioned her out.

"Anthony!" Chickie exclaimed. "I certainly didn't expect to see you. How good of you to come. J.J. will be thrilled. But how are *you* doing?"

"As I told Danni, one day at a time. I had to come. The court is not the same without him. But his health is paramount. Life is too short. I have certainly learned that. He's got to take care, listen to the doctors, and not worry about anything else."

"More easily said than done, as you know, with J.J.," Chickie said.

"I just asked Danni if she might find something for these flowers," Battaglia said.

Chickie turned to Danni. "Let's scout the kitchen, Danni." Turning back to Battaglia, she said, "We'll find something and then I can show you the rest of this palace. We'll be right back."

The women left, but when they returned with a large vase, Battaglia was not in the room.

"Weird," Chickie said, and went about arranging the bouquet in the vase.

A few minutes later, Battaglia emerged—from J.J.'s room.

"Anthony," Chickie said, harshly, "he's not supposed to have visitors."

"Court business," Battaglia said. "Had to have his opinion. I talked, and he wrote on that thing. I needed his thoughts."

Fifty-two

Instead of going to Walter Reed from Ciresi's office, Mort decided to check with Danni first. "What's the word?" he asked.

"He's conscious but weak. Still no visitors allowed, but the doctor says the signs are good even though his speech is very slurred."

"And Chickie?"

"Ten years younger. Anthony Battaglia showed up and sneaked into J.J.'s room while our backs were turned."

"I'll be damned," Mort said. "Like a mischievous teenager. On my end, Littlejohn wants to help his brother any way he can, and it's a good personal-interest story, so I think I'll head to WaPo and knock it out. See you later."

Truth be told, Mort's intestinal system, which was never his strongest feature, had been giving him problems since the confrontation in West Virginia—nausea, cramping and diarrhea. He attributed it to killing a man. He had not slept well either. Weird dreams—maybe it was PTSD. He thought he'd ask Travis about it when he got the chance, or see an internist if it persisted. Or maybe tell his shrink.

* * *

While he was at his desk writing, Mort's cell phone chirped. "Mr. Ahrens," the voice said, "you may remember me, Boris Rosenthal, corporate counsel with NAWES. You gave me your card before you left our office."

"Of course I remember," Mort said, surprised. "What can I do for you?"

"I hate to bother you on a Sunday, but I'm here at our offices, and I really need some advice. I'm calling on one of those unlisted phones."

"A burner phone."

"Yes—I found it in Zeke's desk. I shouldn't even be here, but I was just on another floor of the office earlier sneaking a look at the corporate books. I have a request that's somewhat irregular—no, very irregular—and I got the impression that you were an okay guy, a *lonsman,* who could help me out. This is strictly confidential, so if you say no, I'll understand, and we didn't have this conversation. I can't be involved. Is that OK?"

"I'd be happy to help if I can... without breaking any rules," Mort said.

"I'm deeply troubled," Rosenthal said, "because I'm certain something is going on here that I can't put my finger on, and it has to do with our case before the Supreme Court."

Mort was all ears. "I'm listening," he said.

"It's just that I'm not sure who's involved or how high it goes, but I need someone in the government, someone who's trustworthy, to do some investigation without ruffling feathers. It might even involve someone at the Supreme Court."

Mort leaned into the phone and whispered, even though no one was around. "Why come to me?"

"Because I know you've had experience with the FBI. I was hoping you'd know someone who can be trusted. I think this thing might go pretty high."

Mort thought for a moment. "I have someone in mind, Boris— someone with the FBI. He's tough, but you can trust him. I'll get in touch, and if he contacts you and uses my name, go with it."

"I think Zeke is somehow involved in all this. He knew too many things he shouldn't know, like this is the last week of the Supreme Court. And he knew the vote in our case was tied 4-4 without Justice Richter's vote. He almost had a hemorrhage when he heard the report that there were three kidnappers. In a conference call with Win, he yelled out, 'But there were only two.' How would he know that? Also, he's got great freedom with the company's finances, and there are some things that don't make sense, like large transfers of money. I smell a rat."

Mort furiously typed some notes into his computer, his heart racing.

Boris continued. "I went into his desk—guess that makes me a burglar. But in his old-fashioned Rolodex I found the name and two numbers for that Supreme Court officer who was killed—Brendan Braddock. Why would Zeke have that guy's name? It doesn't add up. I think it might have something to do with Braddock's death. And I would bet that Win is not involved. He's such a straight-shooter. He even wanted to give five million to help meet the ransom demand."

Mort's impression of Zeke had not been positive to begin with. He had thought the man was arrogant and obnoxious. And Mort knew things Boris Rosenthal didn't know—of the bugs planted at the Supreme Court and the FBI's involvement in the case.

Mort said he'd make a call, then got Boris's cell phone number.

Mort was a saver. It sometimes lead to clutter, sometimes came in handy. He searched around and dug out the business card he was looking for. He had the business number on his phone, but it was Sunday afternoon, and he needed a cell phone number. He found it and placed a call.

"Mort, what's up? Twice in one week?" said the voice on the phone.

"Craig," Mort said to his friend, FBI Special Agent Craig Fisher. "I've got a lead into the murder of Brendan Braddock at the Supreme Court, and I think it might be tied into the Richter kidnapping. In fact, I'm almost sure of it. I have some inside information—all still speculative—from the chief legal officer at NAWES, but he can't be the source. And it definitely can't be me. I'm already too involved. Can you run with it? He's standing by, and I have his number. Just mention my name."

"Jesus, Mort," Fisher said. "Let me touch a few bases and run it by the chain of command. I'll keep you out of it."

Mort was pleased that Fisher seemed ready to get involved. But since he was an investigate reporter, he also thought it was fair to pursue leads on his own.

* * *

Fisher called Boris and identified himself.

"I'm afraid I got some of this information illegally," Boris said. "I went through my associate's office. There were also some things he said that he should never have known."

Boris related to Fisher the same information he had told Mort.

"We can protect you in that regard," Fisher said. "You're a private individual. This is not a government intrusion. This is not my case, but I'm certain my boss will know how to handle it. Stand by, and don't worry."

Fifty-three

It was Monday morning—eight days since J.J. had been abducted. The eight justices were in Chief Justice Treller's chambers by eight thirty. There were other places in the court where the justices could have met, but the CJ's chambers were the most spacious and had been swept for bugs by the FBI. As with all their conferences, no one was present except the justices.

She opened with the big news. "Our conference room has been compromised. The FBI found both listening devices and a camera, which means our discussions have probably been recorded and likely disseminated to someone outside the court. For how long, we don't know. But set up from within the court. I can't say more at the moment."

The other justices started talking all at once, surprised by this news.

The CJ held up her hand to quiet them. "We have four cases left before the term ends, and we must decide how to proceed. On top of that, we have J.J's kidnapping, and I believe these events are tied together. Do we strike those cases from the calendar and make the parties start over? Not possible in my mind. Do we pass these cases to the fall? The FBI faces the same indecision that we do. This is virgin territory, and I admit I am at a loss."

The following discussion ranged back and forth on the possibilities. Everyone seemed to have a different view of how to proceed. After almost an hour, Treller finally said, "I think we're beating a dead horse. At first, I was inclined to move the cases to the fall term, but now I realize that would accomplish little. Our positions are set. With what's going on all over the country, we need a final definition in this water rights case no matter what. In addition, should we let a criminal operation, a most serious criminal operation, define the workings of this court? I think not. Thursday will be the final day of the term, and I think we should let the chips fall where they may in the NAWES case."

Anthony Battaglia smiled and said, "Well, that's quite a string of clichés, Chief. But I say we wait until we know more about J.J.'s condition. I know that he is no longer in a coma, but how that translates to the court, I'm not certain. If he can vote, then we can—to add another cliché—kill two birds with one stone. If not, waiting until tomorrow to decide does not impede us. All drafts of decisions are finalized, and we either proceed with nine votes, or eight. Whatever we do is going to make many folks unhappy."

Margaret Lonsdale, the second most progressive member of the court, asked, "Will he be able to vote? What's his condition? Perhaps we can arrange a video hookup as we did during the pandemic and for Justices Ginsberg and Thomas when they were ill? If not, I suggest the balance of the calendar be passed until the fall term."

"I won't be here then," Justice Battaglia said. "I don't want my vote negated because of my resignation. And add in my physical problems. No, I would certainly oppose postponing until the fall. I want my position to be heard, and that's the only proper thing to do."

"We have rendered important decisions in the past with only eight justices voting," Chief Justice Treller said, "albeit because of illness or recusal. There's no reason why we should change a well-practiced process. Television participation is an option, but that depends on J.J.'s condition, and time is short. However, the court is more important than any individual justice, and I'm certain J.J. would concur with that decision."

On a vote of 6 to 2, the justices decided to wait one more day, although no one expected a miraculous change in J.J.'s condition.

* * *

Mort was not surprised to find Travis back in his office and fortified with pain killers but functioning. Travis's first words were, "How is he this morning?"

"Coming around slowly, according to Chickie," Mort replied. "Full of questions, feisty, somewhat confused. Still a long way to go."

"Unless I haven't mentioned it, you saved my life. Don't know how to say thanks. You followed me with a gun in your car, I heard. Are you a reporter or a vigilante?"

"Anything for a story. I wanted to ask you something, though," Mort said. "I've had trouble sleeping. My gut is on the fritz, and I've got headaches and nightmares when I do sleep. Is this normal after a shooting? I mean, I killed a guy. It will haunt me forever. Maybe I could have aimed lower… or shot out a tire."

"Look," Travis said, "you're not going through anything a police officer or a soldier doesn't go through after a killing. Why do you think officers are immediately placed on leave after a shooting? You've got remorse, you've got PTSD, but remember the bottom line. We might both be dead, as well as J.J., if you hadn't pulled that trigger. Think of that poor delivery kid. From what I hear, he was just in the wrong place at the wrong time."

"I know you're right, but still… my gut doesn't seem to understand."

Travis nodded knowingly. "It will take time. DNA confirms that Littlejohn and Abernathy are identical twins and have identical DNA. Littlejohn was another innocent man caught up in this kidnapping. And so were you. In the meantime, enjoy your fifteen minutes of fame. Those moments are fleeting. And thanks again… for my life."

* * *

"What day ish it?" J.J. wanted to know. He spoke slowly, still slurring his speech.

"Monday," Chickie said.

"Whish Monday?"

"The Monday after you were kidnapped."

"Remind me not to stop to help," J.J. wrote on his Etch A Sketch.

"You'll stop anyway. It's just the way you are."

"Where's the Harley?" J.J. wrote.

"No idea, but you won't be needing it for a while."

Between tests, medications and fatigue, J.J. wanted to know everything that had happened during the days following his capture. Chickie relayed everything she knew in slow detail.

"Mort shot a kidnapper?" J.J. wrote. "He's a keeper. Travis OK?"

"Travis is bull-headed. Like you. Mort called earlier, and Travis is back in the office. Still faces a couple of surgeries on his arm."

"And the kidnappers?"

"The FBI is on it. I think Mort has some ideas as well."

"My money on Mort," J.J. wrote.

Chickie smiled and said, "Ours too." Then she kissed his forehead.

"What's with smoochy stuff?" he wrote.

"Time for you to get some rest. Stop worrying about anything but getting better."

* * *

Craig Fisher was quickly authorized to join Tim Richardson's FBI team, which focused on both the kidnapping and the killing of Brendan Braddock. With the information provided by Boris Rosenthal, they felt they were close to solving Braddock's killing. Then it would be a matter of tying up the loose ends.

A surveillance camera at the Immanuel Christian Church and Bible School, a short distance from Deerlick Park, revealed that a recent model Camry had been parked nearby around the hours the medical examiner believed Braddock was killed. The picture was a side view of the car with no license plate visible. According to the camera, the car parked at ten thirty at night and left about an hour later.

"With the information from Rosenthal," Richardson told agent Fisher, "we were able to figure out that to drive from New York to Fairfax County would take about three-and-a-half hours. Even less from Newark International Airport. The local office checked the rental companies, and Hertz rented a Toyota Camry that same afternoon. It was returned the following day with a little over five hundred miles put on it. Just enough for the round trip to Virginia. It was rented with a good credit card and license, and the description of the renter matched Zeke Shannon. But the name on both documents was fictitious. Zeke has a condo in Short Hills, New Jersey. Just a stone's throw from the airport and right across the Narrows from the NAWES office. Very convenient."

"We've got to get Rosenthal in writing, even though I said we'd try to keep him out of it," Fisher said.

"New York, here we come. I'll get us booked today. Who tipped you off to Rosenthal?"

"I promised I wouldn't divulge that."

***

At seven on Monday evening, the two agents met a reluctant Boris Rosenthal at Newark Liberty International Airport.

"You said I wouldn't have to get involved," Boris said.

"You won't," Fisher said. "Ninety-nine point five chances out of a hundred. This is starting to come together, thanks to you."

"It won't be good for the company if Zeke's involved. On the other hand, if it's Zeke," Boris said, "I can end up dead. Especially if he ever finds out I was involved. The guy brags about being a marksman. His wall is full of hunting trophies and sharpshooter medals. He's always going on safaris. 'The Short Happy Life of Francis Macomber.'"

"Who's Francis Macomber?"

"Fictitious character in a Hemingway short story. He ended up dead."

"Well, don't worry," Fisher said. "We'll keep you alive."

* * *

By nine, with Rosenthal's statement in hand, the agents were on their way back to Reagan International in Washington. "Have we got probable cause for a warrant?" Richardson asked.

"More than enough," Fisher answered. "Our next step is deciding how we want this to go down."

Fifty-four

On Tuesday, Mort was back at his desk tiptoeing around "unnamed sources" as he tried to follow up on what he knew but couldn't divulge. He decided to take a fast trip to New York for a follow-up story about NAWES now that J.J. had been rescued. He called Win Abbington directly, and they arranged to meet that afternoon.

On his way to the airport, Mort got a call on his cell and looked at the source. It was Travis.

"I think I'm going to need you as a witness," Travis said.

"For what?"

"I've been brought up on charges for exceeding my authority and unprofessional conduct."

At first, Mort thought he was kidding. He wasn't. It seems that the director of the FBI, George Blessing, had contacted the Montgomery County executive, Flo Nickerson, and insisted that she take the steps to institute an internal affairs investigation of Travis's conduct, not merely because the FBI had jurisdiction over the case, but also because he had launched a rescue mission to West Virginia with only one other officer before the FBI arrived there. He had also exposed Mort— an untrained civilian—to danger. The fact that the mission rescued a Supreme Court justice and brought the kidnappers to justice was apparently secondary. So was the fact that the "untrained civilian" was being lauded for dispatching the kidnapper.

Obviously, Blessing's nose had been bent out of shape when his initial announcement of the capture as a "coordinated law enforcement effort" had been exposed as a total fabrication.

Travis explained, "Flo Nickerson, the county exec, just showed up in my office with Nick Gordon, our attorney general," Travis said. "They were somewhat apologetic but laid out the nature of the complaint. She should have told him to shove it, but she's a politician and running for reelection. Seemed pretty intimidated, so she referred it to internal affairs to get herself off the hook."

"This is absurd. What's involved? What can I do?"

"I appreciate that, Mort, though I never had any doubt you'd do it. Nickerson's visit was followed up by a call from Cynthia Hyams, a commander in internal affairs, who was also apologetic.

"I helped her climb the ladder to commander, on merit. She's a straight shooter. They'll present me with the formal charges, and we'll go before the hearing board. The visit from Nickerson was just a courtesy."

"Some courtesy," Mort said. "What's the bottom line?"

"Well, I was really pissed," Travis said. "At first, I told her to take my job and stick it where the sun don't shine. She got nervous and said it's just a formality. Then I cooled down. I'll go through with it just to get a fair conclusion—and I *will* get a fair conclusion—but then I might just pack it in."

"Well, I'm glad you didn't act on the spur of the moment. Something like that and you might end up with me in Great Capcapon again."

"Very funny."

"Do you need a lawyer?" Mort asked.

"The PBA provides a lawyer, even though I'm the chief."

"I think I can provide one with a lot more clout than the PBA guy. A fellow named Ron Ciresi," Mort said.

"He'd do it?"

"I'm certain he would, if I asked."

They left it at that. Travis would get the charges, Mort would call Ciresi and the proceedings would be strictly confidential with no publicity. They'd have to lay out a game plan and line up witnesses.

The worst that would happen would be a finding of guilty, which would result in a reprimand and a stain on Travis's record. Nothing more. But Mort understood why Travis was "really pissed."

* * *

Conferences for two days in a row were not unheard of in the court, but when both conferences were held in the chambers of the chief justice, it was unusual.

On the morning of the second day, Chief Justice Treller told the gathered justices, "The court administrator spoke with the hospital earlier today, and it's possible to do a Zoom hookup with J.J., if he's up to it. That word has been passed along to the medical staff, and to J.J., I understand. We should know if everyone agrees shortly."

* * *

J.J.'s reaction, when told of the Zoom possibility, was somewhat different.

"No way!" he said. He was still slurring some words and walking unsteadily with help.

"It's the last day of the term," Chickie said. "I thought you would want to participate."

"I do," J.J. said, "but listen to me. I sound terrible. I can hear the words, and they're not coming out right. I haven't been in the court for over a week, haven't seen the last drafts of anyone's opinions, haven't even approved my own. No way. On top of everything, I'm not writing my words on a note pad."

So Chickie had the word passed on to the court that the last day of the session would proceed with only eight justices present.

* * *

When Chickie called Danni to tell her J.J.'s decision, Danni was distraught.

"That NAWES case is *so* important," Danni said. "I'm really shocked. If the Court is 4-4 without J.J., the corporations win. It will be a devastating loss to society."

"You know J.J.," Chickie said. "Proud to a fault. I don't think he'd ever want to be heard slurring his speech or not being physically in his seat."

"He wouldn't necessarily have to talk if he just concurred in the decision."

"Honey, you know that's not J.J. He's either all in, or not in at all. There's always tomorrow, always another term."

Danni called Mort to share the news. She caught him just before he left for New York and his follow-up interview with Abbington.

"That's tough," Mort said. "I know how important that case is."

"Not just to me, but to the nation, to the world, to our dwindling water supply."

"Maybe it's not a 4-4 vote," Mort suggested.

"I'd bet just about anything that I'm right," Danni said defiantly.

"An engagement ring?"

"Don't push your luck, Buster."

"The world will survive either way," Mort said. "Nature has a way of finding solutions. Just have a little faith, be a little patient."

"Et tu, Brute," Danni said, and slammed down the phone

* * *

Danni showed up at Walter Reed an hour later.

"I've got to see him," she told Chickie, pushing right into J.J.'s room.

"Danni," he said, with pleasure in his voice. He was sitting in the armchair usually occupied by Chickie.

"J.J.," she pleaded, "you can't do this. You've got to participate one way or the other. If you won't join on Zoom, then just concur in the opinion which will overturn the lower courts."

He wrote on the pad and held it up. "The NAWES case?"

"Of course the NAWES case," Danni said.

"What about the other pending decisions?" he wrote.

"Nothing is as important as NAWES," Danni said. "You know that. The other cases might already have been decided by unanimous votes, six-two, five-three. Who knows?"

"That's right, who knows?" he wrote. "You want me to be half a loaf?"

"But nothing is as important as having a fair distribution of water rather than putting it in the hands of corporations that are only concerned about their bottom line." Danni bristled. "You know that, J.J.—in your heart and in your entire philosophy."

"I love your passion," he wrote. "But I have to be all in or all out."

Danni slapped her hands together. "Just like every other man in my life! I can't count on you when you're needed most." She turned and walked out.

* * *

On the shuttle to New York, Mort was disturbed by Danni's volatility. He agreed with her in principle, but *you can't always have things your way*, he thought. She had seemed so distressed over this issue that he started to worry about how it might impact their relationship.

At NAWES headquarters, Mort told Win Abbington, "I'd just like some sort of a follow-up for tomorrow's editions, which will be one day before the court ends the term."

Zeke Shannon and Boris Rosenthal unexpectedly entered the office and took seats.

"Hope you don't mind," Win said, "but I asked Zeke and Boris to join us."

Mort and Boris Rosenthal exchanged glances but gave no other indication they had spoken since the previous meeting.

Zeke turned to Mort and said, "The *Washington Post* must have a shitload of money to keep sending you up here on a fool's errand."

Abbington shot him a withering glance. "Enough!" he said.

"But I have to compliment you on your marksmanship in offing that kidnapper," Zeke continued. "Great shot."

"Luck," Mort said. "And I haven't been able to sleep since."

"You get used to it," Zeke said.

"God, I hope not," Mort replied.

Abbington intervened in the sideways conversation. "Obviously, we are relieved that Justice Richter is safe, and we wish him a speedy recovery. His presence on the bench for this final day is welcome, but I hope his frightful episode won't reflect on the case or affect his judgment on the case one way or the other."

"Why would you think it might?" Mort said.

"Because the speculation, the media, and all the publicity suggest that because it was our case at stake at the end of the court's term, somehow we must be involved in his kidnapping. Which is absurd! We respect the integrity of the courts. We do not engage in illegal and barbaric conduct."

"I'll quote you on that," Mort said. "And I can tell you, since it's shortly to be public, that J.J. won't be participating in Thursday's session. That's his decision."

"Hot damn!" Zeke said. "That means we're in like Flynn! Our stock will go through the roof."

Boris shook his head. "I wish I could be as confident as you, Zeke. But I don't have access to all your *confidential* sources."

"You're the one who said all along that we'd win," Zeke snapped.

"What I said is that I think we had the law and precedence on our side and that we *should* win, but you can never be that certain of the Supreme Court. They could adjourn this case to the next term to wait for Richter to return—or who knows what?"

"Not gonna happen," Zeke said. "We win on the tie vote."

Abbington turned to Mort. "I apologize, but you see what I have to put up with? I feel like I'm running a kindergarten."

"Before I leave," Mort said, "there's a theory that the death of Brendan Braddock, the captain of the Supreme Court Police, was somehow connected to your Supreme Court case. Any thoughts on that?"

Abbington shook his head. Rosenthal looked down and did the same.

"Never heard of him," Zeke said. "If that's it, I've got a lot to do."

Fifty-five

In the energy industry, Win Abbington was known as a straight shooter. In his earlier life, the tall, handsome Rhodes Scholar was a bit of a playboy. But the death of his fiancée in an auto crash with Win at the wheel after a night of partying apparently had changed his perspective on life. He played by the rules—humble in his wins, gracious in his losses. It was not out of character for him to offer a large contribution to the ransom demand in the Richter kidnapping, even though it was J.J. Richter who had written the 5-4 opinion in the fracking case several years earlier, a devastating decision that had sent Abbington's corporation to defeat. If Abbington won a contested matter, he wanted to do it fairly.

On Wednesday, nine days after the abduction, Abbington was surprised to learn that two FBI agents had arrived in his reception area.

"Gentlemen," he said, "we have never been so popular. To what do I owe this honor?"

"You may remember me from the day after the kidnapping," Tim Richardson said. "I don't believe you've met Craig Fisher, who has joined me on the case."

They shook hands. Win was smiling, Craig was not.

"I joined the case after the homicide of Brendan Braddock, of the Supreme Court Police," Fisher said.

"That was, to say the least, unfortunate and bizarre," Abbington said. "We were just talking about it yesterday when Mr. Ahrens from the *Post* was here."

Richardson asked, "Are the other members of your executive team available—the men we met when we were here last time?"

Abbington walked to his desk and hit the buzzer twice. Within a minute, both Rosenthal and Shannon entered the office.

"What's up?" Zeke Shannon asked.

Boris Rosenthal avoided eye contact with the agents.

The two agents showed their FBI credentials. "Just a few questions," Richardson explained. Turning to Shannon, he said, "I understand you didn't know Captain Braddock, the Supreme Court officer who was killed in Virginia?"

"Didn't know him at all."

"Then why would you have his name and number in your desk?"

Unflustered, Shannon casually said, "There must be some mistake."

"I don't think so," Richardson said, offering a photograph. "This is a photo of the document in your desk."

"I might have written it down when the story broke," Shannon said, still unflappable.

Richardson stepped closer to Zeke Shannon. "With a phone number? The man was already dead."

"Wait a minute," Shannon said angrily. "I think somebody is setting me up."

He looked directly at Rosenthal.

Agent Fisher stepped forward. "Well, perhaps you can explain why you rented a car at Hertz in Newark on the day of the murder, put on just enough mileage for a round trip to Virginia, and returned the car the next day. With forged documents. I might add, you've been identified by the Hertz agent. We'd also like you to explain how you know inside information about the court, such as the vote in the NAWES case being tied with Justice Richter unavailable?"

The blood rushed to Shannon's cheeks. "I'm going to my office. This is shit. I'm calling my lawyer."

Abbington said, "Zeke?"

Richardson pulled out a document and showed it to Shannon. "Going to your office is not possible," he said, "because pursuant to this warrant, there are agents searching your office at this very moment. Searching your home in New Jersey as well. Mr. Shannon, you are under arrest, charged with the murder of Captain Brendan Braddock. You have the right to remain silent. If you say anything, it can be used against you in a court of law. You have the right to have an attorney present during any questioning. If you can't afford an attorney, one will be furnished to you by the court if you desire. Do you understand the rights which I just read to you?"

"I understand this is bullshit," Shannon snarled. "I'm being railroaded."

"If you'll please turn around," Fisher said. "I'm going to put these handcuffs on you."

A cuffed Shannon was marched to the door where two other agents were waiting.

Richardson turned to Abbington. "You might want to do a fast audit of your books, which we will also do shortly. I think you'll find substantial amounts of money are unaccounted for."

Abbington, flustered, turned to Rosenthal. "Bubba, did you have an inkling?"

Rosenthal replied, "I never trusted that creep from day one."

* * *

A short time later, Mort got a call on his cell. "Just a heads up," Fisher said, "since you deserve to be the first one to know. We just arrested Zeke Shannon, the NAWES CFO, and charged him with Braddock's murder."

Mort was stunned by how fast events had moved.

"It's public information now," Fisher said, "all in the warrant signed by the court. Not only Shannon's name, but his trip to Virginia on the night of the killing and renting a car with phony credentials. We've had some cooperation from the other kidnapper, plus this guy is a recognized marksman. We got a cell phone from the deceased kidnapper in Great Capcacon that ties it all in."

"Craig," Mort said, "many thanks. I'm on it."

"Thanks for the heads up, which shall remain undisclosed."

Mort immediately placed a call to Steve Ginsberg.

"One of the execs at NAWES, the CFO, was just arrested for the murder of Captain Braddock," he said. "I'm on it. Just wanted to give you a heads up."

"Jesus Christ!" Ginsberg said. "You're like a white tornado. Does this tie in to the kidnapping that you already solved?"

"That one still has a ways to go, but I'm working that angle too. This thing has got to go higher up."

* * *

Mort called Danni next. "Are we talking?" he asked.

"I suppose I just have to tolerate you, with your deficiencies," she said. "Like all the other men in my life. What's up now?"

"Apparently it was Zeke Shannon, the NAWES CFO, who killed Braddock."

"Wow. It's still hard for me to imagine Brendan was involved," Danni said.

"It goes higher than Braddock, I'm sure. And I'm trying to work it out. So is the FBI. Braddock couldn't get this far all by himself."

"I just can't believe that Brendan was involved in leaking confidential court information."

"Well, he complained to me about needing money, if you recall. The lure of a big retirement was probably just too much for him. As for leaking confidential court information, remember that Alito draft in the abortion decision that was leaked weeks before it was final?"

"You're probably right, though I hate to admit it," Danni said. "The sad thing is that it won't change the outcome of the NAWES case tomorrow. J.J. won't participate, and I'm certain they're deadlocked 4-4."

Fifty-six

The past week had been particularly traumatic for Anthony Battaglia. Not only was his resignation from the court after a quarter century a deeply emotional event, but it was propelled by pancreatic cancer and a more recent onset of Parkinson's disease. True, the doctors were hopeful of new treatments for the cancer, which had not metastasized, but instead of a summer of leisure and perhaps lectures in a European law school, he was headed soon for the Mayo Clinic.

As his friend and adversary, J.J. Richter, lay in a hospital, the devastating news from his daughter was yet another stab into what was becoming a fragile psyche. Instead of spending the end of the summer vacation period with her, his granddaughter and son-in-law, an Arizona wildfire had consumed everything they owned. And the drought had made their region uninhabitable, at least for the immediate future.

Finally, in the early hours of Thursday morning, he had reached a decision. He thought of his conversation with J.J. at Walter Reed when his friend had said he had to be "all in or not in at all." Once again, J.J. had shown that he was a great wordsmith, and Battaglia realized how difficult it must have been for him to refuse participating in the remaining court cases.

Battaglia showered as the dawn broke, called for an early limo pickup and headed for the Supreme Court. Other than a cursory "Good morning" to his driver, he was silent, wrapped in his own thoughts. He entered the court, took the private elevator used by the justices to the second floor and headed for the chambers of the chief justice, the tapping of his cane echoing in the empty hallway. Treller had not yet arrived, so he left a message for her to call him.

Battaglia headed for the office of the clerk and inquired of a junior clerk, "Is Mr. Bennington in?" It was the last day of the term, Thursday morning, so there was little doubt that Bennington was already at his desk.

Within a minute, Bennington came to the front desk. "Justice Battaglia?" he inquired with raised eyebrows.

"Can we step into your office, Joe?" Battaglia asked.

"Of course."

He got right to the point. "Joe, I am unaware of anything that indicates when one is precluded from recusal in a case."

"I don't know that there is any time limit, Your Honor."

"Good. My research agrees. I am going to recuse myself from the NAWES case. I feel that recent events in my life and elsewhere put me in a position in which I have a personal interest in the case. Does that cause you an insurmountable problem?"

"Recuse yourself?" Bennington said, his mouth literally falling open. "You want to recuse yourself?"

"Yes. Can you handle it before we convene?"

"Your Honor, if that's what you want, we can do it. There are still two hours before the court convenes."

"Not an easy decision, I assure you," Battaglia said, "but it's the right one. Do it, without a word to anyone except on a need-to-know basis. I'll inform the chief." With that, he turned and started to leave, then turned back and extended his hand. "Thank you, Joe, and... I guess we're both retiring today. I'll miss you. Enjoy your retirement. You've earned it."

"Thank you, Your Honor, and back to you. It's been my pleasure to know you and work with you. Good luck."

* * *

When Chief Justice Treller arrived, she immediately called Battaglia and invited him to her chambers.

"Constance," he said, "as difficult as this is, and believe me it's as difficult as anything in my lifetime, I'm recusing myself from the NAWES case."

She turned pale and motioned for him to sit down, which he did.

"Anthony, what is it? At the last minute? Is there something I can do? I don't even know if it's possible. I'm speechless."

"It's possible. The clerk has it in the works already. If it wasn't absolutely essential for my peace of mind, I wouldn't do it, but I have no choice, Constance."

"My God," she said. "This will have all sorts of consequences. Not only here, but throughout the nation. It turns the decision on its head. Are you *absolutely certain* this is what you want to do?"

"Without a doubt. It's the most important decision of my life. I met with J.J. two days ago, and—"

"You saw J.J?" she said, shocked.

"At the hospital, and he said something that convinced me that this is the right thing to do. If you can't be all in, then you shouldn't be in at all. And I can't be all in."

"Anthony, I'm speechless. Let's keep it between us, and the clerk, for now. You may still have second thoughts."

"I won't," Battaglia said. "It's honoring my oath. And you know how important that is and always has been for me. It's as important as democracy."

Fifty-seven

Mort was in the press section of the court when it convened on Thursday morning. J.J. had asked him by way of Chickie to be there and report to him. Mort was amazed that J.J. could have the presence of mind to remain so involved. Mort wished that Danni was there with him, but she had spent a sleepless night on the sofa in their apartment and then headed for the law school. She didn't want to hear the results from the court.

J.J. had told Mort that the last day of the term was always special. The court usually handed down its most important decisions, tweaked until the last moment by the justices in an attempt to achieve perfection. The end of the term also meant that the members of the court would go their separate ways until the first Monday in October when it traditionally reconvened. Some of the staff would have retired, others moved on with words of farewell and gratitude expressed.

Mort was struck, as he sat in the courtroom, by the uniqueness of this particular day. Only eight of the nine justices would be present, and the senior associate justice, the Lion of the Court, was lying in a hospital bed with only a few visitors allowed to see him. The day would also be unique because another justice, Anthony Battaglia, J.J.'s philosophical antagonist and close friend, would be resigning his seat.

Mort gazed up at the ceiling forty-four feet above and smiled as he recalled the tale of Danni, J.J. and the basketball court—"the highest court in the land."

The small gallery was full, and members of the press were packed into their seats on red benches along the left side of the courtroom. The red benches on the right were reserved for guests of the justices; those seats were filled too. The black chairs in front of the benches were reserved for officers of the court and visiting dignitaries.

Mort had arrived very early, and the street beyond the wide sidewalk outside the court was already lined with media trucks and satellite dishes. High security fencing had been installed. Proponents and opponents of the NAWES case noisily chattered and chanted on opposite sides of the fencing as a substantial presence of Supreme Court Police and US Marshals stood by.

Clerk of the Court Bennington, serving his last day after thirty-five years with the court, moved to his desk at the left of the raised mahogany bench, his bald pate shining in the reflection of the overhead lights. He nodded to the marshal of the court, whose desk faced his on the right. They had been part of this pomp and circumstance for many years. The marshal, Geoffrey Taylor, rose, and a hush fell over the courtroom. Mort fidgeted in his seat and leaned forward, although there was nothing obstructing his view.

In a booming voice, Taylor announced, "The Honorable, the Chief Justice and the Associate Justices of the Supreme Court of the United States. Oyez! Oyez! Oyez! All persons having business before the Honorable, the Supreme Court of the United States, are admonished to draw near and give their attention, for the court is now sitting. God save the United States and this Honorable Court." With that, the blue velvet drapes behind the bench parted, and the justices stepped forward to take their seats.

Constance Treller, looking particularly tense, leaned forward and shuffled some papers in front of her. To her right, in the seat of the senior associate justice—J.J.'s seat—the straight-backed chair was empty. To her left, the justice with the next highest seniority, Anthony Battaglia, looked alarmingly fragile, his eyes almost hidden under black, bushy eyebrows.

The first order of business was the swearing in of new members of the Supreme Court bar. These attorneys had qualified for admission to the Supreme Court and had received their notices of admission several months earlier. Seven men and eight women, mostly in their thirties, had the good fortune to be admitted not only on the final day of the term, but on the day when the most anticipated and important decision of recent years would be announced. Clad in dark blue, they had front row seats in a courtroom that only seated four hundred including the press. Several members of Congress were seated along with a few privileged members of the Supreme Court bar, including the president of the American Bar Association, who had flown in from Omaha for the occasion.

The clerk issued a directive that would have been unheard of a decade or so ago. "All cell phones, transmitting devices, beepers and similar instruments are to be disabled until the court concludes its business. Violation of this directive will not only result in your removal from the court but in your arrest and criminal charges." There was a rustling noise as devices were switched off.

The swearing in took about fifteen minutes as oaths were administered and ministerial necessities were completed. There were no other decisions remaining to be rendered, since they had been handed out when the clerk's office had opened, so one decision remained—the NAWES case.

There was the reversal of an order from the ninth circuit court, which had allowed a *habeas corpus* petition to go forward from a convict sentenced to life after the expiration of the statute of limitations.

Bennington then announced the remaining case, "Number one-eighty-eight-twelve, The Environmental Protection Agency, et al. versus the National Association of Water and Environmental Safety, et al." Mort could sense people moving to the edge of their seats.

Constance Treller looked up and paused with a painful expression on her face. She said, "We note the unfortunate absence of the senior associate justice, J.J. Richter, who did not participate in this decision..." She then took a deep breath, pausing again, and added, "...and the recusal of Associate Justice Anthony Battaglia, who has recused himself from participating in this decision."

An audible gasp erupted from the audience. This announcement meant there were only seven justices participating in the decision.

235

None of the justices chose to read from their opinions in this precedent-setting case, and copies were distributed to the press.

The press and media representatives strained to race for the doors, awaiting the conclusion of business for the day. Mort merely sat and looked at his copy of the decision. The appellants had prevailed, 4-3. The circuit court decision was reversed. The Commerce Clause argument favoring the government had been sustained over the argument that the Tenth Amendment gave the jurisdiction in these matters to the states.

Mort thought back to Danni's television debate. She had won again.

Mort walked outside and sat on the steps in front of the court, which were obstructed by iron stanchions driven into the cement. He powered up his phone and called Chickie, giving her the news.

Chickie's voice registered shock. "Really?" She turned away from the phone to J.J. and said, "Anthony recused himself. The appellants won. You won."

Mort could hear J.J.'s weak voice say, "No, the people of this nation won."

Mort wondered what, if any effect, Battaglia's hospital conversation with J.J. had had on his decision to recuse.

Mort called Danni next, but she didn't pick up and the call went to voice mail.

"Headstrong woman," he said, "the court reversed, 4-3, after Battaglia recused himself. Remember, it ain't over 'til it's over."

His cell phone rang seconds later, and he looked at the screen. It was Danni.

Smiling, he let it go to voice mail.

Fifty-eight

Sunday morning, just two weeks after the kidnapping, J.J. was released from Ward 71 in a wheelchair. He wanted to walk out, or at least be able to lean on Chickie's arm, but this was ruled out of the question. His speech had almost returned to normal, and there was just a small bandage on his forehead where the bullet had creased his skull.

Dr. Choupatka and two other doctors were there to say farewell, and J.J. stopped to say thank you to his nurses. Chickie offered them all the flowers that had accumulated during J.J.'s stay. The president had provided a large limousine for the twenty-two-mile trip to Travilah. The limo was guarded by a black SUV with two US marshals.

When the limo pulled into J.J.'s property, he was quick to note that a Montgomery County Police car was stationed at the entrance. "What's with all the security?" he wanted to know.

"Just everybody being overly protective," Chickie said.

"Don't like it, don't need it," J.J. said.

"Well, there may be a lot of things you don't like or need, but you heard what Sanjay said. You're supposed to listen to me, especially when it comes to getting rest, or you'll end up in rehab."

"Even the kidnappers were nicer to me," J.J. said with a smile.

Lupe was waiting on the porch, dressed in her finest dress with Connie excitedly beside her. "Welcome home, Judge" she said.

"Thank you, Lupe. It's good to be home. I'm glad you're OK."

He stooped to pet Connie's head.

"Good girl," he said to the dog. "You tried to protect me. It's good to see you're OK."

"Time for rest," Chickie said.

"Yes, Warden," J.J. answered.

* * *

J.J. slept a good part of the day and then Danni and Mort joined him and Chickie for dinner.

"I owe you a big one, fella," J.J. said to Mort, "but you should never have been there in the first place. Chickie brought me up to date. Do you own the *Post* yet?"

"Please, don't give him any more of a swelled head," Danni said. "His fifteen minutes of fame is unending. He's going to be on *Good Morning, America* next week."

"All well and good," Mort said, "but we still don't know who the brain was behind the kidnapping, although all the speculation has given me plenty to write about. And I'm working on a special story, at Steven's direction, on DNA and its relevance to identical twins."

"Steven?" J.J. asked.

"His new best friend," Danni said, "the managing editor at the *Post*. All of a sudden, our hero and Stan are so close I think they might get engaged."

"If we did," Mort said, without missing a beat, "I bet *he'd* let me get him a ring."

"Touche," Chickie said.

"Ring? I forgot all about the ring," J.J. said, and everyone looked mystified at his remark, except Mort.

"And Travis?" J.J. asked. "What's this about bringing him up on charges? Beyond stupid. When does that get resolved? And when am I going to see him?"

"As to visitation, ask your nurse here," Mort said, nodding his head toward Chickie.

"You can see him tomorrow, if you behave," Chickie said.

"Lupe," J.J. said, "great meal, but not as good as what the kidnappers gave me."

Lupe laughed.

J.J. turned serious. "I just want you to know, all of you sitting around this table, that in that week of captivity I had a lot of time to think. And in the hospital, I had a lot of time to remember how precious life is. You are my family, the ones I hold dearest, and I want you to know I love each and every one of you, and I appreciate all you did these past weeks."

"Only these past weeks?" Chickie said. "That's gratitude for you."

They all laughed.

* * *

J.J. amazed the doctors with his recuperative powers, but feeling better brought out his curmudgeonly side. When he'd been released from Walter Reed, he refused nursing care saying, "I have Chickie, I have Lupe. That's all I need." At home, he started finding that things bothered him that would never have bothered him before. And as he predictably tried to do too much, he became frustrated by his inability to perform tasks as before.

One afternoon, as he and Chickie were walking with Connie through the yard on a sunny day, they entered the barn and J.J. noticed his motorcycle was absent.

"Where's the Harley?" he asked.

"I sold it," Chickie replied.

"You *what*?"

"I sold it," Chickie said matter-of-factly. "It had bad karma for starters, and I knew that if it was still here it would only be a matter of time until you snuck off to ride it."

"How'd you sell it without the registration?"

"Easy. You keep a very neat desk, unlike your chambers, and I found the registration with no trouble. Don't get in a snit. We saved all your stuff that was in what you call saddlebags, and when you're well enough, I'll buy you a new motorcycle. A better one."

"One that you'll ride on with me without bitchin'?"

"If I must, I must," Chickie said and then gave him a hug.

Fifty-nine

On the morning of Travis's hearing before internal affairs, Chickie, Danni and Mort traveled with him to the County Municipal Building in Gaithersburg. In Maryland, these hearings are open to the public and a small group of interested citizens had responded to the public notice. Alison Powers from WaPo showed up.

As they were seated, Danni nodded toward Alison and said to Mort, "She's the reporter you worked with on the kidnapping?"

"More or less."

"She's very cute."

"Hadn't noticed."

"Bullshit."

Cynthia Hyams, commander of the internal affairs division, took a seat at the dais with two other uniformed officers. They nodded to Travis, who was at a table with Ron Ciresi, who was representing Travis without a fee. A court reporter was there to transcribe the proceedings.

"I will read from the document," Hyams said, "since the complainant, County Executive Nickerson, has chosen to proceed in that fashion, as is her right." She then proceeded to read the charges.

"Exceeding his authority and unprofessional conduct. The complainant chose not to be present, stating that she was acting as the representative of the director of the FBI. The genesis of the complaint is that Chief Anderson took it upon himself to facilitate the rescue of Senior Associate Justice of the Supreme Court, J.J. Richter, who had been kidnapped and was being held at a location in West Virginia."

Hyams looked over at Travis, and then continued. "He did so with only one officer from the Montgomery County Police, and in addition utilized the assistance of one Mort Ahrens, a reporter for a Washington newspaper, a civilian with no affiliation with law enforcement, not only endangering his life but also that of the chief himself and his officer. Such conduct is alleged to have far exceeded his authority, interfered with the federal authorities in responding to the emergency, and as such constituted unprofessional conduct on his part. Since the nature of the complaint speaks for itself, Mr. Ciresi, representing Chief Travis Anderson, do you wish to proceed?"

"I certainly do," Ciresi said, rising to his feet, "and I will call Chief Anderson as my first witness." He went through Travis's background, his humble beginnings in Detroit, his military service, his Medal of Honor and other commendations, and his exemplary record and commendations in the police department as he worked his way up to his appointment as chief.

Travis rose and was sworn. His arm was still wrapped in a cast from shoulder to wrist.

"Chief Anderson, you have heard the charges," Ciresi said. "I would like you to respond, please."

"J.J. Richter is like family to me," Travis said. "Not only my dearest friend, but perhaps calling him my other father would be more appropriate. He is a patriot, and a Lion of the Court. When he was kidnapped, I was distraught, along with much of this nation."

Danni and Mort found themselves nodding as Travis spoke.

Travis continued. "Then a ransom demand was made, and the White House was silent as to whether they would meet the ransom demand. Fortuitously, in retrospect, the kidnappers attempted to burglarize the justice's home in search of life-saving medications that he needed. They apparently thought the house was deserted, which we learned after the fact. But the justices' housekeeper, Lupe Ruiz, was at home and knocked the kidnapper unconscious with a frying pan."

The onlookers started to laugh at this description, and Hyams cautioned everyone to remain silent during the testimony.

"She called me, in a panic," Travis said, "and I dispatched cars to the scene and sped there myself. Arriving minutes later, I found the burglar secured and two officers present with the housekeeper and Mr. Ahrens, who had also just arrived and is also virtually a member of the Richter family. The burglar, who was one of what we learned were two kidnappers, disclosed the location where Justice Richter was being held, under questioning by Mr. Ahrens.

"Time was of the essence, the situation was exigent, and I dispatched two officers to take the burglar to headquarters for booking. I then called the FBI, disclosed all the essential information and then departed with Officer Young of my department to the kidnap location. I instructed Mr. Ahrens to stay at the Richter house and was unaware that he was following me in his own vehicle.

"I also knew that minutes were precious, and it would take the FBI quite some time to put together a task force. Since we were advised that there was only one kidnapper at the West Virginia premises with the justice, I realized I could get there first and made the decision to go there. When we got to West Virginia, the situation was chaotic. The kidnapper who was guarding the justice had killed a young restaurant deliveryman and shot Justice Richter, who was wounded and unconscious at the bottom of the basement stairs.

"The kidnapper panicked and ran me down with a van, causing multiple fractures to my body and arm, as you can see. He then fired two shots at Officer Young and hit him in the chest. Fortunately, Young was saved by his Kevlar vest. The kidnapper then directed his attention to Mr. Ahrens, who was there unarmed, and tried to run him over. Fortunately, Mr. Ahrens dove for my shotgun, which had fallen to the ground and fired as he was about to be struck by the van, killing the kidnapper. Mr. Ahrens then ascertained the serious condition of the justice, and at just about that time the federal authorities arrived *en masse* and assumed authority. It's my professional opinion that if we had not acted as and when we did, His Honor would have died. That opinion has been borne out by the doctors at Walter Reed Hospital."

"Why didn't you call the local authorities?" Commander Hyams asked.

"First, I knew that the justice was being held in a small community, and second, frankly, I didn't know the quality of local law enforcement there. I notified the feds and knew that they would respond, but not as quickly as I could. And if they arrived with a large force, it could have been deadly to His Honor. It was an instantaneous, spur of the moment decision. It was what I have trained for all my life in the service and as a policeman—to make quick and difficult decisions based on circumstances on the ground."

There was no other questioning by the IAD panel. Then Ciresi put the two officers on the stand, as well as Dan Harrington of the Supreme Court, and they all agreed with what Travis had testified. Harrington went further, emphasizing the exigency of the moment and the serious injuries as well as the two deaths that had occurred a few moments apart.

Mort took the stand as the last witness.

"Do you normally carry a rifle in your car?" Commander Hyams inquired.

"My fiancée and I go skeet shooting on occasion," Mort said, "and I keep the shotgun in the trunk unloaded with the pellets contained safely. Frankly, my fiancée is a much better shot than I am."

The spectators chuckled.

"But you started to remove it from the car and then chose not to."

"I decided that weapons were for the professionals. I wasn't certain how helpful I could be with a skeet shooting rifle. The shotgun I fired was Chief Anderson's, and it was on the ground after he was purposely struck by the kidnapper."

"Apparently, you are a good enough shot," Hyams said. "I understand that you fired through his windshield, and that saved the day."

"And then I threw up all over West Virginia," Mort said.

Again, laughter.

The board didn't even adjourn to discuss a verdict. They were unanimous in recognizing the urgency of the event and complimented Travis for his leadership and bravery.

True to his word, Travis then resigned as chief of police. He took his prepared resignation out of his jacket with his free hand and handed it to Commander Hyams, asking her to present it to the county executive.

Everyone was shocked. "Why have you chosen to do this?" Hyams asked. "You people are heroes and saved the life of an American icon."

"That's just it," Travis said. "We did what police officers are trained to do. Well, not Mort, who fortunately was there and reacted on instinct. But when the FBI issued a statement that this was "part of a coordinated rescue" and then insisted on bringing these charges against me because they were embarrassed when the truth came out, I realized that I've had it with bureaucracy. I love law enforcement, but I'll find something else."

Sixty

Mort continued to write articles and follow-ups on the kidnapping and the events in West Virginia. There was all sorts of speculation about the mastermind behind the tangled affair. Mort interviewed anyone he could locate who was attached to the case and had several more interviews with Win Abbington about NAWES, the Supreme Court decision and Justice Battaglia's recusal.

Abbington was philosophical. "Win some, lose some," he told Mort. "I'm embarrassed that someone in our organization had a hand in all this, and thankful that Justice Richter is recovering. I know Zeke didn't come up with this scheme on his own, and I hope that they get to the bottom of it quickly. The FBI did find missing funds and some hidden accounts in our organization, plus some offshore corporations, and I have every confidence that it's only a matter of time until we know the whole story."

Boris Rosenthal stayed far away from the interviews.

* * *

"Everyone has their own theory about who's behind it," Mort said to Danni one evening. They were back at home in their apartment, and she was somewhat chagrinned, a new emotion for Danni, over her behavior with J.J. and Mort.

"So much finger pointing," she said to Mort. "Everyone has an idea of who was behind all this, but no one knows. I have my suspicions."

"I'm hoping Craig Fisher might give me a heads up if they figure it out before I do. By the way, in another vein, it looks like J.J.'s gala, his annual after-term barbecue, is a thing of the past, at least this year."

"Don't bet on it. He's nudging Mom about doing something over Labor Day. By the way, I think we should get a dog."

"A dog? Where'd that come from? You know I'd love a dog. What a non sequitur."

"I just think it would make our life more complete," Danni said.

"An engagement ring would make our life more complete. Tell you what, I get you a ring, and we go and get a dog."

"The dog first," Danni said, "and then, maybe—if you're lucky—we'll talk."

* * *

Mort was at his desk the following morning when his cell phone rang.

"Got a story for you," J.J. said. "The governor called, wanted to know how I was doing and then told me that the state wants to give Lupe a medal for her part in the capture of that kidnapper. Said it was the first time anyone ever helped solve a crime with a frying pan."

"Wow, that's something," Mort said. "Someone finally recognized how instrumental she was in this whole thing. I'll call his office to confirm and write the story. Real human interest. Where did the governor get that idea?"

J.J. chuckled. "Don't have a clue."

"Lupe must have been thrilled," Mort said.

"She said no," J.J. said.

"No? Why would she say no?"

"Embarrassed. Not used to being in the limelight. But I told her if she didn't accept it, I'd fire her. So, she said yes."

"I'm on it," Mort said. "And thanks."

* * *

The ceremony at the Maryland State House was J.J.'s first public appearance since the abduction. J.J. and Chickie had traveled the fifty miles from Travilah with Lupe in a rented limo. Danni and Mort drove from Georgetown. Travis, after his final surgery, and his family were there along with several dozen curious citizens.

The Maryland State House in Annapolis, according to Mort's article, was the nation's oldest state capitol and the only one that had ever served as the nation's capitol. The Continental Congress had met there for several years after the Revolutionary War. The rest of his article read:

"A reluctant heroine stood in the sunshine on the steps outside the oldest state capitol in the nation, fidgeting while receiving a Commendation of Valor and a medal from Maryland's Governor Larry Hogan today for her role in solving the kidnapping of Supreme Court Senior Associate Justice J.J. Richter. Lupe Ruiz, a naturalized citizen of Mexican descent and the housekeeper of the justice, brandished a frying pan, knocking one of his kidnappers unconscious while he was attempting to burglarize the home. She then tied him up and alerted the authorities, which led to the disclosure of the location where Richter, the seventy-eight-year-old senior associate justice of the court, was being held in West Virginia. He was rescued a short time later."

Lupe was noticeably embarrassed when the governor asked her, "Did you bring the frying pan with you today?" She responded, "No. Frying pan in cabinet, where it belong. I only do what anyone would do, and praise be to God that the judge now home and safe. He is man who makes America the great nation that it is."

Sixty-one

Mort called Craig Fisher at the FBI to learn whether Zeke Shannon was cooperating with the federal authorities in naming the person who was the mastermind of the kidnapping and Braddock's murder.

"I can't say much," said Fisher. "Basically, there's not much to say. But he hasn't been very cooperative. It's now in the hands of the US attorney in Virginia."

"Who's representing him?"

"A federal public defender."

"Jesus, he was the CFO of a major corporation, and he's got a public defender?"

"Well, all his assets were tied up by the court."

"Family?" Mort asked.

"Mother, two brothers and a sister. They want nothing to do with him since he's charged with Braddock's murder and implicated in the kidnapping."

"Wife? Kids?"

"An ex-wife and son who he abandoned when he came back from overseas with the Seals and then took up with a mistress. I know that there's a pending lawsuit for nonsupport. But that's all I know."

Mort was curious. "Where would that case be heard?"

"Don't know," Fisher said. "Probably in New Jersey where he lived."

"Well, if you hear anything, don't forget me."

* * *

Mort found out that Shannon was represented by Monique Kahn, a public defender. He called and left a message. An hour later, she called back.

"Mr. Ahrens," she said, "what can I do for you?"

"I'm still working the story about the kidnapping of Richter and murder of Brendan Braddock. Can you tell me about where things are at with your client?"

"There's really not much I can say. He's awaiting trial. That should be coming up shortly. The government is seeking the death penalty under eleven-eleven of Title 18, US Code, but that's public information. We're scheduled for a conference next week."

"Where and when?"

* * *

Mort was able to locate the court in New Jersey where the support proceedings had been pending. He called and spoke with the clerk, Asa Demmings.

"These proceedings are confidential," he told Mort, "but I can tell you they have been transferred because the complainant has moved out of state. Without objection from the father, understandably. By the way, your reputation precedes you. Congratulations."

"Thank you. Can you tell me where she moved to?"

"I can. Wilmington. Not Delaware—North Carolina."

"Can you get me an address?"

"I shouldn't, but I will. Just forget where you got it."

After a short flight from Washington, Mort knocked on the door of an apartment on Cadfel Court in Wilmington. A thin, pale teenager answered the door, and Mort explained who he was.

"Mom," the teen yelled, "some newspaper guy wants to talk to you."

Megan Shannon, a trim forty-year-old in a waitress uniform, looked at Mort through the bluest eyes he had ever seen. She was instantly suspicious. "Yes?"

"Mrs. Shannon, I don't want to bother you, but I'm Mort Ahrens of the *Washington Post*—"

252

"I know who you are. I read the papers!" Megan said abruptly. "There's nothing I have to say to you."

"Please, just a few minutes. It's really important."

She turned to her son. "Daron, go to your room." The boy left, silently.

"If there is anything you could tell me about your life with your husband..."

"*Former* husband," she said. "Left us high and dry without the proverbial pot. I've been struggling ever since. I'll never see any money from that bastard, and I've got a teenage son who needs a kidney transplant. On dialysis twice a week, and I'm just trying to earn a living. Besides, I told the FBI everything I know. Twice."

"Please," Mort said, "if you could just spare me a little time. And perhaps I could help your son. We have a lot of contacts."

"I'm already late for work. Tell you what—I'm a waitress at the Pilot House restaurant. I get off at nine. Meet me there at the bar."

Mort left and called Danni to tell her he'd be in Wilmington overnight. There weren't any flights back to Washington that late.

The Pilot House was in a historic section of Wilmington, on Chandler's Wharf. The Cape Fear River flowed swiftly past. Mort decided to have dinner there, made certain that Megan Shannon knew he was there, and she met him promptly at nine. They went out on the boardwalk to talk.

"I know you've been questioned, but if there is anything you can think of in your husband's—"

"Ex-husband."

"Excuse me, ex-husband's life that could help resolve this case. Isn't there someone who he was close to... a friend, maybe, or a buddy from the service...?"

"You know, there is one guy from the Seal Team he adored. I never met him, but Zeke had him up on a pedestal. Zeke eventually went into finance, and his buddy went into government work of some kind. But I can't remember more than that. It never came up when I was questioned."

"His name?"

"Can't remember. I think he had the same name as one of the presidents, but I'm not sure. He saved Zeke's life on one of their missions. Zeke used to say, 'glad for Chad or I wouldn't be here.' That's all I recall."

"Megan, you've been a Godsend. When I get back to Washington, I'll get to work, and we'll find a donor for your son. That's a promise."

Mort walked away and was so excited he called Craig Fisher at home.

"I think I stumbled on the lead that you need," Mort said, "but the price is finding a kidney donor for a young kid."

Sixty-two

The following week, Zeke Shannon's case was on the conference calendar, so Mort attended. A shackled Shannon was led into the courtroom by two US marshals. The federal public defender, Monique Kahn, leaned over and whispered to Shannon.

The district court judge, Eugenia Finley, a pleasant looking African American woman who looked about fifty, was on the bench. They went through the preliminaries and then the judge asked, "Is discovery complete?"

Both attorneys said, "Yes, Your Honor."

The judge nodded and said, "When I conclude the calendar call, we can go into chambers and discuss a trial date."

Mort leaned over the rail to the defendant's table and tapped Kahn on the shoulder. She turned, and he mouthed, "Mort Ahrens, *Washington Post.*"

She stood up, moved to the rail and shook his hand. Zeke Shannon looked over, surprised to see Mort in the court. He was obviously curious.

Mort handed a note with his card to Monique Kahn and whispered, "Can you give this to your client?"

She took it, went back to her seat and read the note. Then she turned around to Mort with a curious look before handing the note to Shannon. After reading it, his head slumped down.

The note read: "No matter what you've done, you have fathered a son, a nice kid who will die unless he gets a kidney transplant. The most successful transplants come from a parent. I also know you have refused to cooperate with the government in naming your co-conspirator. If you cooperate, I think the feds might consider a long sentence instead of the death penalty, despite the charges against you. You'll be dead forever if you choose omerta, but that doesn't make you a hero. You could give your son a chance at life if you cooperate. You have been a hero in your military service. Stop being an ass and do something decent. Be a hero again. Cooperate and you'll probably get the chance to see your kid grow up and be a man. It is time to do something beneficial for someone else, an innocent kid who you have already failed in many ways."

Shannon read the note a second time, then turned and sadly looked at Mort. It was the saddest expression Mort had ever seen. Shannon leaned over and whispered to his attorney.

When the case was called for conference, Monique Kahn stood and said to the judge, "Your Honor, I'd like a few moments to confer with the prosecutor. Just a minute or two."

"Granted, but make it quick, I've got a full calendar."

Monique Kahn walked to the prosecution table and whispered briefly to the prosecutor, who turned toward Mort.

Kahn looked at the judge and said, "Your Honor, I would also like to request that Mr. Shannon, the defendant, be present during this conference."

The Judge looked at the prosecutor, who nodded agreement.

"Unusual," the judge said, "but let's continue this in chambers."

They all went into chambers, Kahn, Shannon, the prosecutor and two US marshals.

Mort waited in the courtroom for fifteen minutes. When no one came back from the conference, he got up and left.

Back at his office he got a text. "You are not only a great reporter, but a great human being. Monique Kahn."

Sixty-three

Chad Kennedy, the president's chief of staff, was dining at a large, circular table at The Monocle on D St. NE. He was joined by the speaker of the house, two members of Congress and a US senator, all males. They had come at Kennedy's invitation and were just finishing the main course. The wine was flowing, and Chad was relishing the moment.

"Even though we lost that water case in front of SCOTUS, I have some great opportunities for you with several corporations based overseas. They are foursquare in recognizing the world's drought conditions. There's still a fortune to be made here, which is one reason I invited you all tonight," Chad said.

"So, they're headquartered overseas?" the senator asked.

"Overseas, and out of the reach of the IRS," Chad replied.

His cell rang and he responded. After listening for several seconds, he shook his head and said, "Yes, sir," and disconnected.

"Gentlemen," he said, "you'll have to excuse me for what I hope is a short time. I've just been summoned to the White House. If I'm not back within the hour, the tab is taken care of and we'll continue this later."

He took a last sip of wine and shook hands with the maitre d' on his way out.

At the White House, Chad Kennedy was directed to the Oval Office. He was surprised that the president was in the Oval Office this late and assumed there was a matter of critical importance.

In the Oval, the president nodded to him and said, "You know George Blessing, of course." Kennedy was surprised to see Blessing there. "These other two gentlemen are Tim Richardson and Craig Fisher, both FBI special agents.

Kennedy nodded and said, "Gentlemen."

"Special Agent Richardson headed the investigation into Justice Richter's kidnapping, and Special Agent Fisher was brought in after the killing of the Supreme Court marshal in Virginia," the president said. "Well, we might as well get right to it."

He nodded to Richardson, who stepped forward and faced Kennedy.

"Mr. Kennedy," Richardson said, "I am placing you under arrest for complicity and for being a principal in the death of Brendan Braddock, a federal employee, for violation of your oath of office, for conspiracy, and for violation of the Federal Trade Act." He then recited the Miranda warnings.

Kennedy was flummoxed. "For what?" he asked. "I haven't done anything wrong. Someone has made a very serious mistake."

"Chad, I'm very disappointed," the president said. "I really thought so highly of you. To use this office to further your own ambitions is far beyond the pale. To say nothing of embarrassing me and the entire administration." He looked down at a document in his hand. "Your co-conspirator, Ezekiel Shannon, has already given a full statement, thanks to the work of these special agents and their team, implicating you in Braddock's murder and your illegal plans to pirate the market in private access to water. A dastardly scheme, Chad. The decision of the Supreme Court laid waste to those plans, and thank God they did."

Kennedy sank into the soft sofa and tried to disappear into it, his face flushed, his eyes squinting with despair.

The president continued. "But your greed knew no boundaries. This was all done at your direction—the bank accounts in the Cook Islands for the kidnappers, one of whom I might mention is now dead and the other one facing a lifetime behind bars. To say nothing of the funds that your buddy Shannon pilfered from the NAWES company.

You set up shell corporations and money laundering from Cyprus to the Cayman Islands, from the Channel Islands to Jersey and God only knows where else. Even tonight, you invited elected members of Congress to a restaurant to inveigle them into this scheme."

"How did you know...?" Kennedy started to say.

Blessing, who had remained quiet up to this point, said, "We have sufficient evidence to be certain of your guilt, Chad. Didn't you ever think twice about how this could embarrass the administration, to say the least?"

"I want an attorney," Kennedy said. "You can't prove a thing."

"Unfortunately for you," Blessing said, "with what we already have, we can prove everything."

Epilogue

After an unusually wet August, Labor Day was a perfect late summer day, the air crisp following a late evening shower. The sun quickly burned off the dampness.

For many years, J.J. had closed out the court term with his barbecue. The invited guests included members of the court, court staff, law clerks and a few friends.

Travis and his family were there, of course, and he was out of his cast and spending a lot of time in physical therapy to restore the full use of his limb. Travis was getting used to his new job as marshal of the Supreme Court Police, Braddock's old job. As the former decorated police chief of a thirteen hundred-person force—far larger than the 145-person Supreme Court Police force—a Medal of Honor winner and rescuer of a kidnapped Supreme Court justice, the job competition had disappeared.

Chickie had been living at J.J.'s full-time since he was released from Walter Reed, spending a good deal of her time stopping J.J. from doing things that his body was not ready for. Despite his good health, he was a seventy-eight-year-old recovering from a traumatic head injury. He had been told to ease back into his regular schedule, which for J.J. meant getting back on his mower.

Chickie had put a quick stop to that and hired a gardener.

Until last year, J.J. had manned the barbecue himself, flushed and exhausted and doing all the cooking. Chickie put a stop to that too. She bought a barbecue about the size of an aircraft carrier, which was now manned by a caterer and his crew. Chickie had also hired a keyboard player, which the guests thought was a pleasant new innovation.

Several of the justices made short appearances, and law clerks and court personnel came for the afternoon.

J.J. was more emotional than anyone had ever seen him when Anthony Battaglia, still using a cane, arrived with his daughter, son-in-law and granddaughter.

"Anthony," J.J. said, and the two men shared a long embrace.

"He looks a lot better than he did on the last day of the term," Mort said to Danni.

She replied, "Probably a lot of stress has been removed, and he has his family here."

"Your Honor," Mort said to Battaglia, "you look a lot better than the last time I saw you."

"I hope it's the proton beam therapy that they are experimenting with at Mayo," Battaglia said. "I had an operation on the pancreas, and part of the after-treatment is this proton beam thing. Early results are encouraging. Fortunately, after the wildfire tragedy my family endured, they're here with me. Just having my granddaughter nearby is the best therapy."

J.J. had little recollection of the actual kidnapping, although he vividly recalled Connie trying to come to his aid. He refused all requests for interviews with the press and even rejected Mort's request for a story. Although he wouldn't admit it, he was relishing the "family time," which had been lacking in his life for over a decade.

True to her word, Chickie took J.J. shopping and bought him a new "bike," as he called it—a shiny, maroon Harley-Davidson Road Glide Special two-seater.

Constance Treller, who was back at her home in Arizona, had suggested by Zoom that J.J. accept a bodyguard from the US Marshals Service.

"For what?" he had said. "They already kidnapped me. What more can they do? Besides, they'll never catch me with my new bike, and I make no more unscheduled stops between Travilah and the court."

"Does this mean," Chickie said, "that you're definitely going back for the new term? You've already given more than anyone could possibly ask of one person."

"As long as I feel competent, that's my home," J.J. said. "And besides, I've got to keep an eye on this new marshal of the Supreme Court Police and keep him on the straight and narrow."

J.J. had insisted on stopping in unannounced at the court earlier that week and rode in on the new Harley with Danni at the helm and him in the second seat. He pounced on his law clerks when he walked in because they were lounging in his office.

"What's going on here?" he barked. "I turn my head for a bit, and you all forgot how to work? Let's get with it. I'm certain there are cert applications pending."

Danni worked hard to suppress her laughter.

But his fake tirade managed to intimidate the newest clerk, a young woman from Georgetown Law, who had clerked in the district court.

When he looked around his office, he roared, "Who the hell has moved my stuff? Now I'll never find a damn thing!"

Danni raised herself to her full five-foot-two and said, "This place was a mess. It's worse than when I was here. So yes, I stopped in one day and straightened up. Nothing is missing. You just can't deal with it because it's neat." The clerks snickered.

Mort's parents arrived at the barbecue about three o'clock. It was their first time at one of J.J.'s events, and his mother was awe-struck. His father, on the other hand, headed right for the food and informed whoever he spoke to that he was "Mort's dad, the young man who saved the judge's life."

Mort said, "It's justice, Dad, not judge."

His father looked at him and said, "Whatever."

Craig Fisher and his wife were there, at Mort's request. He and Danni introduced them to J.J. and Chickie.

"I just want you all to know," Fisher said, "that the case might still be unsolved if not for Mort."

"How so?" J.J. asked.

"Well, knowing Mort, he probably never said anything, but when we were still struggling to find the leader of that kidnap plan, it was Mort who got the NAWES CFO, Shannon, who had absolutely refused to cooperate, to change his plea and let us button it up."

Mort was embarrassed and said, "Pure luck."

"No," Fisher said, "not luck. Finding information we never unearthed, digging and not giving up."

"You never said a word," Danni said.

"I'll tell you about it another time," Mort said.

At about four thirty, J.J. asked everyone to gather near the keyboard player. There were chairs set up in rows by the caterer.

"As long as I have you all here," he said, "can you please be seated? Anthony?"

Justice Battaglia came forward, and Chickie joined J.J. The keyboardist started playing and singing in a smooth tenor voice the song that Elvis Presley made famous: "I Can't Help Falling in Love With You." Everyone was curious and puzzled.

J.J. stepped forward and said, "We have a little surprise for you all. Would Travis, Mort and Danni please come forward."

Danni and Mort looked at each other, eyebrows raised, questioning. They stepped forward. Connie stood next to J.J., tail wagging.

"Life is short," J.J. said, "and these last few months have made me more aware of it than ever. Finally, I have given in to Chickie's badgering and agreed to get married, and you friends and family will be our witnesses."

There was not a sound except for the noise of the caterers.

Chickie said, "He's full of it. He's been begging me since he got out of the hospital."

"I think it was the knock on the head," J.J. said to laughter.

J.J. was wearing one of his famous western shirts, jeans and boots. Chickie was also in jeans, with a soft multi-colored silk blouse.

Anthony Battaglia said, "It's been a long time since I performed one of these. Come to think of it, I'm not sure I *ever* performed one, but nothing can give me more pleasure than to join these two wonderful people. They have written their own vows, and somehow sneaked into town and got a license." He reached into his pocket and took out a folded piece of paper. "Join hands, and repeat after me…"

"As sure as the sun will rise, I will love you,

As sure as the storms of life will rage, I will love you.

I will be your lover, your best friend, your companion,

I will be your warmth in the cold, your light in the darkness,
I will share your dreams.

You are my love and my life, today and forever, and I cherish your love.

Be patient with my imperfections, and be my mentor,

But most of all be my friend, my ally, my equal in all things,

Today, tomorrow, and to the end of life's road."

J.J. and Chickie looked at each other and Battaglia said, "You may kiss."

As they leaned into each other, Mort looked around. There were surprised expressions, many teary eyes, and then spontaneous applause.

Travis and Mort shook hands with J.J., and as Mort leaned in to kiss Chickie, his mother's voice, loud and clear, cut through the air like fingernails scraping on a blackboard.

"So how come you and Morton never got married?" she asked Danni.

"Because he never asked me," Danni said. By now, heads were turning. "It's always about an engagement ring, but he never asked me to marry. So?" She looked at Mort, who felt himself turn crimson.

Mort dropped to one knee. "Danielle Rose," he said, "will you marry me?"

"I've been waiting for you to ask," she said.

"Mister Judge," Mort's mother said, "can we get two for the same price?" Again, laughter.

Using the same vows, in front of the same people, Danni and Mort became husband and wife. Sort of. Without a license, and without a ring.

Acknowledgments

Completing this novel has been a trial of endurance and patience, and would never have been brought to fruition without much help along the way. There are so many to thank.

First of all, my wife Sharon sacrificed hundreds of hours from our marriage when I was toiling over the computer, offering her support, travelling to the various locations to ensure accuracy, and being the first reader of the many discarded revisions to get us to this point. Faithful Katie, our rescue Springer-Spaniel spent many of those hours under the desk, patiently waiting for a pat, or reminding me it was time for her walk, and a treat.

My love of writing has manifested itself in many ways over the years, from the late Prof. Donald Dike at Syracuse University, to those dozens of writers who served as my inspiration, from Ernest Hemingway to the incomparable Daniel Silva, as well as those mentioned here.

David Housewright, the Edgar-Award winning novelist, gave unselfishly of his time with his blistering critiques, which only made my efforts better; I am forever in his debt. Shawn Otto, with his own award-winning writing credits, implored me to reduce unnecessary verbiage and focus on "story and spine."

Best Friend Bill Raker was a tenacious reader and editor, far and above the call of duty. Hon. Paul Anderson, Minnesota Supreme Court (ret.) not only read the drafts but offered valuable suggestions

(I learned a lot about shotguns from him), and the Hon. David Straus, of the 8th Circuit Court of Appeals, arranged a valuable tour of the Supreme Court a decade ago which got all this started, and offered helpful information about the workings of the Supreme Court.

Avi Meshar, the computer maven, patiently endured my many struggles with technology and corrected them, giving much of himself to make me better. Leon Hendrickson of Copy Right Printing, contributed reams of paper to rewrites. I am deeply indebted as well to those accomplished authors who not only read the novel, but offered their endorsement – David Housewright, Shawn Otto, Brian Freeman, Paul Anderson, Roxanne Meshar, Chaunda Scott, Cellin Gluck, and a special shout-out to Judy Rabinor, not only as an author but as a friend.

Then there were the readers, who offered countless critiques and corrections: Jane Katz, a fine author in her own right; Dr. Irwin Hirsch, not only a reader but a personal life-saver; Rick King, and Dr. Paul Dondlinger, who generously offered his time.

My children Peter Miller and Stephanie Handlin have withstood much from me over the decades, but have always been there to offer strength and support. The Theodoratos and Harouche clans and son-in-law Bob Handlin have also been a great source of support.

We have been blessed with the support and friendship of so many, including the best neighbors anyone could imagine – Deb and Mike Shannon; Mark Alevizos and Cathy Curtis; Patrick Klinger and Jennifer Nasifoglu; Mike and Joey Bussiere; Mary Dahlke and the Access to Democracy crew; The Movie Group; Jan and Paul Anderson; Jim and Gayle Carlson; Bill and Wannapa Raker; Ellie Fishman; and Carlos and Genevra Salazar. I am certain there are names I have omitted, but those, like any errors in the text, are mine, for which I apologize.

Finally, the staff at Calumet Editions: editor and designer Gary Lindberg, copyeditor Rick Polad and publisher Ian Grahm Leask, who offered their knowledge and expertise, as well as invaluable assistance. I have learned that the completion of a novel is far more than an individual effort, and I am awed and humbled by all those who touched my efforts along the way.

About the Author

Alan Miller was writing weekly newspaper columns by age fifteen, writing for Newsday while still in high school, graduated college as a journalist, then went to law school, obtaining a J.D., litigated extensively, as well as taught in colleges, universities and law schools, won numerous writing awards including Best Column from the NY Press Assn., wrote for a national magazine, his writing appearing in both periodicals and national newspapers. He has presented at professional seminars both here and abroad, served in several positions in city and state governments, was honored for his articles during the Persian Gulf War (Operation Desert Storm), has been a radio talk show host, and for twenty-three years has been host/producer of an award-winning cable access TV show seen in multiple cities and worldwide on YouTube, has been featured in Who's Who for decades, and authored two non-fiction books. He brings all that experience to bear in "Holding Court," a political/literary/thriller. He resides in Minnesota with his wife Sharon, and Springer/rescue Katie. They have six children and seven grandchildren.